AF191280

For Judith,
who always believed in me, even when I
didn't believe in myself.

Minds like

Midnight Blue

Alina Bachmann

Bibliografische Information der Deutschen Nationalbibliothek:
Die Deutsche Nationalbibliothek verzeichnet diese Publikation in
der Deutschen Nationalbibliografie; detaillierte bibliografische
Daten sind im Internet über http://dnb.dnb.de abrufbar.

Verlag: BoD • Books on Demand GmbH, In de Tarpen 42,
22848 Norderstedt
Druck: Libri Plureos GmbH, Friedensallee 273, 22763 Hamburg

ISBN: 978-3-7583-5126-6

Cover: Maren Nachtsheim
Translation: Alina Bachmann

Chapter 1

Even though it had happened more than 12 years ago, to him it felt like it was just yesterday. The memory didn't vanish, it burned itself down into his mind, and he doubted that he would ever be able to forget this certain day when, until today, he wasn't anywhere near able to repress these memories.

Summer. He has always loved the summer. He loved spending his time outside, to go on adventures together with his dozens of friends, and to stay up longer since the sun shone bright until the evening hours and therefore enlightened the night.

It has always been easy for him to make new friends or to talk to other people, which made him a very appreciated friend and contact person. If his friends wanted to go and play outside, they always asked him first if he wanted to join them. He was popular, and his very short life of six years went normal until this certain day. The day that had changed everything.

It was a regular Saturday morning, like any other, and his mother decided it was time to spontaneously visit his grandmother. Immediately, he packed the most important things he would need for the long journey into his small backpack. His mother added a couple of socks and other clothes since they wanted to stay at his Grandmother's place for two days. Then their trip started.

He was looking forward to seeing the old mansion of his Grandma, which lied between a big, adventurous forest and a playground. He couldn't imagine a place more beautiful than this one anywhere in the world.

The ride didn't feel as long to him as it used to, he could even feel how he grew up and became more and more patient with time. He had learned to wait and therefore time flew by quickly. His tiny heart beat fast, caused by all the excitement he felt when they drove through the forest that led to his Grandma's house.

He loved the old mansion that was covered in ivy where his Grandma lived since he was born. He was fascinated by the huge windows that let the sun get inside the cold-looking house and fill it with light and warmth. Also, he enjoyed the playful garden filled with bushes of roses and a small pavilion next to a tiny pond. He knew that the house with many rooms had lived through better times, but he loved every-thing about it.

The mansion was old, but even though her children have always told her to renovate it so the roof wasn't literally falling down on her, his Grandma refused to do it. She has always said that the house was a piece of history, and it was her duty to protect it. He agreed with her because he was fascinated by the fact that this old house still stood at the same place where it had been built after all these times, even though he only knew parts of the history of the building. One day, his Grandma had said, he would get to know the full history, but for now, he was too young to understand.

After some of his other family members had arrived at the old mansion, they had coffee and cake in the small garden. The adults were happy to see each other again since they all lived in different cities spread throughout the country and barely saw each other anymore. He, however, felt lost because there were no kids his age that he could play with. That's why his mother allowed him to go to the playground nearby, whereupon he immediately stormed out of the mansion and onto the playground.

As always, it wasn't difficult for him to connect with other children and make new friends. Soon, he joined a group of four boys to play hide and seek. He realized quickly that a tiny girl was following him. He eyed her closely and asked her if she wanted to join them, but she denied his question. She had already asked one of the other boys if she could play along, but they didn't want her to. She didn't even know why it made her feel sad, and neither did she know why she liked observing one of the boys so much.

To break the silence that was crawling over them, he asked her for her name; Luana. Her freckled cheeks started glowing out of joy when she told him her name. Before he could tell her his name, his new friends were saying goodbye because it started getting late and their parents wanted to leave. On the inside, she was happy that his friends needed to leave, but on the outside, she didn't show it. The only thing that made her mad was the fact that he couldn't tell her his name. She, indeed, knew it already since she had heard one of his friends call him, but she didn't want him to know that.

When he came back from saying goodbye to his new friends, he asked her how old she was. Shily, she looked at her hands and showed five fingers. To show her his age, he wanted to touch her hands and stick out another finger, a sixth one. So, he carefully grabbed her hand, but the moment their fingers touched, something strange happened.

A quick tingle shot through his body and stopped as quickly as it had started. He realized that he curled his forehead, then his view turned completely black. However, it didn't stay black for long. Almost immediately he could see colors again. Firstly everything was blurred, then it became more and more clear.

Now he wasn't standing on the playground anymore, but in the middle of a street in front of a big apartment building with a garden. He saw a woman who looked astonishingly much like Luana, then he could see her as well. Luana was playing with a tiny ball. Suddenly, the ball rolled on the street, and Luana ran after it without paying any attention to her environment. She didn't see the car that was on the road. But he could see it. He couldn't do anything. Rattling. Screaming. The door of a car. A crying mother. Voices. Multiple voices. Multiple voices that were all talking at the same time. Silence.

His view became blurry again, then black, and in the end, he returned to where he previously stood on the playground. A strange daydream.

He had to blink multiple times until he could think clearly again. Everything happened so fast, she didn't even realize something was wrong. And before he could say anything else or even tell her that he was six years old, her mother had called her. Shockingly, he had to admit that the woman who introduced herself as Luana's mother looked exactly like the woman in his daydream.

They said goodbye but agreed to meet again the next day. Then she entered their car and saw how he looked after them until they vanished behind a corner.

The next morning, he was eager to go back to the playground and didn't want to be late under any circumstances. He couldn't explain his excitement.

Eventually, he sat down on one of the swings on the edge of the playground and waited. After some time, it started to rain, but he didn't want to get back to the mansion; he didn't want to miss her. So, he stayed. And waited. The rain passed, children came and went, but she didn't come.

After some time, he saw a familiar face. It was Luana's mother. She told him that he should go back home because Luana wouldn't come and play with him. She didn't even have to tell him the reason why. He already knew what had happened.

His daydream became a reality.

Luana was dead.

✻✻✻

"You don't look too well," Mrs. Müller said and sighed.

"I never look too well," he answered coldly.

He was tired of wasting five hours of his week in her doctor's office without making any progress.

"You are so pessimistic again," she reminded him, and put on her pink glasses that were hanging on some threats around her neck like a very ugly necklace.

She started to read the journal that he had handed her a few minutes ago and uttered things like 'interesting' or 'strange'. When she had finished the latest pages, she put her glasses down and looked at him sternly.

"I can't see any irregularities in your dream journal. No panic or anxiety, no daydreams, no negative thoughts anymore. You do know what that means, don't you?"

"You can finally release me?" he asked full of hope.

"No", she shook her head. "It means that we need to change something. If you are not ready to open up after more than 10 years, I have to pass you on to another therapist. You do know that I'm very interested in your case, but it would be for the best. I can't help you if you won't stop writing made-up stories in your journal."

Her voice was calm and neutral, but still, it made him feel upset. How should he be honest if no one wanted to believe him?

"Did you have any more of your dreams?" she tried again.

"They are no dreams. They are visions," he corrected her.

He hated this discussion. It was such a waste of time. Throughout the past 13 years, he has become more and more certain that the accident with Luana was no coincidence. It was a prediction, but nobody believed him.

Narcolepsy, PTSD, severe anxieties, and depression – this was what the therapist, whom he was seeing voluntarily at the beginning, has diagnosed him with. Nowadays, he just continued to see her because he had promised his mother to become healthy again and to get in control of his life. This happened before he felt that her time was up.

Again, he saw her dead before it happened. It was just one of the multiple deaths he had predicted. That's why he was sure his visions were real. On the other hand, it just confirmed Mrs. Müller in her diagnosis.

"Ramon," she said softly, trying to bring him back to reality. "You know that the human brain can manipulate memories in a way that makes you think you've predicted them before they happened."

Her voice became sterner.

He gulped.

Of course, he knew her theory was valid, but he had already tried writing down his visions before they became reality to prove to himself that he was not insane. And he was right every damn time. But he didn't tell her. He didn't care that Mrs. Müller probably felt superior with her knowledge. He knew the truth.

"If you say so," he murmured, visibly annoyed by her omniscient attitude.

Yes, he was only 19 years old, and therefore way younger than her, but still, he knew more about himself than she would ever know. He just had to wait for the right moment and the right shreds of evidence to show her that she had been wrong all the time.

It simply couldn't be a coincidence anymore that his predictions have always changed since the day they started. In the beginning, they were triggered through physical contact. Later, it had to be eye contact. Now, it was enough that he saw a human being from somewhere. His predictions became more random and, therefore, uncontrollable.

"The time is up," Mrs. Müller said after checking her watch.

Relieved, he said goodbye and exited her office.

He was free again.

Fortunately, the streets were still empty. The fewer people, the better. Few people meant that his visions wouldn't occure that often or not at all.

Quickly, he entered his car, which was gifted to him by his dad for his 18th birthday, and drove down the two streets that were separating his apartment from the therapist's office. He could easily walk back to his apartment at this time of day, but he didn't want to risk seeing anyone. He preferred being alone.

There were only two reasons for him to leave his apartment anyway: grocery shopping and therapy. The rest of the time, he spent all alone at home. Even though he still had his father, he had moved out as quickly after graduation as he could. He had told him that it was easier for him to focus on work if he lived alone. But the truth was that he was afraid to watch him die as well. This fear ruled over his life, so he preferred being left alone for most of the time.

After he had turned seven, he cut the contact with all of his friends because he had predicted the death of one of them. Only one friend remained: Tim. His best friend. For some reason – that he couldn't explain – Tim has endured him and his odd behavior, which made it impossible for him to burn the bridges between them. Perhaps this friendship was a good thing. Without any friends, he might become mad or insane, but with Tim, he knew that one person in this world got his back despite his visions. It was a welcome compensation for all the hours spent in Mrs. Müller's

office, who treated him like he was lacking something.

Usually, it was easy to find a parking spot in front of
his house since there weren't many cars driving
through his street. That's why he was confused to see
a huge moving truck parked in front of the apartment
building. He couldn't remember that anyone had
moved out of the building; however, he wasn't particularly interested in his neighbors either.

Usually, he avoided meeting his neighbors since the
day he moved into his apartment. He didn't want to
talk to them or even see them. That's why he learned
to fit into the rhythm of the apartment complex.

He knew at what time he could leave his apartment
without meeting anyone on the staircase. It worked
well, up until now and most of his neighbors have
never met him. Occasionally, he couldn't prevent
meeting the old lady from the first floor. He simply
couldn't pretend to be an asshole and ignore her greet-
ings, and for now, these brief meetings always went
fine. But he knew this was no assurance for eternity.

Hesitant, he left his car and tried to sneak into the
building as unobtrusively as possible. Relieved, he
realized that no one was near the moving truck, so he
tried to hurry up.

Again, he managed to enter his apartment on the fifth
floor without seeing a single soul.

Chapter 2

It took a long time until all the moving boxes were brought into the apartment. Therefore tired, she fell on her bed. Somehow, moving felt way easier in the past, which could've been caused by the fact that she used to be a child when they moved the last time, and she didn't need to help anywhere. Now she was old enough to help her mom.

Tired and exhausted, she glanced at her alarm clock that was standing on her improvised nightstand – a moving box – to realize more time had already passed than she thought. She sat up, yawned, and stretched her joints. There was no way she could avoid a hot shower today. It was Sunday and already way too late. She had sweated a lot and felt absolutely exhausted, but this didn't change the fact that she had to get ready for school the next day.

Nobody would care that she was already tired of this town, even though she just spent her weekend helping her mom move here. Her life had to continue normally, and no one would care about her problems. She really couldn't understand why her mom wanted to move away so urgently. And even less why her choice fell on this ugly city when there were so many prettier ones in the world.

She left the shower and wrapped the first towel she could find in the chaos around her body. Before she left the bathroom, her gaze remained on her mirror reflection. She could barely recognize herself. Her skin was pale, and there were visible dark circles around her eyes. Besides that, she still couldn't find anything on her face that was close to being beautiful. Not today.

Today was not her day. She had figured that out first thing in the morning when she had to say goodbye to her best friend Sina for an uncertain amount of time.

They had been friends since forever. The two of them were like sisters, even though both of them were only children. And even their looks used to be quite similar since both of them had long brown hair and freckles. Just her blue eyes made her look different than Sina.

When they grew older, they looked less and less alike, but this didn't hurt their friendship at all. Damn. She wanted to go back.

She didn't want to go to a new school, and even less in the middle of the school year. If it would've been after some sort of holiday or even vacation, it would be okayish. But in the middle of the school year sucked because she would be the center of attention, and she wanted everything but being noticed by anyone. She didn't even want to try to make friends. She just wanted to survive day by day until she would graduate.

"Luna, if you want to be at school on time, get up!" she heard her mother shout.

A quick glance at her alarm clock told her that she was already late. Fuck.

She hurried up and put on the first jeans she could find. She then combined a gray top with her black leather jacket, and she was ready to go. After checking herself out in the mirror again, she had to admit that she looked way better than the day before, so she would not need to put on any foundation or concealer today.

"I'm ready," she screamed, and stormed out of the bathroom.

On her way out, she grabbed her breakfast and a cup of coffee that was already prepared by her mom and left on the kitchen counter. Then she went outside her apartment on the fourth floor.

The way to her new school was definitely shorter than it used to be in her previous home; therefore, she could walk without any problem. In her hometown, she always had to rely on the bus.

In front of the building, she took a deep breath, then she entered.

The entrance door was way heavier than it looked. I wondered how tinier students should be able to open the door if I, a student in 11th grade, had issues opening this damn door. I had to admit that there were people from 7th grade that were way taller than me, though I wouldn't say that I was super tiny either.

So, there I was, standing in the entrance hall of my new school. I had to admit that I imagined the school to be totally different than it was. I was somehow expecting it to be less old and less desolate. But this was great. I liked old things.

The walls of the entrance hall were made of dark, slightly mossy stones, which made the hall look dark but somehow magical. The dark ceiling was high, so it looked like the walls were going nowhere. And if I would've seen a witch flying on a broom, it wouldn't even have surprised me. The whole place just seemed supernatural to me.

In the middle of the round entrance hall stood a tree, and below that tree was an old wooden bench. However, the tree felt so oddly out of place in this dark hall. It seemed like magic that the tree was able to survive here even though its photosynthetic potential couldn't be all too high. Nerd, I called myself out and forced my glance away from the tree, the center of the hall.

I could see some tables and benches on the opposite wall of the entrance door. This was probably where the students were sitting during their breaks and hours off. There were two hallways on each, the left and right side of me. So far, I couldn't tell where they would lead to. But I could already tell that I would get lost in this school on a daily basis. One would need a GPS to find the correct way. Or maybe I just needed one.

I'm directionally challenged, but I had other well-hidden talents. So well hidden that I didn't even know them.

Eventually, I could snap out of my stiffness that was triggered by both my fascination and dislike for this place. I didn't realize that the entrance hall was empty by now; school has started. And since I was already late, I didn't have much time to look for the office where I could get my timetable. But now I was the only breathing creature in this hall, and the school looked way bigger and way more confusing than I estimated. To sum it up, I had no clue where to go next.

Desperately, I made my way to the tree and sat down on the bench. From there, I had a better view of the hallways. They could've at least put up some signs, I complained in my thoughts. Why did we have to move here?

"What are you waiting for?" I heard a voice behind me.

Scared I turned around, but there was no one.
Was I losing my mind, or was the tree talking to me?

"I'm not waiting for anything," I claimed awkwardly and confusedly at the same time.

"And what else are you doing here?" the strange voice kept on asking.
This couldn't be real. I was talking to a tree. A damn tree. This wasn't possible. This couldn't be possible.

"Thinking about the meaning of life. What else should I be doing here?" I asked ironically.

"If you are looking for the student's office, I can bring you there."

While I was wondering if it was normal to talk to a tree and even more, if it was possible that this tree could show me the way, the silhouette of a human person appeared out of the shadow of the tree.

"Before you look at me like you've seen a ghost, no, I didn't come out of the tree. I just came in late and thought you could need some help," he laughed and came closer. "I'm Julius, by the way."

"And I'm going to be late to class on my first day here," I answered coldly.

Julius laughed briefly, then we went to the student's office.

"See ya," he said, and waved slightly.

I didn't say anything but opened the brown, heavy door that parted the hallway from the office.

"Excuse me for being late, but I'm the new student here," I said apologetic.

"This isn't a problem at all. For new students, this school can be a maze," the secretary responded friendly.

She looked through some binders and gave me multiple sheets of paper, like my timetable, but also some information about the school and its rules. Friendly, I said goodbye and made my way back to the entrance hall since it was the only place I felt comfortable going to.

I put my bag on top of one of the tables and took a closer look at all the papers.

The last paper I checked was my timetable. And with the appearance of the school, it wouldn't have surprised me if I would've had classes like *Defense Against the Dark Arts*. Obviously, my timetable was normal, as were all the classes I had.

According to my timetable, I would have history class now. Fortunately, there were some short descriptions of the rooms on one of the papers, so it wasn't that hard for me to find the correct room. Otherwise, I wouldn't have found the room in time, probably. Maybe I wouldn't have found the way at all.

In front of my history room, I stopped and took a few minutes to listen to the voice of the teacher to make sure I was in fact in front of the correct room. After I heard words like "Prussia" and "Wilhelm II", I was convinced that this was the right place.

I was ready to enter the room. I just had to open the door. I just had to put a little bit more pressure on the doorknob. It shouldn't be that difficult, but I simply couldn't do it. So, I stood there in front of the door, debating whether I should enter the room and say something or rather stay in the hallway. I was sure I could do it. I just had to enter and throw myself on the first free seat that I would see. I was ready.

My hand tried another attempt at pushing down the doorknob. I could feel the cold metal in my hands. I just had to use a little bit of strength to open it.

I took a deep breath.

Then I felt some movement from the doorknob and someone else opened the door from the inside. Quickly, I jumped back so I wouldn't get hit by the door.

On the other side of the doorframe was a boy who cringed slightly when he saw me. I couldn't prevent my cheeks from turning red. Confused and annoyed, the boy walked past me and vanished through the next best door.

My cheeks were still red while I was standing between the open door and the dark hallway.

Damn. Damn. Damn.

This could only happen to me.

"And who are you?" the teacher asked me.

"Luna," I answered quietly, so only he could hear it.

"You have to be the new student," he figured out after some incredibly painful silence.

I nodded.

"Come inside and sit down."

I looked down at the ground when I entered and desperately looked for an unoccupied table.

"There is some free seat next to Jane", the teacher said.

But how the fuck should I know who Jane is?

Jane turned out to be the girl with the curly blond hair that was sitting in the last row and chewing on her bubble gum. Uncertain, I sat down next to her, and the teacher continued his lesson.

Fortunately, I didn't see the guy that almost crashed into me anymore.

"Jane, could you maybe show Luna around during the break?" the teacher asked.

Apparently, now the teachers were making new friends for me.

Like me, Jane was not very interested in getting to know me or even introducing me to her friends. Still, she navigated us into the entrance hall and to her group of friends.

In the darkest and loneliest corner of the round hall sat a group of five people. Unfortunately, I recognized the guy from history class as well as Julius.

"Finn," Jane said, and sat down next to the history class guy, who immediately tried to get a bit of personal space by moving more to the side.

Jane didn't seem to realize this; she was way too busy admiring him from her position.

I felt lost standing within a group of strangers, and all I hoped for was that Julius wouldn't talk to me. I couldn't even tell what I didn't like about him, but something about him was odd and annoying.

"Did you find the right room?" Julius asked, and smiled at me.

"Yes. The descriptions on the timetable are quite good," I answered politely.

Without breaking the eye contact, he pushed some of his blond hair out of his face. This steady eye contact made me feel even more uncomfortable than before.

"Were you at least somehow on time?" he desperately tried to keep the already dying conversation alive.

"She even had enough time to stand in front of the door for some minutes," the guy from history class, Finn, entered the conversation (quicker than I had entered the room).

He smiled apologetically at me.

I sighed.

This situation was more than awkward.

"Don't worry. We've all been new here once," Finn tried to cheer me up a bit.

"But probably not in the middle of the year but at the start of the school year. So, you've never been the only new person here," I said.

"That's true. But this doesn't mean that we felt less insecure than you," Finn started. "When I was new here, I was pretty insecure, to be honest."

I eyed him closely.

He didn't look like someone that even knew the words 'insecurity' or 'self-doubt'. He was tall, with dark brown hair, and brown eyes, dressed in all black clothes that looked like they were fashionable and trendy. It was impossible that he didn't belong to the cool and popular people in this school.

Perhaps Jane and I had the same thoughts because she suddenly entered this irrelevant conversation: "This is so not true. From day one, you were talking to everyone and making jokes with the teachers."

"Oh, was this on my first day? I couldn't remember," he answered coolly.

This just reassured me in thinking that he was not as insecure as he wanted me to think.

"What class do you have next?" Finn asked.

I put my bag on the table and started looking for my timetable.

"Biology."

"If you want to, I can show you the room so you don't have to wait in front of the door for that long," he offered politely, and winked at me.

"I think I'm fine on my own," I denied his offer.

"You can show me the way to the gym," Jane said, and grabbed Finn's arm.

As if he did it all the time, he shook her hand off and politely said: "You can find the way on your own, I'm sure of that."

She didn't look happy, so I decided it would be the perfect moment for me to leave.

"I guess I go and look for the room," I quickly said and left.

I still felt them, especially Jane, look at me while I was already gone.

I was relieved when I found the biology room, but even more so when I realized that my last two classes were canceled so I could walk home earlier than expected.

Today was strange, and I just wanted to go back to bed. I didn't want to talk to anyone and just sleep.

Exhausted, I carried myself upstairs when someone talked to me.

"Are you the new neighbor from the fourth floor?" I heard a friendly voice behind me.

Slowly, I turned around.

"We just moved in here yesterday," I answered politely.

"I saw that," the older lady responded.

Confused I looked at her and eyed her long, white hair that almost reached her belly button. Her gray eyes had some sparkle in them, and there were a lot of wrinkles around her mouth. In addition to her friendly and open way of talking, she seemed quite likeable.

"How do you like it here?" she asked.

"It's nice," I lied.

There was nothing I could say about this city. The only thing that I had seen outside of my bedroom was the school. I didn't have the time to go out and explore the town, and I didn't want to do it alone anyway.

"That's great," she said more to herself than to me.

I gave her a quick smile and waited.

I thought she would go back to her apartment, but she didn't. Instead, she stood not more than two steps apart from me and didn't look like she was planning on moving any time soon.

"I like it here a lot as well," she said after some time.

Out of reflex, I nodded.

"But if you are alone like me, you don't see much of the city anymore. So, don't make the same mistakes as me. Go outside. Explore the city. Use the one life that you have and live it to its fullest."

"Sure, I will," I responded.

"If you ever feel alone, keep your eyes open. On the fifth floor, right on top of your apartment, lives a young man, not much older than you. Maybe he can show you around the city", she winked at me like she just told me some kind of secret.

I highly doubted that I would let some kind of stranger show me around.

A noise disturbed the silence.

"Oh, my tea is ready. Have a great day, Luna!"

She hurried back into her apartment, and I had no other option than to stare after her.

How was it possible that she knew my name even though I tried so hard not to tell it anyone?

This thought was in my head for the rest of the evening until I could find some kind of explanation for it. She must've heard my mom call me at some point yesterday. There was no other way she could've know it.

The only good thing that came out of this day was that after the conversation with the old lady, the people from my school didn't feel as odd as before. They suddenly seemed so normal.

At least the people from my school – and I won't call them friends, especially not after a single day – didn't try to play matchmaker for me and some stranger.

Chapter 3

7 a.m. Waking up. Getting dressed. Starting to drive. Wasting another hour of my life again for therapy without the chance of any success. Working. Avoiding all contact with other humans. Going to bed.

Since I graduated from school, my daily routine hasn't change that much. I got used to it. I had to get used to it if I wanted to avoid seeing somebody die.

I would lie if I said I wasn't afraid to form relationships with other people because, at some point in time, I was certain I would see them die. And I couldn't stand this feeling anymore.

I was tired of planning my life around my visions. I was so sick of not being able to live the way I wanted to live, and maybe I was exhausted. Exhausted by my life.

On some days, I even believed Mrs. Müller with her diagnosis. Maybe throughout the years, I had gotten a bit depressed because I wasn't sure how long I could continue living like this.

"How did you sleep?" Mrs. Müller looked at me the way one would look at an injured puppy.

"Bad," I grumbled quietly.

It was probably the first time since I started therapy that I'd answered one of her questions honestly. Even

Mrs. Müller must've realized that because I could see how a slight smile was twitching over her face.

"That's a great start," she said with a lowered voice. Maybe she was right and it was a proper start, but only for her; not for me.

"Did you have any more nightmares?" she continued with her questions after the silence that filled the white, cold room became unbearable.

I had to think about that question for a few seconds. If I was being honest, I couldn't even remember my dreams from last night. The only thing I could remember was having a weird feeling that kept me awake at night. It was an unfamiliar feeling that I couldn't describe in words, and I didn't know if it was a negative feeling either. However, it kept me awake, whatever that said about me.

"Not really," I answered, and observed the wrinkles that appeared on her forehead.

Before she could blame me for not being completely honest with her, otherwise, therapy wouldn't make much sense if I won't open up to her – especially since we had already made some progress in the right direction, according to her, and I had started to accept my problems – I added: "I can't remember my dreams recently. I slept poorly, but it wasn't my dream that kept me awake, I had trouble falling asleep."

The wrinkles on her forehead didn't vanish completely, and her glances seemed to be very critical, however, she looked happier than before.

Maybe I should stop trying to fight therapy. Maybe Mrs. Müller was right about everything. Maybe she was right I wasn't normal, and I needed help.

How could I even be okay?

I saw more people die in front of my eyes than others would see in their whole life. Maybe it was okay to not be okay. To be weak. To admit to having problems. Maybe it was okay to be confused. Maybe it was okay to cooperate during therapy, and it wouldn't mean being weak or anything like that. Maybe that was being strong?

Wasn't it strong to face your anxieties and admit to having problems in the first place? Wasn't it strong to work on yourself when the natural protection mechanisms of your body have failed and you couldn't repress all the emotions you've felt anymore?

I could even be happy about my body's horrible protection mechanisms because one ends up with more problems if the body was always repressing all the memories and feelings. I read some articles about dissociation on the internet, and this really didn't sound like it would be fun.

"I had such a strange feeling," I continued while looking at the ground.

From the corners of my eyes, I could see that Mrs. Müller's face lit up. It was the first time the therapy was successful, and I was cooperating with her.

"What kind of feeling?" she wanted to know.

I desperately tried to remember the feeling I had so I could somehow try to describe it or even figure out if it was positive or negative.

It took some time, but after some minutes, I could find the concentration that I needed to remember. I was thankful Mrs. Müller let me think in silence without asking any other stupid questions, like she always did when silence overtook the conversation.

I put my hands on my forehead as if it would make it easier for me to remember things, and started to breathe slowly and focused. It would probably be easier to remember if I would've had chewing gum. I once read that chewing gum could help one to remember things more easily. Of course, I could remember such bullshit, but I still couldn't remember the feeling that kept me awake at night.

I tried to breathe even slower and massaged my forehead, which was covered in black strains of hair. Then, finally, I remembered that strange feeling. It was a feeling of connecting, or a connection with somebody or something. A feeling that made my heart beat faster and my pulse race. A feeling of activity. Of being active. Of doing something.

The harder I tried to remember the feeling in more detail, the blurrier the memory got. So that in the end, I wasn't even sure if I was connected with anyone – it would be hilarious if it was that way anyway – or if there was another cause for my state of mind.

"It was a strange feeling," he started talking even though he wasn't ready to say anything yet.

Mrs. Müller looked at him with her eyes opened wide and her eyebrows raised. She was waiting for him to continue talking, but he didn't.

Silence.

Then, after an eternity, he raised his head like he was in a trance and looked Mrs. Müller straight in the eyes. He didn't know at all what he was doing. He had planned to be silent for as long as he was still unsure about what to say or how to explain that certain feeling. But something inside of him took over and controlled him.

"I had the feeling as if everything would end soon." As soon as these words left his mouth, his head fell on his chest and his eyes were closed.

Not even Mrs. Müller could respond to him, she was way too confused about all the things that had happened during this therapy session.

✳✳✳

"I feel like I was driven over by a truck," I greeted Tim, who has just entered my apartment.

"I'm also happy to see you," he said, grinning while throwing himself on my sofa.

I chuckled, shook my head, and took place next to him.

"So, what's popping?" he asked.

"Why do you think there is anything special going on?"

"Ramon, you probably won't believe me, but I know you for quite some time now… I realize if something is wrong."

"You probably know me better than I know myself," I said and sighed.

"That's you talking. I wouldn't have said it, but now that you said it, I can't argue with that," he laughed.

Sometimes it was hard to not be jealous of him. He was always so happy and cheerful. If it weren't for me, he could even be popular and have lots and lots of friends. But here he was. Wasting his time with me when he could go outside and do all these things regular people our age would do.

Instead, he drove to my place when I asked him to, was always ready to pick up my calls, and all in all, he was there for me whenever I needed him. I couldn't imagine a better best friend than him, but still, there were times I felt incredibly guilty about being friends with him. Tim could reach so much more in his life, and the only thing preventing him from doing so was me.

"I had a super odd therapy session today," I started explaining what was going on during that hour of therapy.

Additionally, I told him everything, even the one thing I didn't tell Mrs. Müller because I didn't feel comfortable sharing that information with her, knowing she would probably misinterpret it.

While my head was resting on my chest, I started to black out, but I could see one thing clearly in front of my eyes: Luana's face.

"Do you think it was another vision?"

Tim tried to understand what was going on.

"It was the weirdest vision I've ever had," I confirmed his theory.

"But she is dead. She can't die again," I continued, and observed Tim, who was staring at me with his eyes wide open. He looked shocked.

"Do you think you are about to die?" he asked surprisingly seriously, and it took me a few moments until I could realize that he was actually worried.

"I don't know… It's all so confusing. First, the weird feeling – "

"– The feeling you're about to die," Tim interrupted me.

"Then my odd behavior, and then Luana – "

"– Who has already died."

I just nodded silently.

"This does sound pretty much like dying, doesn't it?" I murmured quietly.

Tim didn't say anything.

He just looked at me in silence. It was uncommon for him to lack words to say. Since I knew him, he was always talkative and sarcastic. This was the very first time I saw him like that. The first time I could tell, he was desperately trying to find something to say. But it was understandable. I, myself, didn't know what to say or what to think either.

Every single one of my visions had led to the death of the person that was in it, but Luana couldn't die anymore. She was long gone. She was the first main character in one of my visions. It was the vision that started everything.

What if everything started with Luana, and now everything would end with her as well? It almost sounded plausible that another vision of her face would mark the end of my own life.

"Shit," Tim screamed after some time, he probably had the same thought as me.

"What are we going to do?" he asked me.

I shrugged.

"I don't know."

Silence.

"I really don't know… That's why I hoped you could tell me how ridiculous I sound and that it's all just bullshit."

I tried to sound calm, but I failed miserably. All I could do was hope that Tim didn't realize how shaky my voice was.

"All we can do is wait now, can't we?" Tim asked.

"I don't know."

This time, there was no chance he could overhear the shaking in my voice.

"But don't you think you would foresee your own death differently?" Tim thought out loud.

I didn't say anything because my answer would be another 'I don't know' which would not help the situation at all. Also, it felt like he was talking more to himself than to me anyway, so I didn't want to interrupt his monologue.

"I mean, you foresaw every death in extreme detail. Why should this differ when it comes to your own death? Also, maybe it's a good sign you saw Luana. Not everything has to be bad all the time. How could you even think about the feeling of having a connection with someone, and now you are so sure you are about to die? And are you certain you didn't just feel a special connection with Luana? I mean, it was her face you saw…"

His thoughts burst out of him, and again, I felt guilty about burdening him with my problems. My whole life was a burden. I was a burden. And if I would die now, everything would become worse. His reaction to my problems only proved that it was valid to distance myself from other humans as much as possible. No one deserved a friend like me. No one deserved to be burdened like that.

After checking his watch, Tim realized that he would again be late for one of his appointments. I could tell he didn't like the thought of leaving me alone for today, but I tried to subconsciously reassure him that I would be fine. Maybe I even needed to be alone to sort my thoughts.

It was not until Tim was gone that I realized how quiet it really was in my apartment. Usually, I didn't notice how lonely I was because my apartment has never felt as silent as it did in that moment. I didn't even feel like turning on the TV for some background noise. So, I decided to quickly grab the full trash bags that I had forgotten this morning and bring them down. After that, I could go to bed and sleep or something like that.

I opened the door to my apartment and carefully checked if I could hear any noises from the staircase. Nothing.

Quickly, I looked out of the window to see if anyone was on the street, but there was no one as well. The streets were completely empty. I didn't expect it to be different. It was 4 p.m. Most of my neighbors were still working at this time, except for maybe the old lady from the first floor. But she wasn't a problem for me. I could handle her.

I rushed down the stairs because I always needed to be aware of the fact that I could run into other people on the staircase. Even though it had always worked out so far, there was no guarantee it would always be that way in the future as well.

Unfortunately, I lost some time because I struggled to open the trash cans since I didn't want to take my time to put down my trash bags. In my thoughts, I cursed a lot and decided I would always take my time to open the trash cans properly in the future. I was about to go back inside the house when I heard a voice.

Quickly, I rushed back to the trash cans and hoped that the person who belonged to that voice didn't notice me. It must've been a visitor since the voice didn't sound familiar to me at all.

The voices came closer, and I tried to calm down by telling myself that there was no chance anybody could've seen me hide behind the trash cans. If they could see me, however, it would become a very awkward situation since I was ducking behind a trash can, trying not to be seen. If someone didn't know my story, they would expect me to be a creep.

While I was waiting for the voices to fade so I could get out of my hiding spot, I made amends with the fact that today was simply not my day. I would be able to go upstairs to my apartment eventually. But the voices didn't fade away, not even after five more minutes of waiting. Sometimes the original voice was interrupted by another voice, but none of the voices sounded like they were about to vanish into the house any time soon.

I tried to fight the urge to eavesdrop, but eventually I gave in. I didn't know the context of the conversation, but I could understand that these people weren't friends.

One of them was a girl, and the other was a boy, but it was impossible for me to tell their ages just by listening to them. They must've been older than children, but probably still younger than me. Both voices sounded unfamiliar, which confused me a little bit since I was sure I could tell the different tenants of this apartment complex apart just by their footsteps. But all of a sudden, the image of the moving truck that was parked on the street came to my mind.

There were new tenants. I didn't know these people, and neither did I know their voices. It was possible that one of these two people lived in this building and couldn't enter because they were trapped in a discussion with the other person.

I started to become impatient. It felt like the fight would never end, and I really didn't want to picture anyone else finding me between the trash cans. I would look like the biggest stalker ever and would have to move apartments. Maybe even towns. And I really didn't need any additional stress in my life.

The longer I had to wait, the more curious I became. I wanted to know who was debating in front of our front door. Who even wanted to loudly discuss anything in the front yard at 4 p.m.? 4 p.m. was such an odd time to arrive back home... Damn, why didn't I think of it before? It must've been teenagers that came home from school.

If I would ever make it upstairs again, I should write this down urgently. In the future, I would need to be aware of the fact that I could encounter people at a time when I used to feel safe.

Even though everything in my head was fighting against it, a small part of my brain thought it was good enough to check out the people whose voices I was hearing. Carefully, I pushed my head through the gaps between the trash cans to get a better view.

As I had already guessed, there was a girl and a boy, both aged between 16 and 19 years. I wasn't completely sure about their age since I've always been horrible at guessing people's age.

The guy was tall, sporty, and his blond hair was styled perfectly. I couldn't see his face because his back was turned in my direction while he was facing the girl that was standing in front of him.

The girl was almost one head smaller than the guy. She had long brown hair and ... No, that was impossible. This couldn't be true. I was going crazy. There was no other explanation than me being insane.

Out of shock, I lost my balance and almost knocked over the trash cans. The girl... She looked exactly the same as Luana, and weirdly enough, there was no doubt in me that it wasn't her.

Chapter 4

After yesterday, I wasn't keen on spending another day in the school building. Accordingly, I woke up listless. I didn't even bother putting any effort into doing my hair or my choice of clothing. There was nobody I wanted to impress at school, and I didn't need to impress myself.

"Join us, newbie!" Julius shouted from the other end of the entrance hall when I entered the building.

Annoyed, I walked in the direction of the only people in this school that I had talked to.

"First of all, you'll never shout through the whole school that I should join you. It's still my decision whether I want to join you or not. And secondly, you'll never call me 'newbie' again because it makes you sound stupid," I hissed at him.

"No need to get your claws out, kitten."

He laughed, however, it felt like he gained some respect and realized that he couldn't talk to me like that.

"You're back," Jane figured out unhappily.

I just nodded in silence because I had no clue what exactly she wanted to communicate by saying that.

"How should we call you, by the way?" Julius wanted to know.

I would prefer to not even be talked to by him, but I didn't say that out loud. Some thoughts were meant to stay in my head. I decided I would try to be as friendly as possible with him until I would find other friends because something told me I would never get rid of him otherwise.

"Just call me Luna."

"So. Your name is Luna," a familiar voice repeated my name.

Out of reflex, I turned around.

"Finn," I figured out.

"Why didn't you tell us your name yesterday already?" he asked.

"Because yesterday you guys were too busy talking about me waiting in front of history class," I answered neutrally.

"Okay, fair enough," he started and smiled.

"This is probably not the best way to get to know someone," he laughed, and scratched the back of his head.

"Happens."

I glanced at my schedule to figure out where I would have to go next.

"Awesome, I have art class too," Julius exclaimed with joy.

Great.

As already expected, he didn't leave me alone for the next two hours, and even for the rest of the day, he was always by my side. Like we were glued to one another. I've never been that annoyed by anybody that quickly. Especially after he insisted on bringing me home after school, I lost my temper. I couldn't even pinpoint what annoyed me, but he simply annoyed me. Something in the way that he behaved made me believe that he probably wasn't unsuccessful with other female students, but that wouldn't change the fact that I simply couldn't stand him.

I tried to explain that I didn't want to spend that much time with him, but this just seemed to confirm his belief that he was great and wonderful, and that I was totally into him. I had no clue how he could understand my annoyance that way. He was definitely wrong. But the fact that he insisted that I liked him made me furious.

Eventually, I was able to make my way up to the fourth floor. This was too much to handle for just one day.

✳✳✳

After some time had passed, I realized that school was different if you were friends with Finn. People were looking at you differently, and in general, it was easier to talk to the other students in our year.

Jane and her other girlfriends were kind, but I guess that was just because Finn personally forced them to be polite. He was the only person in my year who was close to me calling him a friend. The others were strangers. Strangers that I would sometimes interact with in superficial conversations.

However, one could say that my start at the new school could've been worse. And even though everything was working out somehow, I felt lost and misplaced. Like I didn't belong.

Sometimes, I even felt sorry for Finn since he – and Julius but I won't count him – was friendly from the start and believed that the moody person, aka me, could be fun to hang out with even though I gave him plenty of reasons to not think that way about me. If it wasn't for Finn, I would probably be an outsider without a group of 'friends' to hang out with during break times. It's not that I would've minded, but… It was better to hang out with Finn and his friends, I had to admit.

As some time had passed, I had encountered the other tenants in our apartment complex, and every single one of them seemed friendly and welcoming. I was fascinated by the people in this city since they were super different from the people in our old town. I barely knew our neighbors back there, and if I knew them, I never said more than a 'Hi' as a greeting.

Here, it was almost impossible to not be caught up in a short conversation about just anything. I didn't have to talk to the woman living on the third floor for long until she told me that she owned a small Mexican restaurant on the other side of town and even invited me to come there. The couple, living on the second floor, was together for almost eternity. That was why they decided to become parents of a small dog since it didn't work out for them to have a baby. Besides them, I already knew the old lady from the first floor since my very first day here.

The only person in this house that I didn't know was the young man from the fifth floor, and I started doubting his existence. I didn't care much about him, but it was strange that the old lady talked about him, and I had never seen him. And the stranger a thing or a person was, the more interesting it became. Confusing people were more interesting than normal ones. But after not finding any evidence that he existed, my doubts grew stronger.

It was Friday, the 13th, and I just walked home from school. My mother wasn't in town because she was on a spontaneous business trip. I was actually looking forward to the weekend.

Finn had already promised me to come by on Saturday because he knew that I wasn't feeling 100 percent comfortable in the new apartment yet; this feeling would be even worse now that I was alone at home. The first evening and the first night I had to spend alone, though.

On my way home, the sky had already become cloudier and darker, so I was certain it was about to rain. I even hurried up so I wouldn't have to walk through the rain and eventually become wet.

In front of the main entrance to the apartment complex, I looked into my bags to find my keys. When I couldn't immediately find the keys, I started to become more and more panicky. I couldn't have forgotten my keys. That was impossible. This couldn't be happening. My mom would never leave me at home unsupervised again, but what was even worse was the fact that I had no clue where else to go.

I frantically emptied the pockets of my jacket, but all I could find were some used tissues and an empty package of chewing gum. No key.

Slightly stressed I walked around the building, but it looked like nobody else was at home. The couple from the second floor was on a trip for the weekend – they had told me about that last week – and the other windows of the building were dark. There was no light.

Since it was already dark outside because of the upcoming rain, I would expect people to have their lights turned on to be able to see. No light, no people. And that meant no one could open the door for me and let me inside. Desperately, I went back to the entrance and leaned against the front door. After some time, I realized that I was sliding down further and further and eventually found myself sitting on the dark and probably dirty doormat.

In the meantime, it had started to rain. How predictable. The rain started as a drizzle, but eventually it rained cats and dogs. I could feel how I got wetter and wetter since the little roof on top of the door wasn't meant to keep away all of the rain. My clothes were cold and stuck to my skin. My hair was completely soaked, and my makeup was probably running down my face. I looked pitiful and not pretty at all.

It got colder and colder, and I wondered how long I would have until I would die of hypothermia. A glance at my phone told me that I had been sitting in the pouring rain for over an hour, and I had no clue when or if someone would find me. If I wouldn't have had my phone, I would've lost all track of time, but a look at my battery warned me that it wouldn't last for much longer. Desperately, I rested my head on top of my angled knees, so I couldn't see anything anymore.

"What horrible weather to sit outside," an unfamiliar voice said.

Slowly, I raised my head to try to figure out who was talking to me, but it was impossible to say for sure since the light was bad and all I could see was the silhouette of someone.

"Pfff," I just answered.

"Or are you going for a near-death experience?" the stranger wanted to know.

Even though I didn't feel like laughing at that moment, I simply had to laugh.

"Neither," I responded.

"Should I let you inside?" the person asked, and almost sounded worried.

I nodded, stood up, and made space so the stranger could open the door. I only realized who I was talking to while I was following the stranger through the poorly lit staircase.

There was no one in this building that I didn't know. Only the guy from the fifth floor. My stranger must've been the mysterious guy from upstairs.

When I arrived in front of the door that led to my apartment, my worst fear was confirmed. I hadn't simply left the key in the lock. I must've forgotten it in the apartment. Suddenly, all my hopes of spending the night in my room vanished.

Damn. This was not my day.

"Shit," I cursed.

"Are you okay?" the stranger asked.

"Besides the fact that I'll spend the night on the doormat in front of my apartment, I'm fine."

The stranger laughed for a second, then he got quiet as if he had to think about what to say next.

"Don't you have a spare key below the doormat or something like that?"

"Nope. Apparently, my mom didn't think about how dumb her daughter could possibly be," I responded and sighed.

The stranger hesitated.

"Do you want to come upstairs? I can give you dry clothes. If we're lucky, we can reach the landlord. Maybe he has a key to your apartment," he proposed slowly.

While we were talking about dilemmas in philosophy class, I would've never imagined that I would end up in a dilemma like that. I didn't know that guy; he could be a murderer or something like that.

I had learned as a child that I should never follow anyone to their home. But on the other hand, I needed to get out of my wet clothes. I wasn't keen on catching a cold. And there was the possibility of being able to receive help from the landlord.

If I would sleep in front of the door, there was no chance of getting back into the apartment. And the most convincing – and least important argument – I was curious to see the strange guy from the fifth floor, and now that I had finally met him, I wanted to know what he looked like. Who knew when or if I would ever see him again if I would stay in front of our locked door.

"Do you have the phone number of the landlord?" I asked.

"Does this mean you'll come upstairs with me?"

I nodded and followed him up the stairs.

"Do you need dry clothes?" he asked without any emotion in his voice.

"I don't know," I answered more insecurely than anything.

I let him take my bag out of my hands, which were holding on to it as if my life depended on it. While he was doing that, our fingers touched for a brief moment.

"You feel very cold," he discovered.

"Do you need a hot shower to warm up again?" he asked.

I didn't respond, but I let him push me in the direction of the bathroom while he handed me some of his dry clothes.

I locked the bathroom door behind me and carefully stepped under the shower. I still had no clue who that guy was or what he looked like.

All I could tell from the way his bathroom looked was that he lived alone.

I only realized how cold I was while standing under the shower. Even the normal water temperature felt way too hot. The warm water ran down my arm and left a trace of heat behind. However, it got better quickly. When I was done warming up, I got dressed and hung up my wet clothes so they could dry.

The stranger brought me a mug full of tea after he saw me leave the bathroom and gestured that I should sit down on his couch.

"I couldn't reach the landlord, unfortunately. But if you want to, I can try again in like 30 minutes," he started.

Finally, I could take a closer look at the mysterious neighbor. He had a young-looking face, younger than I had expected. It made guessing his age impossible, though. I couldn't even tell if he was around my age or older (I mean, he must've been older since he was living on his own). Additionally, he had black hair that was a little bit shortened on the sides of his head but longer and curlier on top of his head. To sum it up, it was the most basic haircut one could imagine for a guy around my age. His hair seemed a little bit messy since some strains of hair curled up on his forehead, but it looked like it was exactly the look he was going for. His eyes were a huge contrast to his dark hair. They were blue. A bright blue that made you doubt if they were blue or grey. He was wearing huge glasses that made him look even younger and nerdier than he probably was.

All I could tell was that he didn't look like a criminal or a murderer. He looked innocent and confused. Clueless somehow. But he didn't look bad. More like the opposite.

"Thanks," I whispered, and smiled at him.

"No problem. You're not the only person that has ever forgotten their keys."

He smiled as well.

"You too?" I asked confused.

Somehow, I couldn't imagine something so ordinary and, at the same time, so stupid happening to this guy. He was everything but ordinary.

"Yes, even I had the experience of leaving my keys in the apartment and not being able to reach anyone. The only difference is that I had to sleep in front of my door," he said, and slowly ran his fingers through his hair.

"At least you didn't have to worry about someone being a potential murderer."

He laughed.

"True. But did you really think of me as a potential murderer?" his voice became more serious in the end.

"A little bit," I admitted. "I mean, I don't know you. Today is the first time in my life that I'm talking to you, and until I came out of the shower, I didn't even know what your face looked like. I don't know anything about you, not even your name. Of course, I must be extremely careful," I tried to explain my point of view to him without being offensive.

His facial expression changed in a way that I couldn't read. However, I would understand if he was feeling offended. Nobody wanted to be judged as a potential murderer.

Silence overcame us, and the stranger looked like he was fighting with himself about what to do next.

"My name is Ramon," he said cold and dismissive.

"I'm Luna, by the way," I just said because I didn't know what else to say.

Again, we were quiet.

The chill and almost fun atmosphere was completely gone, and it felt like the ice age had come over his cozy living room. The silence in the room started to feel incredibly uncomfortable, so I frantically thought of a way to escape.

Finn.

"I think I quickly call my boyfriend," I tried to break the silence. "He isn't my boyfriend, like a boyfriend. He is just a regular friend-friend, but he is a boy…"

I stuttered and immediately realized how ridiculous I must've sounded by clarifying that I wasn't dating Finn. Ramon probably couldn't care less about my dating life, and even if he did, it was none of his business.

Still embarrassed about my behavior, I cleared my throat and added: "However, he might be able to pick me up."

"Okay," Ramon just said.

Nothing more.

Inexplicably, this reaction made me mad. I completely embarrassed myself in front of him due to my insecurities, and all he could respond was 'okay'.

Okay.

OKAY.

To avoid him seeing my anger, I stood up and went into the hallway of his apartment before I grabbed my phone to call Finn. It was only when I wanted to turn it on that I remembered my empty battery.

"My battery died," I said as casually as possible while going back into his living room.

I had no clue what caused his mood to change like that, but if he thought he had to be cold and dismissive, I could simply do the same. Somehow, his behavior didn't fit his appearance.

"Do you know the phone number of your friend-friend by heart?"

I thought about his question and was about to shake my head when I repeated the question in my head again.

"Are you making fun of me?"

"Never. I wouldn't dare to do that," his voice was full of sarcasm.

I observed him carefully and tried to read from his facial expressions if he was being dismissive again or if he was back to being friendly.

"What I dare to say is, however, that these wrinkles on your forehead make you look at least 15 years older," he added.

Now I was sure that the coldness in his voice was gone, and he was loosening up again.

"Damn, I wish someone would've told me three years ago. Then I wouldn't have needed a fake ID to buy alcohol," I countered.

He chuckled, which proved my theory of him not being dismissive anymore.

"I think you can use my cable to charge your battery," he said, and plugged his cable into my phone. Not much later, my phone was charged enough for it to be turned on again.

Relieved I looked for Finn's number in my contact list and called him. The phone beeped five times until he picked it up.

"What's up?" he asked and sounded out of breath.

"I could ask you the same thing. Are you okay?" I wanted to know.

He sounded like he really had trouble breathing. But maybe I just wanted to not focus on my stupidity for some more seconds.

"I'm fine. I just came home from jogging. But tell me, what's wrong with you?" he requested.

"Promise me you'll not laugh at me or tell anyone else."

"I promise," he said, and I could picture him sitting on the other end of the call with a wide grin.

He always grinned widely when he realized something made me uncomfortable. While I was panicking, he was always calm. But maybe he just liked to grin because he grinned a lot, from what I could tell.

"I surpassed my stupidity. I left my keys at home," I started.

"Shit. What are you doing now?" he asked, and I could hear that he was trying to suppress a laugh.

"Now I'm standing in the hallway of my neighbor, and I have no clue how I should get back home," I explained.

"Should I pick you up?" he asked immediately.

"That would be awesome."

"When does your mom come back from her trip?" he wanted to know.

"Sunday afternoon," I sighed.

"Okay, give me a min," he said, and I could hear that he was asking his mother if it was okay for me to sleep over until Sunday.

"It's fine. I'm coming to pick you up now," he hung up so fast, I couldn't even respond anything.

Not too long after the call had ended, the doorbell rang. Ramon opened the door, and Finn ran upstairs. It confused me a little bit that he bothered coming up all the way until the fifth floor, when it was so much easier to wait in the car.

"So, you are Luna's … "

Ramon started and paused for a moment as if he was choosing his next words carefully, "Friend."

He ended his sentence and winked at me in a way that only I could notice.

I was grateful he wasn't calling Finn my 'boyfriend' or even worse, my 'friend-friend' because then I would've had to explain myself and I was in enough trouble for today.

"Yes, that's me. I guess," Finn responded happily. Then he turned to me: "Shall we?"

I nodded.

When I followed Finn to the door, I quickly whispered a brief "thank you" to Ramon.

"No problem. And have fun with your friend-friend," I could hear him say before I followed Finn down the stairs.

"Was this guy the mysterious neighbor the woman from the first floor meant?" Finn asked me curiously when we sat in the car.

"Yes, it was the neighbor," I responded.

Of course, I had told Finn about the awkward encounter with the lady from the first floor. He was the only person I would talk to about absolutely everything, which also included odd encounters with neighbors.

"He seems to be a nice guy," he stated.

I laughed.

"If you ask me, he has some severe mood switches," I murmured.

"What did he do?" Finn wanted to know.

I already expected him to ask further questions, but I didn't want to talk about it at the moment, so I briefly tried to sum up his change in behavior.

"Hm…" Finn said, "He seems to be a mysterious guy."

He laughed.

"Who knows what skeletons he hides in his closet," I joked.

But one thing I had to admit, Ramon did look handsome somehow.

"Really? You think he looks handsome?" Finn looked at me with open eyes.

Damn. Did I think out loud?

"Eyes on the road!" I demanded to distract him from the awkward situation.

Immediately his eyes wandered back toward the road.

"Real talk, why do you think he is handsome?" he asked further.

I thought about it for a moment, then I responded: "I don't know. He just doesn't look like everybody else, I guess."

"He looks unremarkable."

"So what? I'm unremarkable as well and that never bothered you."

"That's something else," he rumbled, and stared overly concentrated on the road.

We stayed quiet for the rest of the trip, but as soon as we arrived at his place, our weird conversation from the car was already forgotten, and he was back to normal.

He introduced me to his parents, whom I didn't even know until that day, even though it wasn't the first time I was visiting him. In general, it felt strange that I'd never met them before since I was hanging out a lot at Finn's place lately. They seemed to be pretty busy people.

The weekend at Finn's place was fun and a nice variation in comparison to the previous weekends that I spent mainly alone. I was spending a lot of time at Finn's place during the week, but it was mostly to study for the upcoming exams. Unfortunately, this weekend had to pass like every other weekend.

On Sunday afternoon, Finn drove me back home, and I decided I should finish the homework Finn and I didn't do in the last two days – which was all of them. Before I started doing my homework, I threw Ramon's clothes in the washing machine.

After they were washed, I made my way upstairs to the fifth floor. He probably already missed his clothes and maybe even regretted lending them to me.

I knocked on the door, so he knew I was standing in front of his apartment and not in front of the door downstairs. But nothing happened. Nobody opened. Even though I was sure he was at home since I heard footsteps in his apartment not so long ago.

I knocked again; this time louder, so I could be sure he heard me.

No reaction. Again.

"Ramon. I know that you are home," I said while I knocked on his door for a third time.

Finally, I heard fast steps heading in my direction. Then the door opened.

"What do you want?" he asked obviously annoyed.

He observed me skeptically.

Grrrr. Pettiness got the best of me. Two people could play this game, and I could play it better than he could ever.

I put on my friendliest – almost creepily friendly – smile and said: "I just wanted to bring back your clothes. It was super nice that you lend them to me. I even wash …- "

I couldn't even finish my sentence because, while I was friendly rambling, Ramon grabbed his neatly folded clothes and closed the door in front of me. He didn't even thank me for bringing them.

My plan to kill him with kindness, so he had no other choice than to either feel guilty for being an ass or to be friendly as well, didn't work at all. But I didn't need to deal with that.

It didn't take long for my pride to come back to me, and I turned around and walked downstairs without looking back.

It's not like he would've seen it or even cared, but I felt a bit better about myself after this grand exit. I felt a little less humiliated. If he thought he needed to treat me like that, fine. I would treat him the same from now on.

Chapter 5

I Was an idiot. A huge idiot. First, I couldn't stop myself from taking her into my apartment, and then I even told her my damn name. But what else was I supposed to do? I couldn't have walked past her and entered the staircase without paying any attention to her.

I mean, I could've done that, but that would've been pretty shitty of me. Maybe it would have been the better alternative for everyone, though.

But the worst part was not taking her into my apartment and endangering her to my visions. No, the worst part was me dumbass telling her my name. Something that … personal.

A name is some kind of connection between two humans. Knowing someone's name meant that you knew the person or at least wanted to meet them again. Of course, I would love to see her again to further investigate the connection between her and Luana, since not only did their names sound similar, but they resembled each other visually as well. But I couldn't risk it. I didn't want to watch her die a second time. I simply couldn't do that.

It had been years since I had told someone my name – which was probably because no one had asked me for it in quite some time – but I didn't plan on changing that. And then came she. It was so ridiculously dangerous. I could've had a vision so easily.

So many thoughts were filling my head. I needed to change something. Urgently. So, I decided I needed to be colder and dismissive toward her. It wasn't easy because I could tell by her facial expressions that my behavior hurt her, and I didn't want to be an asshole, so I changed back to being friendly. She would be picked up, and I would never see her again. Especially not when I would be more careful to avoid her in the future. Or even move towns. Or just houses.

So, when she knocked on my door a few days later, I decided to ignore it, hoping she would give up and just go back home. But it felt like she knew that I was there. There was nowhere for me to hide from her, so I opened the door. Even though it wasn't particularly nice – and it was so damn difficult to be cold and untouched by the situation – I didn't say a word. I remained silent, let her do the talking, grabbed my clothes, and went back into my apartment. I closed the door behind me and took a deep breath.

It took so much of my strength to be like this because I usually wasn't an asshole. More like the opposite; I cared too much for people too quickly. And just like that, I had a bad conscience. Even though I knew it was the best for her. For me. For everyone.

Again, I realized how quiet my apartment was. It was lonely. As lonely as my life.

Maybe I should check on her. I could open the door and check if she was still there. I could apologize. I could even try to explain to her why I behaved the way I did, and maybe she would be understanding. Maybe she would also understand why it would be better for her to stay away from me, or she would make the decision that she wouldn't care about the dangers and occasionally talk to me if we met on the staircase.

I carefully opened the door, but I was too late; she was already gone. She decided to walk away without knowing the other options. Because I didn't tell her anything useful. Because I prevented her from knowing all the possible decisions she could've made.

Now I felt even worse than before.

Why was everything I was doing always wrong? Probably because there was more to a situation than simply being right or wrong, and sometimes it was even harder to distinguish than other times. In the same way, dreams and reality were blurring into each other, sometimes right and wrong could become a big blur as well.

Maybe Mrs. Müller was right, and my visions were just dreams that seemed a bit too close to reality. Or maybe I was the problem, and I had issues distinguishing my dreams from reality. Maybe after all, I was just mentally ill. Was that the hard truth? There was nothing that would debunk this theory, was there? The sound of the doorbell interrupted my thoughts. Confused, I went to the intercom to listen if someone was saying something.

"Ramon, it's me," Tim said.

"Can you get the mail?" I answered, and still confused pressed the button that would open the door downstairs. He was way earlier than I expected him to be.

It didn't take Tim long to reach the fifth floor, and he really brought the mail. In his hand, he held two letters, which he almost shoved into my face as a greeting.

"Thank you," I whispered.

Tim was such a huge help in my daily life. And it bothered me so much that there was no way I could ever repay him. There were days when he went grocery shopping for me because I didn't feel well enough. My fear of having a vision ruled my whole life, and Tim was the one person paying for that.

He also had the key to my mailbox, so he could grab the letters during his visits. It was really helpful, so I didn't have to lose any time on the staircase and could avoid meeting people more easily. With Tim's help, I could even avoid encounters with the lady from the first floor. He would do anything to prevent me from meeting anyone, and I... What exactly was I doing for him?

Except for keeping him in my life, there was nothing I did for him. I probably was a really shitty human and an even shittier friend. But to be fair, if there was anything I could do to change my current living situation, I would do it without hesitating. Simply so I could give back what he did for me.

"Do you want to read the letters now or later?" he asked curiously.

"They are probably not that important anyway," I said.

"I'm not sure about that. How often does your Grandma write you a letter?"

I raised my eyebrows without even knowing it.

In answer to my unspoken question, Tim handed me one of the two letters so I could see the name and address of the sender.

To my surprise, I had to realize that they were in fact identical to the ones of my Grandma.

Confused, I stared at the envelope until I couldn't detect anymore where the letters started and where they ended because everything became a blurry, un-recognizable mess.

"My Grandma never mails me," I murmured.

"That's exactly what I've thought as well," Tim answered.

"Do you think something bad happened?" I asked unnecessarily.

Why in this universe should Tim know that?

"I hope not."

My hands were shaking when I opened the envelope. Immediately, I could sense the smell of my Grand-ma's favorite perfume. Now there were no doubts anymore; she must've written this letter.

I carefully unfolded the blue paper and started to read while I tried to ignore the fact that Tim attempted to secretly read the letter as well.

Dear Ramon,

you will probably be confused because I never write to you but do not worry. At the end of this letter, you will understand everything.

How reassuring.

When you receive this letter, you must know that my time on this earth will come to an end. It might have already ended then.

What does she mean? Why should her time be over? She wasn't that old, and as far as I could tell, she was perfectly healthy. Or could she mean something other than death?

You will probably have a lot of questions, which I, unfortunately, will not be able to answer. At least not in the way you would deserve.

Again, what was that supposed to mean? Everything in that letter confused me even more. Maybe I should call her and demand an explanation. It would be so much easier to understand if she wouldn't write in a goddamn riddle. Why couldn't she write something more understandable? It would make it so much easier to follow her thoughts.

That is why I will leave something behind for you, which should be able to explain everything to you. Be patient and hold on.
It will feel almost like I will explain everything to you, even though I will be gone from this earth until then. How do I know this, you might wonder? Well, I cannot fully explain myself since it would cost too much time. Time, which I do not have. But I will try to summarize the situation.
There are more things on this earth that you do not understand and even think of as being impossible. You have always been a special boy, Ramon, but you know that already.

The only things making me special were my visions but how should she know? It was impossible she could know about them because, in my family, I had only told my mother about them, and she took this secret to the grave. But for the tiny chance that she could've known about my visions… Was she trying to tell me that I wasn't hallucinating? That everything I saw was real, and I wasn't insane, at least not yet? Maybe she could've helped me to live an ordinary life.

And in the way that you had a gift, I did too.

Okay, no doubt, she definitely knew about my visions. But who told her?

But this is not the only secret I kept from the world. The whole history of our family is full of secrets. And these secrets lured them into town. Beware of them! They are dangerous. They will come and get me and look through the mansion.

That is why I ask you politely to stay away from the mansion after my passing. They will not hurt ordinary humans because they are of no use to them. But you are not ordinary; they will harm you. You are only allowed to get to the mansion after you receive your inheritance and can answer all your questions. Then, and only then, can you stop them.

Stop who?

I have to hurry now. I can hear them already.
Best wishes,
Your Grandma

"Wow, that's what I would call a surprise," Tim said, and whistled impressed through his teeth.

"What the …– "

That was all I could say after this letter. It felt like my head was empty.

Silence.

Somehow, neither Tim nor I could figure out what to do with this letter. I would've even thought of it as a prank if I wasn't 100 percent sure that the letter was, in fact, written by my Grandma. But there was no doubt about her being the sender. She must've written the letter.

"I'll call her," I said all of a sudden.

But before I could get anywhere close to the telephone, Tim jumped up and blocked the way in front of me.

"Stop! You can't do that. Who knows what kind of people your Grandma talks about in her letter, and if they really wanted something from her, they might want you too? And I bet they have ultramodern technologies, so they might be able to trace the call back to you and …– "

"… and then one day they'll ring my doorbell?"

I snorted scornfully.

"I just don't think your Grandma would want you to call."

Tim had just ended his sentence when my telephone started to ring. I smirked briefly about this coincidence, then I picked it up.

"Ramon?"

I could hear the voice of my father on the other side of the phone.

"Dad? What's up? I thought we already talked yesterday, am I wrong?" I answered confused.

Usually, he called me once per week. He was a pretty busy guy who never took his time to rest from work, and that was why it was always hard for me to call him; he just wasn't there a lot.

"You're not wrong. Listen, kid, something happened…" he started talking, and it was just then that I realized his voice sounded shocked and sad at the same time. Without further asking, I knew what must've happened.

"What happened?" I still asked.

"It's about your Grandma, " he said.

Damn.

Her death was just another piece of evidence that the letter was real, and written by her. She didn't lie about passing away; she could somehow tell that it was her time to go. And now she would leave something that would help explain not just the letter but everything to me.

Finally, I would be able to understand what was wrong with me or why I've always been different than the others. I would get in control of my little 'problem' and be able to start over. I would be able to live the ordinary life I had always dreamed of. No visions anymore. No therapy. I could be around people, I could go grocery shopping, or just go for a walk outside. I could get to know other humans and even travel. I would move, maybe even out of the country, and completely start over somewhere else where no one knew me.

Whatever it was my Grandma would pass on to me, it gave me hope. Hope I never knew I had. But at what cost? Did she really have to die so I could start living? My happiness would always be built on her grave.

My father cleared his throat, then he continued talking.

"She died this morning," he ended his sentence.

"Shit," I cursed.

That was all I could say. Even though I knew what had happened beforehand and was prepared to hear the news… It wasn't easy to accept what had now become reality. Even though I was prepared, it still felt different now that it was said out loud. Because when something was said out loud, it became real, and if it was real, then she was irrevocably gone forever.

"I'm so sorry you have to find it out like this," my father continued.

"It's okay," I tried to calm him down.

It seemed like he was upset enough that he didn't even realize the shaking in my voice because otherwise he probably would've commented on it or – what I thought was equally probable – he thought it was okay to be weak.

My father had always been more sensitive than others, which was why he had hoped I would not become like him. He hoped I would grow mentally stronger and be able to suppress my feelings and emotions. I had to become strong enough for the both of us. That's why our relationship was cordial but also a bit distant, which didn't change anything about the fact that he loved me more than anything else (especially since the death of my mother).

"I want to drive to the mansion tonight. Your aunts come as well, and I thought... Maybe you want to join us?"

I already dreaded this question. Now I was trapped in a dilemma. On the one hand, I would love to go back to the mansion. I mean, this place was the paradise of my childhood and the only place in this world where I always felt safe. Additionally, I would love to say goodbye to my Grandma in person. She has been a wonderful woman and an even better role model.

She always took her time for me and was always by my side. Since my mother's death, she has become like a second mother to me. When I struggled with nightmares, she sat down on my bed and read fairytales to me out of an old storybook. Even though I was already nine years old, it calmed me down to listen to these stories from a better and unhurt world.

On the other hand, however, was my Grandma's letter. She had warned me from God knows who and begged me not to get any closer to the mansion. And I believed her. She wouldn't make up stuff like this. Not now. Not before her precisely foreshadowed death.

Also, I hadn't been to the mansion since Luana's death. My Grandma always came over to our place. I never visited her.

"I don't think it would make sense for me to suddenly get there. I haven't been there in years..." I started.

"Don't worry. It's perfectly fine," my father said gently. "If you need someone to talk to, you can always call me", he offered.

Then we said our goodbyes. He had a long way to drive, so he needed to prepare everything for that journey.

I sighed when I put my telephone back on the little drawer cabinet.

Tim gave me a questioning look.

"She is dead," I answered shortly.

I couldn't and I didn't want to say more about it. It was a fact. One that you couldn't find any euphemisms for. She had died. She was gone. Erased. Forever. Like almost everyone else I had ever cared about.

By now, I should've gotten used to the fact that every human that was important to me would die sooner or later. It was almost a miracle that Tim and my father were still alive.

"Exactly like she predicted it," Tim said more to himself than to me.

I needed to convince Tim multiple times that I was feeling okay according to the circumstances before he left me alone.

Immediately, I went into my bedroom. It was by far the smallest room in my apartment and consisted only of my 140-cm bed and a huge bookshelf that stretched along two walls. There was no space for more furniture.

Before I let myself fall on the bed, my hand unerringly grabbed one of the books. I sighed and took a closer look at the book in my hand. To be fair, it wasn't really a book. It was one of the uncountable number of travel guides that I owned.

I liked travel guides, and maybe I was the only human on this earth that didn't buy them for traveling but for reading. I read them simply because I knew I would never be able to travel to these countries, but in my mind, I've seen them all. I was allowed to dream, and in this case, dreams were all that I had. I was allowed to dream about the white beaches, the blue oceans, the colorful houses, and the foreign cultures; and if you closed your eyes and thought about what you just read, it almost felt like you were there yourself.

At least I thought so. I couldn't know how traveling would really feel.

But if my Grandma was right and I could get my life under control, then... I realized that I smiled at the thought of it. Maybe my life would be normal soon. Or at least closer to normal than before.

***

"How are you doing today?" Mrs. Müller asked at the beginning of the session, like she always did.

It wasn't particularly creative, but I could understand it was a desperate attempt to get myself to answer honestly. Since the session I saw Luana, I've closed up even more than before, which made her struggle even harder trying to engage me in a conversation. She didn't even bother hiding her disappointment about my behavior.

"I've felt better in the past," I answered, because I was sure she would already know about the death of my Grandma. Lying would only make things worse.

"I'm so sorry about what happened to your Grandma," she said empathetically.

"We all die one day."

My answer was cold and short. I didn't need her pity. In general, I didn't need anyone's pity. Why would we pity the relatives of someone who had died anyway? They weren't the ones who lost their lives.

The relatives have lost a human they might've loved, some people try to fill this hole that was left for the rest of their lives and start to drink or smoke, but the point was that they could continue living. Their life wasn't over, even if they decided it was.

They could still do all the things they wanted to do, and the only thing that prevented them from doing so was not the death of a person they loved; it was their own choice.

The people who weren't spiraling downward, will eventually find other humans that they can laugh and cry with. They'll simply replace the dead person.

The person that died, however, cannot do anything or decide anything. They were ripped out of their life, mostly surprisingly and way too early, and maybe even had some unfulfilled dreams and wishes but failed to fulfill them because of their death. Then they have to observe how they are being replaced, how the other relatives are fighting each other for money and inheritance, or simply growing apart because the dead person held them all together.

Both parties suffer equally, but it won't change the fact that death is inevitable and will happen to all of us. And especially people around me were at higher risk of dying early. This fact made it even harder for me to understand the sudden pity from Mrs. Müller.

Mrs. Müller, however, interpreted my answer differently and concluded everything according to her diagnosis of me.

"Did you have any nightmares or suicidal thoughts recently?" she wanted to know.

Sometimes it felt like depression was her favorite topic. She loved talking about it so much that I wondered if she secretly was the one who was depressed and not me. Her behavior didn't feel normal to me, but then again, what even was normal?

After I answered her question more or less honestly, the time was already up. That was probably the best thing that day.

When he arrived home, a package was already waiting for him in front of his apartment door. He took a closer look until he realized there was a small letter glued to the side of the box.

Unfortunately, I couldn't give it to you in person, but I have to go back to work. Your Grandma wanted you to have this asap. P.S. I didn't open it, but it seems to be important.

He recognized the handwriting of his father immediately and realized that he was sad he didn't see him briefly. Even though he always tried to tell himself it was for the best to keep him away, it was the first time he could feel how much he really missed his father.

He clamped the package below his armpit and entered his apartment. He was pretty nervous when he got the scissors from the kitchen. He knew that no matter what was in the box, it would be the key to an ordinary life. He took a deep breath and started to cut the package open. He was surprised by how well his Grandma sealed the package, making him feel that whatever he was about to find in the box must be helpful.

Also, she wanted to make sure that only he would be the one to open the box. Suddenly, he felt hopeful. It must've been important to her, and if it was important, it must've been able to answer all of his questions.

Only a few seconds separate him from the content of the package. What would he find inside? It could be a letter, a diary, books, or other documents. Something that would explain everything.

When he unfolded the endings of the box, he couldn't hide his grin anymore. His life would make a 180-degree turn, that was for sure, and no matter what was in that box, it would help him do so.

He carefully picked up a thing that was wrapped in blue velvet and unwrapped it.

In his hands was now a thick book. He could only see the back of the book, so he was excited when he turned it around to read the title: *Princesses, fairies, and pirates - my favorite fairytales.*

Chapter 6

"And then he just shut his door right in front of me," I ended the story of my last encounter with Ramon.

"If you ask me, he's not worth being angry about," Finn said while running his fingers through his hair. "Actually, you shouldn't even waste a single thought on him," he continued.

I swallowed.

I knew he was right, but something deep inside of me prevented me from simply forgetting about him. He was confusing, and confusing was interesting. Period. I couldn't do anything against it.

Also, it wasn't like I would like him a lot or some-thing like that. I just thought he was kind when he was friendly and annoying when he was cold toward me. Okay, I thought he looked handsome, even though I knew that his big glasses in combination with his younger-looking face would not be to everyone's lik-ing, but there was something about him I couldn't put into words that was attractive. Something about him was special.

Still, it didn't mean anything that I thought he was handsome, because I found Finn and even Julius handsome as well – and the last one, I really couldn't stand.

"Waste what on who?" Julius, who just arrived, tried to enter the conversation.

Speak of the devil, or in this case, think of the devil?
I rolled my eyes. I really didn't need him here.

"No one," I answered shortly.

He almost looked disappointed after Finn didn't explain the situation, even though he was looking at him with a questioning glance. If he wasn't that clingy and annoying, I would almost feel sorry for him.

"Are you ditching English again?" Finn asked eventually, and I was thankful for this change in topic.

"Not today. I just arrived, and I thought I say 'hey' before I dive into the exciting world of Shakespeare."

Then he said goodbye and went to his class.
I couldn't understand why Finn was good friends with him. I couldn't even stand him for 10 seconds without having the urge to leave the room.

"Okay back to the topic," Finn began. "Is there anything that prevents you from forgetting about him?"

"The fact that he lives in the apartment on top of mine?" I answered his question with another question.

"You only saw him once until now. That can't be a coincidence."

"Maybe I don't see him but sometimes I hear him," is what I wanted to answer.

However, I realized this might've sounded dumb and desperate, so I swallowed these words and instead answered: "You are right."

"I know," he said with a wide grin.

"Mh," I just said, and lifted my backpack onto the empty seat next to me.

I started unpacking my history book and my pencil case.

"Homework," I answered to Finn's questioning glance.

After he observed me for some time while I analyzed the speech of some Prussian king – or was he an emperor? – I didn't really think about it much, and they all share the same name anyway, he broke the silence that filled the whole entrance hall.

"I know what will help you," he said suddenly.

I raised my eyebrows and looked at him.

"I take you with me to a housey."

He grinned, waiting for me to answer.

"A housey?" I repeated.

"A house-party. You know, it's where people meet at someone's house and …"

"A house-party?" I repeated with such disgust in my voice that it surprised even me.

"Come on, it will be fun," he tried again.

"I'd rather eat snails than partying."

"You won't regret it, I swear," his voice had a begging undertone.

"But I can't dance, and I don't like parties," I tried to convince him from my point of view.

"You'll enjoy it. 100 percent. Trust me."

He looked at me expectantly.

Nervously, I pressed the button on top of my ballpoint pen, so the tip went out and back in multiple times. Should I really try to go to a party? I mean, yes, I didn't have anything better to do, but did I really want to waste my Friday evening at a party of someone that I didn't even know with people I mostly despised under circumstances I hated?

"Okay, I'm in."

I had no clue why I accepted his offer, but my mouth had answered before my brain could even realize it. There were so many arguments against this party, but something deep down in me wanted to go anyway. Maybe Finn was right, and I wouldn't regret it after all.

"Really?" he asked incredulously.

"Yeah, I have nothing better to do anyway."

The school bell rang, which meant the break has started.

"Great, I'll pick you up at 8 p.m.," he said, and jumped up.

"Finn?" I called him almost panicky, when he was already on the way to the exit.

Immediately, he turned around.

"What's up?" he asked, and looked as deep into my eyes as possible with the distance in between us.

"What should I wear?"

I could see the tension in his face vanishing.

"Just wear whatever you'll feel most comfortable in. It'll look good anyway," he said, and smiled at me encouragingly, then he left.

I really wasn't looking forward to this party, but it was just fair to accompany Finn after all the things he did for me. Every Friday I had two hours off, and he hung out with me in the entrance hall of the school until the bell rang, even though he could already go home. I wished I could also go home, but I had two not so tempting hours of art class with Julius ahead of me. Fortunately, time flew by quicker than expected, and the next thing I realized was that I was on my way home.

When I arrived at home, the first doubts were hitting me. Was it really a good idea to go to a party? If I would not go today, I would never know, and it was a bit too late to cancel. So, I took a quick shower and put on the first best clothes that I could find.

At 8 p.m. on the dot, the doorbell rang and I made my way downstairs.

"Nervous?"

Finn greeted me.

"I'm almost pissing my pants," I answered ironically.

"You don't even know if you know anyone at the party, and you are that cool about it? Is there anything that makes you nervous?" he asked while laughing.

I thought about it for a second. I really wasn't nervous at all, even though I didn't know where the party was. Probably, because I already expected to hate it, and I was even less motivated to find friends for life there.

"Spiders," I answered after a longer break. "Spiders make me nervous," I repeated. "And presentations," I added.

"Spiders?" he laughed. "Who would've thought..." He said this more to himself than to me.

"Where are we even driving?" I eventually wanted to know.

"I already wondered why you haven't asked, yet. We're driving to Jane's place."

I sighed.

Of course. Why did we have to go to a party of hers? Under normal circumstances, I would probably be the last person she would invite.

"Are you sure she'll be okay with me being there?" Suddenly, I was certain I had made the wrong decision. The evening was doomed to fail.

"Sure, without you, I'll leave, and I don't think she wants that," he said confidently.

However, he was right about it. Everyone knew that Jane was into Finn. She would prefer having me at the party over Finn not being there at all. Still, I didn't feel comfortable with the thought of only being allowed at the party because of some kind of blackmail. I would prefer being driven home, but I didn't say a word, mostly because I knew Finn and he wouldn't have driven me home anyway. This was probably his only chance to get me to party, so he would not accept a no.

I just quietly looked out of the window and accepted my fate. It was already dark, and the landscape was barely recognizable because the road was poorly lit.

"We're there," I heard Finn's voice close to my right ear.

I flinched and realized I was so deep in my thoughts that I didn't even realize Finn had already parked and even left the car. Now he was standing in front of the open passenger door, waiting for me to leave the car as well.

"It's too late to turn around," he added.

Quickly, I unbuckled and stumbled after him to the front door. Jane opened the door, and it was impossible to tell what she was thinking. Maybe she was good at hiding her discomfort with me being there because she was too busy trapping Finn in superficial conversations.

She led us, more Finn than me, to the living room, where a lot of other students of our year were already dancing to the music. It was ridiculous seeing all those stiff teenagers move to – to what were they moving? It was obviously not the rhythm of the song that was played. I probably wouldn't look better than them, but that was why I didn't even bother trying to dance. A short break in the music turned the whole room silent for a quick moment.

My glance wandered around, and I realized how luxurious everything looked. I didn't even know Jane's family was rich. I didn't know anything about Jane except that she liked chewing gum in history class and that she was into Finn. But I didn't know anything about her personally or her family. Another reason why I felt so utterly out of place.

During the break in between the songs, the people on the improvised dance floor didn't move. They seemed like they were petrified, but when the next song started to play, they screamed wildly, almost as if it was their favorite song. After they behaved similarly for the next, the second to next, and the song after that – actually, they behaved like this for every song – I almost started to like these people. Their behavior was weird but funny. Somehow.

Jane eventually vanished for a second and left Finn some room to breathe, but we both knew it wouldn't last forever. Again, the song changed. Again, the people on the dance floor screamed like it was their favorite song. The only difference was that I started to listen to the lyrics for the first time.

Apparently, Finn was doing the same since it didn't take much time until he commented on the lyrics. After I thought I understood something along the lines of drinking and emptying glasses, Finn screamed, even though he was standing right next to me, but because of the music, he was difficult to understand: "That's what we're about to do today."

"I don't drink," I screamed back at him.

It was difficult to be louder than the music. As much as I loved music, this was way too loud for me.

"Are you sure?" he wanted to know, and started moving to the rhythm of the music.

I nodded.

"But it would help you forget about your Rafael."

"Ramon," I corrected him.

"See, you can still remember his name, and this is what we're going to change tonight."

He looked at me challenging, and I gave in.

I let him drag me to the drinks, and without asking me what I wanted to drink, he started filling my glass with the first alcohol he could find. He probably expected me to back off if he would let me decide for myself.

After he handed it back to me and filled his own glass, he dragged me closer to the dance floor.

"As already said, he doesn't deserve you thinking about him. He doesn't even deserve that you remember his name. He isn't relevant to anyone here."

"What is your problem with him?"

"I don't have a problem with him. I simply don't care about him, and you should do the same," he answered neutrally.

"You pretend like I'm going through a breakup," I said, and laughed about how ridiculous the situation was.

"Only because you behave as if you do," he countered.

Could he be right? Did I really behave that oddly? Without further thoughts, I decided to take the song a bit too literally and started emptying my glass.

I made a face. This stuff tasted horrible, but somehow there was comfort in thinking everything would be better the next morning.

"Is it that bad?" I could hear Finn next to me.

"No, it's fine. Everything is fine," I answered hastily and continued drinking.

After some time, I got used to the taste, and it didn't taste as badly as before.

"And now we should dance," Finn shouted when he realized I was done with my drink.

I gave up on fighting his ideas. He had promised me I would have fun at this party, so I trusted him and tried to move as inconspicuously as possible to the rhythm of the music. I probably looked ridiculous, but at that moment, I didn't care. I just wanted to be someone else, even if it was only for a tiny moment. Someone who danced, even though she looked like a fool, without being ashamed of it.

When the song was over and the people next to us screamed excitedly because the next one started, Jane reappeared. Finn noticed my not-so-excited glance and laughed for a second but stopped when Jane was trapping him in another conversation. Again, I felt like I was third-wheeling. Again, I regretted coming here. Finn looked at me apologetically while Jane tried to drag him away.

"You can go. It's fine," I told him, and sat down on the modern looking – and probably expensive – couch that was standing in the corner of the huge living room. From here, I had a great overview.

It didn't take long for Finn and Jane to reappear in my view. Jane had dragged him into the middle of the dance floor. I could only imagine how Finn must've felt at that moment. He could probably picture 1,000 better situations than being there with her.

How many times did he tell me how annoyed he was by her? How many times did he laugh about her behavior and the fact that almost everyone could tell that she was into him?

My glance trailed off and wandered around the room. I couldn't even tell how many people were at this party, and suddenly I felt so lost on this large couch. I felt lost at the whole party. No one paid any attention to me, and the only person in this room that I actually liked was occupied.

Of course, I couldn't blame Finn for my situation, especially regarding his situation. He was probably feeling more uncomfortable than me right now. But I would still prefer being home and watching TV shows. Again, I saw Finn and Jane and couldn't stop myself from observing them for some time. Because of the poor lighting situation in the room, I couldn't tell if they were talking or just dancing.

After some time – I was seriously shocked about how long I observed them – both of them went away to get another drink. Even though the table with the drinks wasn't far away from the couch that I was sitting on,

Finn didn't check on me. He didn't even look around to see where I was.

This didn't feel like him. Maybe he didn't know I was there, because otherwise, I had no explanation for his behavior. He always behaved like the brother I never had. He always made sure I wouldn't get lost – as he claimed – especially when we were surrounded by a lot of people, like here, for example. But today he was different, and I didn't know what to do about it. So, I decided to look away.

From the corner of my eye, I saw them drink together and laugh and then drink some more. Then Jane dragged him back to the dance floor. I gulped. I was about to lose my best and only friend to the girl that he told me not to worry about. The girl that he even made fun of. Didn't he want me to feel better? Now I felt even worse than before.

When I thought it couldn't get any worse, I became a witness of them making out in the middle of the dance floor. From this moment, I was done with the party and with Finn. I wasn't jealous, I just didn't like watching them, and I felt a bit betrayed. So many times did he joke about Jane and reassure me that he would never want anything other than friendship with her. Of course, he could do whatever he wanted to do, but I didn't need to witness it.

Has this been his plan all along? Dragging me to this party to make such a shitty move? I had to focus to not start crying.

"Bad day?" Julius asked who suddenly appeared next to me.

Besides the fact that he was the last person I wanted to see at the moment, I was still way too focused on the stuff that was happening on the dancefloor, and even though I didn't want to, I couldn't look away.

"Oh, I understand," I heard Julius murmur. "That shouldn't prevent you from making the most of the night, though," he continued talking.

Why was he so nice to me, even though I have been nothing but impolite and hostile toward him?

"Why are you being so nice?" it slipped out of her mouth without her realizing it.

He looked at her and ran his fingers extra slowly through his blond hair. It felt like he was doing this to buy himself more time to answer.

"Would you prefer if I start ignoring you again?" He answered her question with another question.

Quickly, she shook her head.

"No, it's fine like that," she stumbled and couldn't prevent turning red.

"See? You should stop questioning everything. Just be happy and live in the moment."

She looked at him and had to admit that he was right.

"Do you know why I'm so popular?" he continued.

When she shook her head, he answered: "Because I don't question everything. You should try doing the same."

She knew for a long time that she was too strict with herself and that she was always worrying too much, so she decided to listen to him and engaged in a longer conversation with him.

Derek was one of the most popular guys of her year, and almost every girl that she knew wanted to get closer to him than just staring at him from the opposite side of the room. He was shamelessly good-looking, intelligent, and especially one thing: unreachable. At least for someone like her.

He had a lot of friends and spent most of his time with his friend group, which didn't let anyone new into it. She, however, only had one friend that could even be her sister, judged by their similarities in looks and everything. And especially because he had so much more prestige than her, she was even more confused that one day they ended up being at the same birthday party.

It was Sina's 14th birthday party, and she had justified that invitation by saying that their parents were friends, and she trusted her blindly. Why shouldn't she, they were best friends?

At the party, some of his friends came to her and told her that Derek wasn't uninterested in her. She didn't believe them. Why should he like her when he could have everyone? She wasn't dumb; she was skeptical at first. Why should she trust his friends, whom she had never talked to before?

She decided to simply ignore these comments until the party was over. It didn't work.

She finally broke when one girl from her class – whom she liked until that day because she had always been nice to her – told her the same things as the others. Even though there was nothing bad about the things they said, she suddenly felt so much further away from everyone. It was as if they were all looking down on her.

A strange girl – until today she didn't know who it was – warned her that they were only trying to prank her, so she left the party earlier than expected. She felt reassured in her opinion and the fact that she shouldn't trust anyone. She felt betrayed by everyone and by no one; empty.

Derek apologized for the behavior of his friends the next day via SMS. It really felt like it was important to him to leave the whole situation behind them. He was being kind, so they texted for a while longer. At school, his behavior toward her didn't change.

She convinced herself that people could change their behavior in such a short amount of time. She believed it, and if she wished for it strongly enough, it might come true in the future. It could've been one of these movies where the cool football captain falls in love with the quiet, introverted girl because he could see things in her that no one else could see. But this was no movie, and he didn't play football, and they weren't in America.

She started meeting him in their free time up until the day when she made one severe mistake; she started trusting him. She told him her darkest secrets that no one, except Sina was supposed to know. She told him everything that bothered her in her life, and he talked about himself as well. Until today, she wasn't sure if any of his words were true, but back then, it meant the world to her that he opened up.

The next day, she regretted everything. She regretted trusting him. She regretted even talking to him after his behavior had changed so quickly. She should've been more critical than she was. She had believed him. She had hoped so badly that he had changed. But he stayed the same.

He still was the guy that made fun of everything and everyone outside of his friend group. He used her to make fun of her and told her secrets to everyone in school. He had never changed, and he never would; that was all she knew.

However, she didn't know why he did it. It was not like it would make him any more popular because he already was popular enough. The only thing that had changed was not his life but hers. He was the cause of her trust issues and why she disliked everyone, who was being too nice too quickly. She became a completely different person thanks to him.

The reason why Julius was nice to me this evening, however, was different. Julius has always been nice to me; I was just too shaped by my past to trust him and his intentions. Of course, sometimes he was annoying, and he had a weird kind of humor, but my biggest problem was that I couldn't accept that some people were friendly because they were simply good people. There wasn't always a bad intention when someone was being nice.

Julius wasn't a bad guy. He just met me at the wrong time in my life. Because one thing I had learned from my past; if it is too good to be true, then it oftentimes isn't true.

I suddenly turned red with shame. I've been so nasty and disrespectful toward Julius in the past few months just because he reminded me of someone in my past. Just because of my prejudices against him. Just because I couldn't let go of what had happened. I treated him so much worse than he deserved because I simply couldn't trust him, even though he had never asked for my trust. He was simply being kind to me. Julius wasn't Derek, and it was time that I had to accept that.

"Thanks," I murmured quietly.

I was almost sure the music swallowed my words.

"For what?" he asked, against my expectations.

"For being nice even though I don't deserve it."

He looked at me confused but silent.

Maybe he could sense that I wasn't in the position to open up much more. One day, I swore to myself, I would tell him about my past and explain my behavior toward him, but not today, and especially not now. Maybe not even this week. But one day I would explain it to him, when I was ready to talk about it which could take some time since it would mean I would have to cope with my past. But for now the wounds were still too fresh. The betrayal still hurt.

"Do you want to drink something?" Julius asked after some time, still observing Finn and Jane from our space on the couch.

Without thinking for too long, I nodded. Just because some things in life didn't work out the way I wanted them to, didn't mean I shouldn't have fun at this party. And in the end, I did have fun.

Maybe this evening was a great start for me. A good start for accepting my past because it was the past; I couldn't change it anyway.

So, I did forget things that evening. I didn't forget Ramon's name, and I didn't forget about Derek, but I forgot to think about either my past or my future for one evening. It was the first time in my life that I could focus on living in the moment, and this meant the world to me.

Chapter 7

When I saw the title of the book, all of my dreams and hopes burst. How could my Grandma do this to me? First, she promised me answers to all of my questions, and then she sent me a storybook. She couldn't be serious about this.

Immediately, I stormed to grab my phone to call my dad, but he just confirmed my dark predictions; there was nothing else my Grandma had left behind for me. I agitatedly typed Tim's number – which I knew by heart – into my phone just to delete it immediately. I couldn't always call him if something in my life didn't go the way I had planned. This time, I would handle my problems by myself.

So, I grabbed the book and sat down on my couch. But even after checking it out multiple times, it was the same book that my Grandma always read to me when I was a child. What did she want to achieve by sending me this book? It couldn't answer all of my questions, could it?

Carefully, I shook the book, hoping that maybe another letter or something else would fall out of it, but again, I was disappointed. Nothing. Again, I grabbed my phone. Next time, I would not call him and ask for his help, but today I just needed him.

In case Tim was annoyed by my calls, he was really good at hiding it. Like always, he sounded cheerful and happy when he picked up and promised to immediately come over. It didn't take long for him to arrive at my apartment.

"So, where is the book," he said excitedly as a little kid before Christmas and stormed into my living room.

"It's there."

I signaled with a quick movement of my head that the book was lying on the couch table. His eyes were wide open when he took the book and carefully turned it around multiple times.

"Did you shake it?" he asked.

"Yes," I answered, and sat down on the sofa next to him.

"And did you read it already?" he wanted to know.

"My Grandma has always read the book to me."

"Something has to be written in here," he started.

"There has to be some purpose in the book."

Again, he turned the book in his hands.

"Maybe we have to read it page by page," he murmured.

"But I know all of the stories by heart. My Grandma always … – "

"Exactly, she read the stories to you," he interrupted me. "But how many times did you read the book yourself?"

I was exactly where he wanted me to be.

"Never," I admitted.

"You know the stories in the book, but you don't know the individual pages. Maybe there is some code hidden in the book or something like that," Tim completely trailed off with his ideas.

"Yes, of course, of course. That's it," I said as ironically as possible.

"As long as you can't prove the opposite, I'll stick to my theory," Tim claimed.

"You can do that," I just said, and observed Tim staring at different pages, searching for suspicious-looking letters or numbers.

To be honest, I didn't exactly know what he was looking for, and maybe he didn't even know it himself, but after he checked a few pages, he lost his patience and gave up.

Before he was on his way back home, he asked me if he could borrow the book for some time. I didn't know what he wanted to do with the book, but whatever it was, it was probably more helpful than everything I could do with it, so I agreed.

It was early in the morning – and by early, I mean really early since I was used to getting up early for my therapy sessions – when the sound of my ringtone interrupted my sleep. Only half awake, I tried to make my way through my dark apartment while groping the wall, looking for the light switch. Eventually, I made it to the landline while still being incredibly tired, but at least I could shut up my phone by accepting the incoming call.

"Hello?"

I yawned without knowing who was on the other side of the line.

"I think, I found something," I heard Tim's excited voice.

"Hm?" I just murmured.

"In the book," he started. "I found something in the book which could be pretty helpful."

Suddenly, I was wide awake.

"What did you find?"

"It's hard to explain. I don't know exactly what to think about it, but I think we're on the right track to get answers. It's for the best if you come over and check it out yourself."

Coming over? Me? These words didn't seem to fit very well together. I couldn't simply drive to his apartment now. It was very early, and there were probably no other people on the street, but still, I didn't feel comfortable with the thought of it. I didn't avoid humans for most of my life just to risk everything now by going outside at a time that didn't fit my schedule.

"So, are you coming?" Tim asked again.

"I-I-I don't know if this is such a good idea," I stuttered and got quieter and quieter at the end of the sentence.

"Just look at it as the beginning of your new life," he said with a lot of strength and motivation in his voice, so I had no other choice but to come over. And maybe he was right, and I needed to change something if I wanted to start over. What would be a better new beginning than to do something I've never done before?

"I'm on my way," I muttered, and hasted down the stairs to my car. Almost as if I was afraid that I would change my mind if I wouldn't leave fast enough.

At this time of the day – or the night – I didn't need to worry about meeting other tenants on the staircase. Neither did I need to worry about my choice of clothes. The only one that would see me in my not-so-eloquent looking jogging pants was Tim, and he was the last person that would judge me because of that.

"Good morning," Tim greeted me happily.

"It's not even 4 a.m.," I complained quietly.

I then followed him into his apartment. His apartment was smaller than I had expected. Actually, I never really thought about Tim's apartment. All I knew was that he had no issues with money – he earned way more than I did, but this was probably also caused by the fact that he was able to have a real job – so I kind of expected him to have a bigger apartment. However, he lived in a small, and minimalistically furnished studio apartment. But then again, it suited him.

"You can sit down," he offered while looking at a small sofa in one of the corners of the room. From there, I could observe every corner of the apartment, which only made me realize how poorly I knew Tim since this was the first time I had come over to his place.

"You'll never believe me if I tell you what I found," he started.

Immediately, he got all of my attention.

"Show me!" I demanded and eyed him.

It seemed like he had been awake all night to study the book, at least the dark circles below his eyes made me think that. I really hoped that all of his work wasn't for nothing.

"You've always said that your Grandma read the book to you," he said while turning over page by page.

"Yes," I confirmed.

"But have you ever thought about her not reading everything to you?" he asked without looking at me. He was still super focused on the book.

"What do you mean?" I asked confused.

He didn't answer. The only noise that filled the silence was Tim still looking for something in the book.

"Tim?" I asked after some time had passed.

He couldn't make me feel excited like this and then be quiet.

"Here," he said, proudly showing me a completely black page.

"What's that?"

"I asked myself the same thing but then I did that," he said while turning another page.

Curiously, I stared at the page, but I had to realize that it looked exactly the same as all the other pages in the book. The same black letters on the same, slightly yellow-stained paper.

"That's nothing special," I muttered disappointed.

"Exactly my thoughts. But then I started to read the titles of the stories."

I looked at him confused.

Why should I care about the titles of the stories?

"The clairvoyant," I read out loud. "It sounds like a normal title to me."

"But now read the story," he demanded.

Again, I looked at him confused, but I started to read the story in silence.

In a world like ours lives a clairvoyant. She had supernatural abilities and could precisely predict certain events. That was why other humans feared her. But she was feared the most by herself.

"How should this help me?" I wanted to know.

"Don't you feel a connection to this?"

"Nope?" I answered skeptically.

Did he really expect me to feel a connection to a fairytale that was written to entertain children?

He scratched the back of his head and sighed briefly. Then he pointed his finger at the last sentences of the fairytale.

Like the following stories, this one really happened. After all, these are the dark pages of this book. Or am I wrong that supernatural creatures exist, Ramon?

"T-t-that's my name," I stuttered and stared at the last sentences of the story.

"Yeah, whoever wrote this book knew that you would end up reading it."

"Or it's all just a coincidence," I tried to find a rational explanation for this.

"Ramon," Tim said as neutrally as possible, "you have been through so much in your life, do you really still believe in coincidences?"

"So, I'm clairvoyant?" I said more to myself than to him.

"I don't think so. That would be too easy. Also, the issues the clairvoyant has in the story are different than yours. "

"But what am I?" I asked again.

"I think we'll soon figure it out, and then you can start over, and get to know other people, and go outside. The first steps, you made today, and from now on, we will work on finding a solution for your problems," he said super euphorically.

"I will be normal," I said uncertainly.

I didn't really buy it, but apparently, this was convincing enough for Tim.

Chapter 8

"Luna, you are late again!" I heard my mother shout. Looking at my alarm clock, I had to realize that she was right, and I was again late for school. Damn. Quickly, I got ready even though I was everything but motivated to go there. I just wanted to avoid certain people today.

Today was Monday, and therefore the first day after the party where I would encounter Finn again. I had no clue how to behave toward him and Jane, and I wasn't very keen on finding it out either.

Out of breath, I stomped into the kitchen and sat down at the table so I could face my mother.

"Do I have to go to school today?" I asked, and looked at her as sufferingly as possible.

"Do you have a fever?" she answered my question with another one.

I just shook my head.

"At least try to go to school. If you still feel ill, you can come home later," she offered empathetically.

"Mh," I responded, and packed my breakfast into my bag. By thinking about going to school today I suddenly lost all of my appetite. Then I went to school.

Maybe it was even a good thing that I overslept. Like this, I could avoid meeting Finn before school. Usually, he and his friends always hung out in the entrance hall, waiting for class to start.

I even joined them on the days when I wasn't too late, but unfortunately, I was really good at being late in the past few months. Today, however, the entrance hall was as empty as it was on my first day of school.

Relieved, I made my way through the poorly lit hallways. Before I entered my classroom, it hit me that I was about to have history class. History class with Jane.

I was on time when I entered the room and fell down on my chair like a wet bag of sand.

"Good morning," Jane greeted me friendly.

"Morning," I answered shortly.

I was not in the right mood to deal with her fake friendliness. Usually, she was only nice to me as long as Finn was around. During history class, she ignored me most of the time. That's why it felt obvious to me that she wanted me to do something for her.

"Soooo, you're really good friends with Finn…" she started.

I looked at her and raised my eyebrows, waiting for what she was about to say next. From here, I had no clue as to where this conversation was going.

"Do you think he likes me?"

I looked at her confused.

Why should I know that? Until a few days ago, he made fun of her clinginess, but even I had too much empathy to tell her that. Also, I wasn't even sure what was true or false since last Friday. Maybe he did even like her.

"Sorry, but I don't know," I said after a longer break. I had answered her question, and the conversation would be over or so I thought.

"I don't know either. I think he likes you," she whispered while the teacher was writing down something on the blackboard.

"What do you mean?" I asked perplexed.

"He talked a lot about you, and everything sounded so positive."

Silence.

"Of course, he likes me. We're friends, after all. It would suck if he wouldn't like me," I answered as soon as I found myself to be in control of my words again. She seemed to be pleased with that answer. Even though I could see that my words did not fully calm her down, the strict glance of the teacher could prevent her from asking further questions.

When the bell rang, I packed all of my things in my bag as quickly as possible. My plan for the break was to avoid everyone, and to do so, I headed in the direction of the restrooms.

The restroom was the only place in this school that I tried to avoid as much as possible. There were multiple reasons why I did so. The smell and the dirt were already enough reasons to stay as far away as possible from there, but the main reason why I didn't want to use the toilets was the queue in front of the restroom.

There were definitely not enough toilets, and one or two of them were always closed because they needed maintenance.

So, if one wanted to use the toilet, it would take the whole duration of the break. And this was my plan. I would not be in the entrance hall, and I would not be able to see anyone that I didn't want to see that day. Happy, because my plan had worked, I went to biology class five minutes after the break had ended until I heard someone call my name in the hallway. I walked faster and reached the room before the other person could reach me.

Biology class passed, and I still had no clue what I should do for the next break. Luckily, my teacher was ill, so I could go home earlier and didn't need to hide anywhere – especially not on the toilet again. But before I could exit the entrance hall, I felt a hand grab me by the shoulder. Reflexive, I turned around and looked into the brown eyes of Finn, which were – as I had to realize as time passed – not just brown but actually they were only brown around his pupils while the rest of his iris was slightly greenish. However, it was really hard to recognize the green as green.

"Hey, is everything alright? I tried to talk to you before biology class, but somehow you didn't respond," he wanted to know.

"Sorry, I didn't hear you," I murmured not very convincing, but he didn't seem to be bothered by that.

"How did you get home from the party?" he asked as if everything was fine between us.

"Julius drove me."

Again, I tried to answer as briefly and reservedly as possible.

"Julius?" he repeated with an odd undertone in his voice while raising his eyebrows. "Why did he take you? You could've told me that you wanted to go, and I would've brought you home."

"You were a bit occupied," I answered, and avoided all kinds of eye contact.

All of a sudden, I felt so uncomfortable around him. Was it possible that I overreacted? He was allowed to do whatever he wanted and with whom he wanted, but somehow it hurt me more than I would've thought it could hurt me.

"Oh, that's what you're talking about," he suddenly remembered. "You could've saved me from that."

He laughed and scratched the back of his head.

"You didn't look like you wanted to be saved," I answered drily.

"But you don't seriously think I'm into her, do you?" he wanted to know, and for the first time since I met him, he sounded a little bit insecure.

"I don't know what I should even think anymore, but I can tell you what Jane thinks about this. She really likes you and now hopes that you feel the same about her."

I was surprised that I was suddenly standing up for Jane.

"Just don't toy with her feelings," I added, then I turned around and went home.

I could hear him respond that he was not into her, but that wasn't my problem. He got into this situation all by himself. It was none of my business.

Even though it comforted me a little bit that he wasn't that much into Jane, I still tried to avoid Finn the next day as much as it was possible. As expected, it was hard since we had the same friend group, and he was more or less my only real friend in this school. But I didn't want to waste another break on the toilet because it was simply disgusting and a little bit childish. So, when break time came, I sat down next to Julius instead of Finn.

Sometime later, I tried to interact in a conversation between Jane and her girlfriends, which was way more difficult because they only talked about celebrities that I either didn't know or didn't care about.

Either Finn didn't realize that something was wrong or he was afraid of talking about it. His way of dealing with the situation was to act like nothing had ever happened. Maybe he hoped that things would go back to normal if he would behave that way, but unfortunately, life wasn't that easy. And I was way too resentful.

The following weeks were similar, and I became more and more distant toward Finn. In the meantime, I got used to Jane and her friends and even joined their conversations without feeling left out. I also got along with Julius after I stopped treating him as if he was the enemy. It was almost shocking for me to figure out how easy it was to get along with people if I was just nice to them.

Finn gave up on talking to me which hurt me a bit, but that was just how life could be. Everything would eventually come to an end.

Jane, Julius, and the other people I talked with invited me to multiple parties, and what was even more shocking about that was that I actually went. My mom was happy that I changed so much. She always want-ed me to have a lot of friends and have all of the typi-cal teenage experiences in my life. Also, she could justify to herself that moving was a great idea because I've never been that socially active before.

I heard the voice of my mother dully. She was proba-bly on the phone again. I realized that recently she was often talking on the phone, but I didn't know to whom. Just after I couldn't hear her voice anymore, someone knocked on my door.

"I'm not hungry," I screamed, hoping that this was the answer to the question she was about to ask.

I just wanted to be left alone today. And even less did I want to sit at a table and play happy family with my mom when I just didn't feel well. School was shit, and even my homework was more annoying than usual. I didn't need my mom to worry about me. I didn't need anyone to care for me. All I needed was space.

"Then I'll eat this alone," I heard a familiar voice.

My glance wandered to the now open door. I could see Finn with a big McDonald's bag standing in the doorframe.

"You look like you had a shitty day," he said, and sat down on my bed next to me like he always used to do before our fight.

"Thanks," I just said.

I didn't know what else to say.

He just smiled at me.

"What?" I asked after some time had passed.

"Nothing. It's just great being back here."

I would lie if I claimed that it didn't feel odd at all to be with Finn like that. But on the other side, he was exactly what I needed at that moment. Of course, I missed him. However, my ego was too big to admit that.

"I'm so sorry," I blurted out.

"What exactly are you sorry for?" he asked, looking me deeply into my eyes.

I always found it scary when people were able to look into other people's eyes for such a long time. I never did that. When I talked to people, I tried to move my glance over the whole face and never solely focus on the eyes. It made me feel uncomfortable to look into other people's eyes like that, and it made me uncomfortable if people looked into my eyes like that too. I could never bear eye contact for too long because it always felt like the other person would see more than just my eyes. As if my eyes were about to give away all of my secrets if you would just look at them for long enough. Maybe it was just too intimate for me because I was afraid that someone else understood me better than I understood myself.

"I'm sorry for ignoring you and avoiding you because of some bullshit," I answered slowly and tried to withstand the eye contact.

"Okay, apology accepted," he said happily and jumped up. When he saw that I was confused, he added: "You should've known that I'm not into Jane. Otherwise, I wouldn't have made fun of her that often."

I sighed.

I would probably regret my next words for centuries, but this didn't stop me from saying them out loud: "She actually is a nice person. Maybe you would see it too if you would spend more time with her."

"I never said that she isn't nice. She simply isn't my type. It was great being here, by the way, but I have to go now."

He winked at me before he walked away.
This was by far the weirdest conversation I ever had with anyone, if one would exclude Ramon. Because no one would ever be as weird as him.

Sometimes I wondered what my life would be like if we hadn't moved towns. I would probably watch TV with Sina and eat ice cream because that was what we always did if any of us had a bad day (and thanks to Derek, we had a lot of them).

I wouldn't say that my life had gotten easier because we moved, but it became different. I would've never been able to imagine how it would feel to be disappointed by your best guy friend and then return to being normal after the fight was over. I never had any guy friends. I actually never had any other friends than Sina. And I didn't talk to guys either. I simply wasn't good at doing that.

Meanwhile, I had figured out the reason why Sina had a lot of bad days, even though she didn't want me to know back then. It turned out that she had stayed friends with me solely because her mother asked her to do so. Otherwise, she would've ended the friendship earlier. Me moving to a town far away came in quite handy for her, and as soon as I was gone, she became part of the 'cool' friend group in our class. Sometimes I wonder if she was the reason for Derek's behavior back then, because, as far as I knew, they quickly became a thing after I had left. Suspiciously quickly. At least that was what my mom told me. I didn't know how their little love story ended because my mom didn't tell me, either to protect me or because she didn't know it. One thing I did know; I never wanted to see Sina ever again. Never ever.

So, thinking about it, moving towns wasn't the worst thing that had ever happened to me, and actually, I was kind of glad that we did it. I finally found true friends. I didn't need anyone to eat ice cream in front of the TV anymore because I didn't have bad days like that at all.

It was stunning how one single move could change my whole life, and even though I used to be so mad at my mom for accepting her new job offer, I had to admit that I was doing alright. More than that.

This ugly city did me good. These odd people did me good. I myself finally did me good again. Maybe I found myself or I invented myself. Whatever it was, it felt right to be here. If there was something like destiny or fate, then this must be it.

Chapter 9

Since my visit to Tim's place, a few days have passed, and until now, neither he nor I could get behind the secrets that were hiding in the storybook. Every day, I read a few pages in the unfamiliar part of the book, which was back at my place by now. But most of the stories were about demons, shadow creatures, and other supernatural things that weren't even close to what I was. Even though my abilities were exactly as dark and cruel – at least for myself.

Like the previous days, I hung out in my bedroom to read and analyze the pages of the book. After I had read more than half of the dark and unfamiliar part of the book, I decided to skip a few pages and pay closer attention to the titles of the stories. By now, I was convinced that something in this book must be helpful. And I didn't have to look for longe until I found a page that looked like it could contain some answers for me.

I immediately called Tim to tell him about what I just found. Fortunately, he didn't want me to visit him again. Instead, he promised to drive to my place as soon as possible. He was out of breath when he arrived in front of my door.

"You'll never believe what I found," I bubbled out excitedly. I usually never was like that.

"Show me."

"There is a chapter in the book, which has a pretty odd title. It just says, 'my grandchild' and I have the theory, no wait, I feel that this is about me."

I feel that this is about me? Wow, I really sounded as weird as Tim sometimes was.

He looked at me with a wide and hopeful grin.

"But what does it say in the story?" he wanted to know.

"I don't know yet. I'm too scared to read any further," I admitted.

Now that I was closer than ever to understanding what was going on with me, I was scared that whatever it said in the book would just be another disappointment. What if everything was just a waste of time? I was scared of finding answers that I didn't want to hear or answers that I wouldn't be able to put into practice. Just because we would have answers wouldn't mean I could start my new life immediately.

"Then let's not waste any time and read it," Tim said, interrupting my thoughts.

I showed him the page, which even looked a bit different from the other ones. It was odd that we didn't see it sooner. Then we started reading the text.

Once upon a time, there was my grandson. He was young, but even then, he knew that he was different than the other boys his age. He was special. Not just special in being an individual but a different kind of special.

He could see things that no one else could see and that had not even happened so far. He had a unique ability. So unique that he was the only one who would ever have it. He was able to look into the future of people, but not just that. At the same time, he had the ability to change it.

*He and just he is the **Guardian of All Good**.*

He will realize that he has special abilities when he is still a little boy. It is uncertain how he will notice them, but I'm sure he will figure it out himself. When time passes, his abilities will become more and more obvious and harder to repress, but he will be able to handle them, I count on that. Once he realizes that his powers are all coming out of himself, he will learn to fully control them and use them as he wishes. They are a gift, not a curse. One day he will be grateful, but until then, the road will be rocky.

If he is fully in control, he will be able to move things just with the power of his mind. He will also be able to control the future of individual humans, or he will decide to not do it. It will be his choice.

"Woah," Tim was astonished, "do you know what that means?"

"Yeah, Guardian of All Good is just a euphemism for murderer because I killed all of these people?!" I answered.

"I didn't mean that point. It says you'll control your predictions and be able to have a normal life."
Tim was happy like a little child, and it was hard for me to drag him back to reality.

"It doesn't even tell me how."

"So what?" he said stubbornly. "You don't need instructions as long as you have me."

Against my will, I needed to smile.

"Man, I'm so glad I clung onto you even though you tried to get rid of me back then. I would've missed out on so many things," he added quietly.

Then he jumped up and went into the kitchen.

Confused, I observed that he took a glass off the shelf.

"I'll buy you five new glasses if you manage to push this one from the table," he said, and demonstratively put the glass in the middle of the table in front of me.

"How should I do that? The text stated that I'll only be able to do that when I'm familiar with controlling my abilities. And I'm so far away from doing that," I moaned.

"Bullshit. It's time that you stop looking for excuses. Just try it, and if it doesn't work, you just try it again until you can do it."
Before Tim could start his pep talk about positive thoughts and motivation, I tried to squint my eyes and fix the glass with my glance. There was my target, and somehow, I should be able to move it. Just focus.

I tried to remember how I felt when I was about to have a vision. Usually, I felt my body twitching, and my forehead wrinkling until everything was turning black. Then my vision would start. It has always been this way since my very first vision. And every time I thought about this vision, I was shocked at the things I was able to do even at such a young age.

The story called me the Guardian of All Good. I wasn't good. I was the villain.

✳✳✳

Every day, Tim came by my place after work to check on me, and every day, I had to disappoint him because nothing had changed even though I practiced every second I could spare.

I realized that I lost faith in myself, and even worse, I realized that even Tim started to lose faith in me. If he didn't believe in me, who else should?

Maybe it was the first step toward my new life that I had to stop having these doubts. I should become my own Tim. I should motivate myself, and I shouldn't depend on someone else to motivate me. So, I decided to practice and believe in myself. And if that wasn't enough, I had to remind myself of my Grandma's words because she apparently knew about my abilities, and if she knew that, she also knew that I would be able to control them one day. Maybe I had to change myself first before I could change my whole life.

"Okay, change of plans," Tim said when he sat down on my couch.

When he saw my confused glance, he added: "I will make something happen."

"And you want to do what exactly?" I asked skeptically.

"Easy. I'll move in here for a few days and provoke a vision," he explained.

"Why would you want to do that? That's bullshit," I blurted out.

"If you see me die, we'll know how and therefore can prevent it. And then your vision will be invalid."

"How should this help us anyway?"
I still didn't understand what he wanted to do, and why he wanted this to happen.

"You wouldn't put that much pressure on you, and your thoughts would be clearer. Also, you would be able to focus more on how, when, and where your visions are happening, so you can use this knowledge when you focus the glass," he ended his explanation and looked at me, waiting for me to say something.

"This plan is bullshit," I repeated, and I couldn't prevent my voice from sounding harsh.

"Why? Can you name one good reason to not do it?" Tim wanted to know.

"I can not only name one good reason for that. There is no guarantee that my vision is going to be invalid any day. I don't know how long the time frame is between me having the vision and the person actually dying, or if there is some time limit that you need to pass to survive for good. It's all way too uncertain. You could die and I don't want to support that. I don't want to be the murderer of my best friend," I was in a rage.

"I know that you would never kill me," he answered quietly.

"Damn. I can't control who I kill and who I don't," I started, "I didn't want to kill my mom, for example." Now I almost screamed.

Before Tim could answer, our conversation was interrupted by a loud clink. Immediately, I looked at the table. Where there was a fully intact glass just a few seconds ago, was now nothing but 1000 small pieces. I didn't just push the glass off the table; I made it explode.

"I knew you could do it," Tim said, and already looked for some kind of broom to collect the broken pieces of glass.

"Did I do that?" I stuttered confused.

"Yes," Tim said happily. "Yes, that was all you."

Still astonished by everything, I observed Tim cleaning everything.

"Did you see how dangerous I am? Today it's just a glass, but maybe one day this is going to be your head or something like that," I tried to convince him of my opinion.

Tim just started laughing, and it took him some time to become calm enough so he could explain to me why he was even laughing in the first place.

"I never planned on moving in. To be honest, I hoped that I would trigger a reaction. I didn't expect the glass to immediately explode, though."

"You are a genius," I said surprised.

I had never thought that he just wanted to pressure me to trigger some kind of reaction. This plan was genius, and even more important, it worked. I had found new motivation, and Tim had found his faith in me and my abilities.

Additionally, we were one step further than a few days ago. We now knew that the book was right about me. My abilities were far beyond just visions. What exactly I was able to do, we would have to figure out in the future. This was enough stress for just one day.

The next day, it was Saturday, my doorbell rang at 12 p.m. Confused, I went to the intercom to hear if someone would say something.

"Good morning, Ramon," I heard Tim's cheerful voice.

"What do you want here at this time?" I asked.

"It's a surprise," he just said, because I had already opened the door for him.

Tim randomly showing up at my place could only mean that he had another plan for me. Especially since yesterday, I've realized that I should never underestimate him. Whatever he meant by 'surprise' could only mean that he had another idea to test my abilities, and I wasn't sure I was ready for that.

"You are still in your pajamas," he noticed surprised, when he entered my apartment.

"Yes, I didn't plan on leaving my apartment today," I answered.

"Then you better hurry! I give you 10 minutes to get ready. Today, we go into the city center," he said demanding.

I knew I had no other choice but to listen to him, he could be very convincing sometimes. So, I went to my closet to get properly dressed.

"Wear something nice," he shouted after me.

Up until today, I never thought about whether my clothes were nice or not because, for me, they only fulfilled the purpose of preventing me from being naked. Now that I tried to find some clothes that somehow looked nice, I felt slightly overwhelmed. I had no clue about fashion or the latest trends. Neither did I know what Tim would consider nice. It was obvious that he meant I should not wear jogging pants, but what exactly were nice clothes anyway?

Before I could drift off into a philosophical debate with myself, I figured I would just grab the first clothes I could find. Tim wouldn't complain about my outfit anyway, as long as I was ready to go outside with him.

"That's a good start," Tim said, and eyed me skeptically.

Maybe the dark blue hoodie in combination with black jeans (my black hair) and the black shoes was not exactly what he had pictured, and maybe the colors didn't fit particularly well, but I didn't care about that.

"Take some money with you. We start your new life today," he decided.

In case he wanted to go shopping with me, I was prepared to disappoint him. I never went out of my apartment to buy clothes because I could simply order them online without seeing anyone. Also, I didn't expect Tim to be the kind of person that liked shopping. It was so untypical. Then again, I should not make the same mistake as yesterday. I should not reduce Tim to the things that I knew about him. Of course, I knew him pretty well, but I didn't know all of him because I never really met him outside of my apartment in the last years.

Our little journey to the city center could've also been summarized as a short trip to hell. There were hectic people, screaming children, and loud noises – so everything I tried to avoid for most of my life – everywhere. In moments like that, I appreciated the silence and loneliness in my apartment.

A bit lost, I followed Tim through the crowd of people without questioning his intentions. Unerring, he was walking toward a little shop that sold accessories and kitchen gadgets.

"I still owe you five glasses," he answered when he saw my confused glance.

"No need to take me with you," I murmured quietly, but still followed him into the store.

The idea of bringing me to the city center was completely dumb, but I could've said that from the beginning without using my abilities for that. In fact, it didn't take me long to have my first vision.

After the usual tingle twitching through my body and the blackout, I knew what was about to happen. The only thing I didn't know was who would be the target. Somebody who was somewhere close to me and wanted to do something in the city center would be very unlucky. This person was in the wrong place at the wrong time, and soon their life would be over.

Today it was the cashier in the little store that we had entered. He was a young, bald man who I briefly saw when Tim paid for the glasses.

Shocked, I stared at him. It was nothing new for me that my predictions scared me, but this time it was different. The feeling of being shocked turned into a feeling of disgust against myself and distraction. It was all my fault that this guy would die soon, even though I didn't want him to die. But it was too late now.

"Are you okay," the cashier asked worriedly.

"Yes," I whispered.

Tim made up some excuse for my behavior, then he led me out of the store.

"RAMON!" Tim screamed next to me.

I had no idea how often he had shouted my name until I reacted. Neither did I know why I didn't hear it.

"Please," I begged him, "please, let us go home."

Chapter 10

After all the time I spent in this city, I should've gotten used to the weird but likeable people that lived there. But so far, I haven't, because every time I thought things couldn't become any stranger, I was proven wrong.

I was on my way to school (late as usual) when I saw someone approaching me from the corner of my eye.

"Hey," I heard a voice through my headphones.

I decided to take them off and listen to what the person that seemed to know me had to say. Confused, I stared into the green eyes of Jane.

"Hey," I said with a questioning undertone which, however, didn't seem to bother Jane.

"Can we talk for a second?" she asked politely but seriously at the same time. So that I didn't have a choice but to talk to her, even though I wasn't very keen on missing the beginning of my philosophy class because of that.

"I have some kind of problem, and I think that you are the only one that can understand it," she started. That caught my attention because there was not a single problem I could think of where I could give her useful advice. Still, I stayed quiet and let her finish.

"It's about Finn," she said, and I noticed a slight shaking in her voice.

"What about Finn?" I wanted to know to disturb the silence that came over us.

If there was any hope, I could make it to class on time I couldn't stay here in silence for too long.

"Yesterday, he came to see me at my place and told me that he wasn't interested in me because I'm not his type," the shaking in her voice became stronger and stronger, and I realized that her eyes filled up with tears while she at the same time tried to prevent them from rolling down her cheeks. If one took a closer look, one could tell that somewhere in her, something had broken.

"Out of nowhere?" I asked critically.

I almost couldn't believe that Finn would behave that oddly. He always wanted what was best for everyone. There was a reason he had always been nice to her, even though he had always been uninterested.

"Yes, out of nowhere. I think it has something to do with you … "

"I swear, I have nothing to do with it," I interrupted her before she could accuse me of manipulating him into letting her down.

"That's not what I wanted to say. But I already told you that I think he likes you because since you are here," she took a quick break as if she had to choose her next words carefully, "he changed somehow."

"Oh," I just said, and was surprised at how much sympathy I felt for her.

It must've been horrible to be in love with the same guy for two years and to look forward to every inter-action, every word you spoke. And then someone else came by, someone strange, and got along better with that person.

"Would you prefer if I would take my distance from him?", I asked without knowing if I ever had the intention of doing so.

"No, no, no. Hell no. I don't want to be in the way of your friendship. It would just make me feel better if I would know that you aren't interested in him like that," she explained.

"Interested in him?"

I laughed.

"No, I'm absolutely certainly not interested in him."

"Thanks," I heard her murmur.

"I could try to talk with him about that again," I offered. "Maybe we can modify his idea of what's his type and what isn't."

"No", she answered and shook her head. "Maybe I needed this. Now I can let go of the idea of us ever being something and can start turning toward other things, better things. Everyone needs a new beginning every once in a while, and I guess it's time for me to let go."

I had to smile.

I liked her idea of letting go, and maybe I had already done that by now. Maybe I had finally found closure and accepted my past.

When I joined my friends in the one corner of the entrance hall where we always hung out – we wanted to spend the afternoon in the city center – I saw Jane sitting next to Julius instead, like always, next to Finn. She shot me a victorious look, and I grinned back.

"Did I miss something?" Julius asked us.

"No," we both said in unison.

"Careful, not that you'll become friends," Julius joked.

Could he be right about that? Were Jane and I about to become friends? Up until now, I saw her more as an acquaintance from school than a friend, but maybe now that she was getting over Finn, we were able to turn this involuntary rivalry into a friendship.

"Maybe we already are," Jane answered and smirked.

"Did you miss that as well or is it just me?" Julius asked Finn.

Finn, who was surprisingly quiet and reserved, twitched as if he was so absorbed in his thoughts that he didn't realize someone was talking to him.

"What did I miss?" he stuttered which was really odd since he was always so certain in everything he was doing. Something was wrong, and I couldn't imagine that the situation with Jane was the only reason why he behaved that way.

"Apparently you even missed my question," Julius answered. "What's wrong with you today?" he finally said what everyone was thinking.

"Nothing. What should be wrong?"

He ran his fingers through his hair and suddenly seemed so awkward.

Was he anxious? But he always was the calmest person I knew.

"Well, you seem pretty out of it," I said, and looked at him seriously, hoping he would finally tell us the truth.

"Maybe. I just had a very unpleasant encounter," he said annoyed.

"With who?" Julius asked.

"It seems like I can't avoid your questions anyway," he sighed. "I had the last two hours off, so I only came back to school because of you guys and guess who I saw in front of our school?"

"Your creepy ex-girlfriend?" Julius asked.

"Your uncle?" Jane guessed.

I could feel everyone looking at me, expecting me to make another guess.

"I have no clue," I said insecurely.

"Wrong, wrong, and …", he looked at me when he continued talking, "you are the only one that could've guessed it."

"Me?" I repeated even more insecurely.

Why should I know who he encountered? I didn't know his uncle nor his creepy ex-girlfriend, nor had I any idea who else would put him in such a bad mood or who would want to stand in front of a school if they weren't even a student and therefore didn't belong there.

"Yes, you. It could be rather interesting for you," he answered neutrally.

"We can all go and take a look," Julius offered and the rest of us followed him, even though Finn wasn't very happy about this.

He offered us multiple times to explain everything if we would simply take the back exit, but we all agreed that we preferred looking at the person ourselves.

And then, when I thought it couldn't get any more awkward and crazy, I was proven wrong again. Because in front of our school were two people that I didn't expect to be there and whose presence made my heart jump all the way down into my pants.

Chapter 11

After this rather peculiar trip to the city center, I strictly avoided all of Tim's surprises. Of course, he has never wanted to harm me; he just wanted me to confront myself with my biggest fears to be more successful quicker. And if it wasn't me, it would've probably worked. However, I felt so incredibly guilty about my visions – I didn't want to say that I wasn't guilty – but life would be easier if I didn't feel that way.

If Tim wasn't by my side, I would have given up my dreams about living a normal life at the latest after the trip to the city center. But Tim didn't give up on me and tried to find new tasks for me every day.

I still couldn't control my abilities at all. There was barely any success, and if something ever happened, it was so insignificant that we couldn't tell if it was me or just the wind. Although the biggest secret about my ability was kind of solved, I still had so many questions. Not just about me and my visions but also about the book, its author, and the strangers my Grandma warned me of. But even though I read the book every day, I couldn't find anything about these things.

The author of the book was still unknown, and so were the strangers. My Grandma had told me that the book would answer all of my questions, and if she was right about everything so far, why should she be wrong now? I just had to be patient and try to connect further with my powers, and maybe some of the answers would come all by themselves. It might've sounded naïve, but I was ready to believe that everything would happen when it was the right time for it to happen.

When I was younger and my Grandma read the stories from the book to me, I would've never expected the significance the book would have in the future. Although she only read the unspectacular beginning of the book, I still heard her voice in my ear when I read the part she had left out. I pictured her sitting next to me and reading the book to me out loud, like in the old days.

The only difference was that the stories had changed a bit. They weren't about fairy tales or other made-up stories anymore. They were stories about creatures that really existed. There probably was a reason my Grandma had only read the beginning to me, she might've found me too young for the truth (which has always been her favorite answer to all of my questions related to our family history or the old mansion). Actually, it felt like some kind of sadism to let your grandchild kill people for so many years until one decides to inform him that he was 1.) not insane and 2.) a mass murderer.

If I would have gotten the book a little bit earlier, I could've started to learn how to control my abilities earlier, and so many people would've stayed alive.

Additionally, my Grandma could've helped me with everything in person. But there must've been a reason for all of this. Maybe she just wanted to protect me. From myself.

Although some time has passed, the success was still left out. I totally gave up on moving things via telekinesis but there was some slight success in controlling my deadly visions.

Eventually, and with a lot of begging, Tim managed to drag me out of my apartment into the real world. My second trip among people was to a less crowded place; Tim had learned from his past mistakes, and we gained a lot of insight into how my visions worked. Since there were fewer people, the probability that I would kill someone was smaller from the very beginning, but since I didn't even have a vision, we concluded that they were triggered mainly by stress or if I felt pressured or highly uncomfortable.

If I was able to avoid stressful situations in the future, maybe I would be able to avoid my visions as well. However, I had no clue how to do that, but it was at least some kind of beginning to understand what was going on with me.

"I have another idea," Tim said one evening when he visited me.

"Again?" I protested a little bit.

I was still very exhausted from our last trip, which wasn't even a week ago.

"Yes, and this time we raise the difficulty a little bit," he said and smirked suspiciously.

"I don't want to go back to the city center … " I started, but Tim interrupted me with a declining gesture.

"That's not what I mean. It's something even better but more difficult. But you won't have any trouble with it, I guess."

"Then tell me what I'm supposed to do," I sighed.

"You are going to," he started, and smiled as widely as a five-year-old child that just got a package of gummy bears, "visit your father."

I looked at him with my eyes wide open. I had expected everything but that.

"No," I complained immediately.

"You can't make me do that. I didn't keep my distance from him for so long. That wouldn't be fair. Impossible. I'm not doing that," I blurted out.

"But you already got so much better, and we know how to avoid your visions in theory," he was almost beseeching me.

"No, I mean, yes, we know so much more about me, but we still don't know everything yet. All we have is a theory, but we don't know if we are right. I just don't want to risk the life of my dad, which I tried to spare for so many years just for some experiment. In general, I don't want to risk anyone's life ever again."

"But I'm sure you can do it," he tried again.

"Never. Tim. Never. Can't we start a little bit slower?" now it was me who almost beseeched him.

"But we already started slow. What do you think should be your next step?"

Damn, he was right. We had started off incredibly slowly, and I didn't have any better idea than visiting my dad, but I just didn't feel like I was ready yet. And I hated the idea of losing another beloved person, and even worse, ending their life for them.

"Maybe I don't have any better idea, but I'm begging you to think of something else. I'm just not ready for that," I tried again, "I would do anything to avoid visiting my dad for now."

"Oh, so that's what it's all about. You should've told me from the beginning," Tim was surprisingly okay with the situation, which could only mean that he already had another plan.

"Anything you say... I have a better idea, and I know that you are ready for that," he said and smirked at me.

Chapter 12

"**D**o you know them?" Julius asked, eyeing the two strangers skeptically.

She had to look twice because, at first glance, she didn't recognize him. In comparison to their last encounter, which was almost half a year ago, he had changed drastically. His hair was still looking unstyled, but in a way that it seemed like they were supposed to look like that, but his face somehow seemed different.

It took her a moment until she realized that he had exchanged his glasses for contact lenses, which made his blue eyes even more of an eye-catcher than they were before. But his body language had also changed. His aura was somehow more confident, and a little bit happier.

She, on the other hand, just came back from PE class and didn't think it was necessary to get out of her leggings and into her regular jeans. Her oversized T-shirt, which she had tied to a knot so it ended right over her belly button this morning, hung loosely and wrinkly because she didn't find the time to tie it again. Her hair was completely messy, and her face was still red from all the exercising. It was a classic case of I-feel-cooler-than-I-actually-look. But now that she has seen him casually leaning next to the school gate, all of her previous coolness has vanished.

"It's complicated," I answered Julius after a long break.

"Does he stalk you?", Jane wanted to know, but I ignored her and slowly walked in the direction of Ramon, who was staring at me from the moment I walked out of the building.

I had no clue why he was here or why I even walked toward him like I was hypnotized, but something inside of me – and I highly doubted it was my common sense – took control over my legs and made me walk toward him.

"That took you a while," he greeted me like we were supposed to meet here.

"What?" I asked perplexed, and eyed him skeptically.

I realized that his unknown friend was gone by now, and even my friends didn't follow me here; we were all alone. More or less. As alone as you could be in front of a school.

To answer my question, he just laughed and slowly ran his fingers through his hair without messing up his perfect look. How was he doing that?

"Why are you here?" I asked again, hoping to finally get an answer.

"Because I want to talk to you," he said softly.

"With me?" I repeated confused, and suddenly I felt so awkward.

If I had known I would meet him today, I would've changed clothes after PE class, and maybe I would've tried to cool down my face so I didn't look like I had run a marathon, even though all we did was play stupid ball games. But now I was looking my worst, and I was standing next to him, who looked relatively normal, even really good. Damn.

He just nodded.

"Ohm," I said. "Actually, I'm already hanging out with my friends," I continued my sentence and looked down at me: "Otherwise, I wouldn't have dressed like this."

"Too bad but then we can talk another time," he stretched the words while talking.

"Or I just tell them I'll join them a little bit later," I proposed without further thinking about what I had just said.

My friends weren't particularly happy, especially Finn didn't seem to like this at all; however, none of them complained. Jane even winked at me before I went away and said that I needed to introduce my strange companion to her one day. I couldn't tell if she was serious about that or if it was just a joke that you would make among friends.

"Before you start with whatever you have to say, can you first tell me how you found out to which school I'm going to?", I wanted to know when we started walking through the nearby streets.

"Sure, my best friend Tim hacked into every school to see the list of all their students," he answered seriously.

Shocked and confused about this level of honesty, I stopped walking.

When Ramon noticed that, he burst out laughing.

"That was a joke. I saw it on your Facebook profile," he explained after he finally stopped laughing. After all the weird pictures I had posted on there, I wasn't even sure if him knowing about my Facebook profile calmed me down more than his previous explanation.

"Oh god. I already thought you were … "

I stopped talking for one single reason; I had no clue what I had even thought he was in that moment.

"A murderer?" he suggested a fitting ending for my sentence.

"No, not quite. A creep fits better."

It was only after I finished talking that I realized he might've alluded to our first encounter. It had been such a long time ago that it almost surprised me that he could still remember.

"I can live with that," I heard him say quietly.

The longer I walked through the streets with him, the weirder I found his behavior the last time we met. If he was such a friendly and chill guy, why did he behave like such an asshole?

"So, to come back to the topic, I wanted to talk to you because I behaved very shitty toward you," he started.

"You noticed that early," I blurted out. "Oops, I didn't want to say that," I admitted in shame.

"It's okay. I deserve that. However, I want to apologize to you. I can't give you a good explanation for my behavior, at least not now, but you can trust me that I regretted everything the moment I shut that damn door," he explained while still sounding so chill about everything, it was driving me insane.

Why was he like this, and why was I so awkward? I didn't even know what to say to that. What did he expect of me? Did he want me to forgive him? Probably. Otherwise, he wouldn't have the need to apologize. Still, I was confused about his sudden change of mood again.

"Do you accept my apology?" he wanted to know after the silence became unbearable.

And if he didn't appear so chill today, I might've thought there was a little bit of insecurity in his voice.

"Yes, I do. You said you couldn't tell me the reason for your behavior, but what exactly do you mean by that?" I asked uncertainly.

"Mh. I expected you to ask this question," he started.

"Then why didn't you tell me the reason from the beginning?" I interrupted.

"Because there are certain things that other humans just can't cope with, and I first need to be sure that you can."

As so often, I just looked at him in confusion until I could get out a critical "Ah yes".

"And what do you expect now that I accepted your apology?" I dodged a cyclist that was dangerously close to the sidewalk – meanwhile, we had arrived at the city center – so I couldn't see Ramon's reaction to my question.

"I don't know, but maybe we can be friends or something like that," he answered and turned to the left to enter the pedestrian zone.

"So, friends," I repeated automatically.

"Does this sound so strange?" he asked chuckling, and eyed me closely.

"No. Actually, it doesn't sound strange at all," I murmured, and my voice became quieter at the end of the sentence. I was surprised that it really didn't sound strange at all.

We walked a little bit longer through the pedestrian zone and talked about everything and nothing at the same time. I learned that he had been liveing alone for over a year by now and that he got his first own car as a birthday present for his 18th birthday. I had to admit I was a tiny bit jealous because I surely wouldn't get a car for my birthday. When we passed a small store for all kinds of accessories and gadgets, the mood shifted a little bit. After Ramon looked at a sign that was taped to the door, he became quieter and more thoughtful.

"Pls, not again," I thought.

The last time he was that quiet, he shut the door just in front of me, which wasn't particularly polite. And even during our first meeting, he had these phases where he suddenly became cold and distant. Why was he like this? Maybe we could even become good friends if he wasn't that complicated. This change in mood made it hard to figure him out and even harder to find the right words to say. Everything I could say right now would sound dumb.

"Are you okay?" I asked carefully.

He twitched for a second, as if I had interrupted his thoughts.

"Yeah, I'm fine, but I think it's time for me to go back home. Also, your friends are waiting there for you," he stumbled a bit.

It took a few seconds until he sounded as confident as he did when we started our walk.

"So, see ya," he said.

"See ya in six months," I joked, and noticed that he had to laugh a little bit about it.

"I think you should totally invite him to my party this weekend. That would be such a great opportunity to integrate him into our friend group," Jane suggested when we were on our way back home.

"I don't know if that would be such a good idea," I hesitated.

I didn't even know if Ramon was the kind of guy who would want to go to a party.

"But you are friends now," she tried again.

"That's bullshit, you barely know each other," I heard Finn complain next to me.

He wasn't wrong about it, but I somehow liked the idea of Ramon and me being friends.

"But you didn't know her at first either," Jane responded.

1:0 for Jane.

"I, however, never asked her to be her friend. It just happened, and I was always nice to her. What I want to say is that he's unpredictable, and this *friendship*," we could tell that it was hard for Finn to pronounce, "won't change a thing about this. He'll always be unpredictable. And I have no clue why he wants to be your friend so badly, but I have a weird feeling about this. Something about him is off."

"No need to be jealous. You should give him a chance and get to know him better. I'm sure he is perfectly fine, otherwise Luna wouldn't be friends with him," Jane defended Ramon.

"Right Luna?" she wanted to know and interrupted my thoughts.

I had stopped following that conversation at some point.

"Ohm. Sure," I stuttered and hoped I was saying the right things.

"See?" she continued talking to Finn.

"There are no excused for you," she now said to me,

"you'll invite him to my party and then we can all judge him better."

That very same evening, I decided to get done with it. If he would say no, I would surely survive that, but if I didn't even ask him, I was certain, Jane would be disappointed, and I wanted to avoid this, especially now that we started getting along well.

My heart beat faster when I went up the stairs to the fifth floor. Was I excited? No ... Maybe a little bit, somehow, but not because of Ramon but more because of the fact that I was inviting him to a party. The whole situation was – and no one could deny that – incredibly weird and uncommon.

Carefully, I knocked on the door. Maybe I would be lucky and Ramon wasn't even at home. Slowly, I counted to ten, intending to walk away once I would reach ten, but I had just made it to seven when the door was opened.

"Hey, what's up?" Ramon greeted me and looked at me expectantly.

Maybe he was ready for anything but me.

"Nothing special," I answered casually.

Then I realized that this must've sounded super dumb since I was the one standing in front of his door. I immediately blushed.

"I just wanted to ask you something," I continued before he could even say anything.

I still wasn't happy with my choice of words, but at least I didn't sound like a complete fool anymore.

"Do you want to come in?" he asked, and stepped to the side.

Thankful, I entered his apartment and followed him into the living room. It reminded me a little bit of our first encounter, the only difference was that we were now friends and I wasn't soaked by the rain. When he sat down on his gray couch, I sat down as well.

"Okay," I cleared my throat, "maybe you'll say no anyway and think it's a stupid idea because I think it's stupid as well ..."

"Just ask me first, and then I can tell you if it's stupid or not," he interrupted, and smiled at me amused.

"Okay," I said more to myself than to him. "A friend of mine, Jane, throws a party, and she suggested that you could come with me, and that's why I'm here."

"Aha," he said stretched, and eyed me with small eyes.

Silence.

He didn't say anything, and I didn't want to add anything. I had already said enough.

"I think I'll come with you," he said, and his face lit up a bit.

"Really?" I asked surprised.

After all this time of silence, I really didn't expect him to agree to come with me.

"Yeah, really," he confirmed and smirked.

"Cool," I just said, until I realized that I had neither told him the date nor the time of the party. After I had given him all the information he needed, I excused myself by saying I needed to finish my homework and therefore escaped from this slightly awkward situation. If I would be as weird on the day of the party as I was today, this could become a really uncomfortable evening.

✽✽✽

It was a lukewarm Friday evening at the end of April; the first exam phase of this semester was over, so there was no reason for me to not go to this party, even though I thought about ditching it multiple times in the last few hours.

Eventually, I decided against faking a disease (or even my own death) but going there because it would be positive to face my fears that often influenced the way I interacted with people. I've been to so many parties in the last time, why exactly should I be afraid of this one?

Since it was too late to cancel anyway, I decided it was time to get ready. I spent so much time overthinking this stupid party that I completely forgot I had only one hour until I was meeting up with Ramon.

Even though there was no real reason for it, I spent almost an eternity trying to find the perfect outfit for this party.

Usually, I never had any trouble figuring out what to wear; I just threw on the first clothes I could find. Most parties were held in the dark anyway, so no one would see me or my outfit and therefore not care if I would look stupid. Overthinking an outfit for any event just felt like such a waste of time and money, but today it felt like I had no clothes in my closet. At least none that I would feel comfortable wearing.

I could stop myself from calling Finn and complaining about my problem because he would probably just laugh at me, and I would do the same if it wasn't me in this exact situation.

Eventually, I decided to combine my black jeans, a white top, and a denim jacket; nothing innovative, but a glance at my watch told me that there was no time to change my outfit anyway. I was already four minutes late when I stormed out of the apartment. Everything was as always.

The party was supposed to start at 8 p.m., but since the drive, despite being in a car, would take some time – especially if we didn't use the GPS and had to rely on my poor sense of orientation – Ramon and I met half an hour earlier than we would've regularly met.

Although there was this unwritten rule that you should show up at the earliest one hour after the party had officially started, which was propagated through American teen shows, I never really cared much about it. Firstly, because we lived in Germany and not America, and secondly, I really enjoyed the beginnings of parties. I even preferred them over everything else. It was quieter, and you could have some nice conversations while the music was only running in the background and most people were still normal and sober. Of course, I could understand that there were a lot of people who disliked these beginnings, like Finn, for example.

He thought of this calmness as cringe-worthy and awkward. No one would be dancing or drinking at the start of the party, and everyone was just waiting for someone to start with either of these things so everyone else could follow them like puppies. Maybe the reason why I particularly liked these beginnings was that I was neither a talented dancer nor a huge drinker.

"Sorry, for being late," I said out of breath when I arrived downstairs.

"No problem. I'm not here for a long time either," he said and moved his head in the direction of his car.

"Shall we?"

I nodded and followed him to the car, which was parked on the other side of the street. The drive was nowhere near as cringe as I feared after our last conversation. As soon as the engine of the car had started, the radio started as well, and it didn't take Ramon long to start singing along with the songs on the radio.

I had to figure out that he wasn't the best singer ever, but he didn't think of himself as being talented as well. He was just trying to enjoy himself, and that made me feel comfortable, so I started singing along.

"We should form a band," he screamed in joy, trying to be louder than the music.

"Sure. Can you play any instrument?" I asked and lowered the volume of the radio a bit, so I could understand him better.

"Nope, but I could try playing the triangle," he answered.

He had to break at a red traffic light before he looked straight at me and asked: "What about you?"

"No, nothing. Not even the triangle," I shrugged.

"These aren't the best conditions," he figured out.

"We could try being an acapella group," I offered.

He shook his head playfully disgusted.

"I prefer playing the drums or the guitar. At least I always wanted to learn these instruments when I was a kid."

"But you should know," I said very seriously, "no one ever cares about the drummer."

"That's very discriminating of you, you know. If I think about it, I doubt that our band has any future," he answered with the same intonation as me.

"That is absolutely unfortunate, but I'm certain that such a talented lad like you'll find another band," I tried going for the same seriousness in my voice, but this time it was really hard to repress my laughter. Eventually, it was Ramon who started laughing first.

"Lad? I don't know why, but this makes you sound so British, innit?" he said while still laughing.

"If you find it that funny, I might consider adding it to my everyday vocabulary," I said and looked at him challenging.

"Please don't. Otherwise, I'll have trouble taking you seriously," and with these words, he turned into Jane's street.

When we arrived at Jane's place, it was still very empty, which surprised me since we arrived a little bit later than we had planned. Happily, she opened the door and led us into her huge living room. Meanwhile, I was pretty sure that Jane's family must've been at least from the upper class, which made it even odder for me that we got along so well.

We didn't find time to talk more with Jane because the doorbell rang another time. It didn't take Jane long to come back, followed by Finn and Julius.

"Alcohol is where it always is," I heard Jane talk to them, which made them walk toward the alcohol. Still, Finn managed to glare at Ramon in disgust. The past had already proved that Finn wasn't a huge fan of Ramon because of the way he had treated me. After our first encounter, I had suffered a lot because of his mood changes, and Finn hated seeing me like that.

For some reason, I had still hoped that he would be able to forget this for one moment. And even if he wasn't able to do that, he could've at least greeted me briefly, as Julius did. I didn't expect them to become best friends immediately, but he could've at least tried to be nice.

Slowly, the other guests came in, and the dance floor started to get more and more crowded, which was my signal to secure myself a spot on the couch.

"I'm sorry," I said to Ramon after we sat down.

"What are you sorry about?" he asked, and looked at me with raised eyebrows.

"I'm sorry that I brought you here. This must be so lame."

He sighed shortly, then he shook his head.

"You don't need to apologize. Just the drive here was worth it," he said, or at least that was what I thought he had said since the music was now turned to full volume, and I wasn't completely sure if I could understand everything he had said, and I was too shy to ask if he wanted to repeat it.

We were sitting on the couch in silence for quite some time, the music was way too loud for a proper conver-sation, and even if it was quieter, I had no clue what to say. Suddenly, he felt as closed and inscrutable as when we first met. Something about him was differ-ent. He wasn't like anyone else I knew – no, I don't just mean his bipolar behavior – and I couldn't put my finger on what exactly was different.

It wasn't like he was distant. He stopped being distant the day our friendship had officially started, but still, it felt like he was trapped in his own thoughts. I couldn't even get close to guessing what he was thinking at this moment. It was like he was mentally so far away from me, despite being physically close.

"Is everything okay with you? You look bored," Finn asked, and sat down next to me.

"We aren't bored," I answered a bit hurt because, deep down, I knew Finn was right.

"Well, then everything is fine. Still, you should come and dance with us. Otherwise, you're missing out on all of the fun," he invited us.

I shot Ramon a questioning glance, he just shrugged.

"Here you are. Jane is looking for you," Julius entered the conversation. "She thinks we should all dance together in a huge group," he added. "You don't seem like you have anything better to do anyway," he figured out while looking at Ramon and me before he vanished again.

Discontented, I followed him leading us to Jane and the others. Finn was, in fact, right, and I enjoyed dancing a lot. Suddenly, I felt so stupid about my attitude at the other parties in the past. Except for my first party, I always tried to avoid dancing or drinking. I preferred standing with my friends until they started getting too drunk. That has always been my signal to lay low and chill on the couch. Mostly, I didn't stay long, and the days after, everyone would always tell me what I had missed, but I didn't care. It wasn't important for me to notice everything.

It was obvious that she couldn't dance well; however, no one here could dance. She felt confident, losing herself in the music and moving the way she wanted. Her eyes were full of joy, there was a special shine in them, something she thought she had lost long before. Her friends vanished in between the songs to grab some more alcohol, still, she never was alone.

She didn't drink anything, but she seemed somehow changed. It was like the evening triggered something deep down inside of her. Something only she could understand, and no one else would ever be able to see it except for her.

It was crazy how well I felt that night. It was like I finally let go of everything that had dragged me down in the past.

The more time passed, the more drunken my friends got, especially Finn was noticeably wasted. Unfortunately, I had to realize that he wasn't able to walk straight anymore. In total, his attempts at walking looked more like staggering. I was confused because he never was like that. I always thought he was under control of his drinking. Someone who knew his limit and never drunk more than that. I couldn't stand looking at him like that, so I decided it was time to bring him home. Luckily, Ramon felt the same and offered that we could drive him home together.

After Finn protested, he finally gave in and let Ramon carry him to his car. I could feel the worried stares of the others when I climbed into the backseat next to Finn.

"Does he need a bag?" Ramon asked while he was looking for one in his trunk.

"I don't know. I've never seen him like this," I answered panickily.

I was completely overwhelmed by this situation.

"I'm perfectly fine," Finn said in a drunken slur.

"Unfortunately, I don't believe you," Ramon answered, and gave him a plastic bag.

"Thanks," Finn murmured, and accepted it defiantly. Then we started driving away.

"Should we rather bring him to a hospital?" I asked after Finn had thrown up multiple times.

"How many times do I have to tell you that I'm fine?" he screamed.

"That doesn't sound like a bad idea," Ramon answered to my question.

"Where is the next hospital?" I wanted to know.

"Good question," I heard Ramon murmur.

"Let's stop here for a second. Then we can google. Also, I think Finn needs another bag," I suggested.

Ramon immediately stopped the car on the side of the road.

So, there we were, somewhere on a lonely country road that no one would drive on at this time of the day anyway. Immediately, I jumped out of the car to look for another bag in the trunk while Ramon tried to google the way to the closest hospital.

"Can you maybe google if there is anything else we can do for him? Maybe we can open a window or something like that," I screamed from outside the car.

"It says we should protect him from the cold," Ramon shouted back, "as long as Finn is still conscious everything is fine."

Slightly calmer, I entered the car so we could continue our ride.

"You two just do what you want anyway," Finn babbled offended. "But I swear I'm fi… ," his head fell on his right shoulder and his eyes were closed.

"How long do we have to drive?" I cried out.

"We're almost there," Ramon said, and I could feel him driving a bit faster than before.

With shaking hands, I was trying to check on Finn's pulse. It didn't work very well.

'Get yourself together', I demanded and tried again. Luckily, Finn still had a pulse, and he was breathing as well.

"I'll go inside and get a doctor, and you stay with him," Ramon demanded, and ran in the direction of the hospital's entrance. Being stressed out like that, I didn't even notice that we had arrived.

"You are such an idiot," I whispered with tears in my eyes. "Really, I wish I could hate you for what you are doing to me right now. But I can't."

Now, I couldn't stop my tears anymore.

"Why are you like that?"

I sobbed and pressed his hand in mine hoping I would feel any kind of reaction from him. But there was none. I should start focusing on the positive things; he was alive. He was breathing, and he still had a pulse. Surely, he was in a critical condition, but he wasn't dead.

Ramon would find a doctor in the hospital and would come back any second. Everything would be fine. If it wouldn't be so incredibly difficult to convince myself of that. I closed my eyes to escape the situation for a brief moment, but it didn't want to work. I checked his heartbeat, which was fine, a little bit faster than usual but fine.

"I dare you to leave me," I said while my hand was still resting on his heart.

"How much did he drink?"

I heard a strange voice say after the door of the car was opened.

"I have no clue," I sobbed.

Quickly, Ramon helped the doctor unbuckle Finn, then they vanished. Ramon had to answer some more questions, then we were allowed to drive home.

"Everything is going to be fine, okay?" I heard Ramon say but somehow these words weren't enough for me. I couldn't believe them anymore. Not after I had seen Finn like this.

"I talked to the doctors. It's not their first drunk teenager. They know what they are doing. And since he is still breathing and everything, the doctors are certain he'll be alright in no time. They have seen worse, okay?" he continued.

"B-B-but he seemed so weak," I stuttered.

"But this doesn't mean he'll die. Believe me, I've seen a lot of people die in my life, and Finn doesn't look like he is about to die."

I was probably way too shocked by everything to question what exactly Ramon was saying. Because I just nodded and stared out of the window. Ramon understood that I wasn't ready to talk about anything and respected that, or he simply didn't know what he should say. Either way, I was happy to be driven home in silence.

"Thank you for everything," I said weakly when we arrived in front of the door to my apartment.

"No problem," he said, nodding friendly.

Was he waiting for me to say something else? I wasn't feeling like saying anything tonight. I just wanted to go home and sleep, and hope that Finn would get better soon. Because it was so easy to forget the value of a person when the person was around you every day. You started taking this person for granted. This was my problem too. I took Finn for granted, and now that he was in a situation where I couldn't help him or care for him, I realized how important he was to me. I couldn't bear losing him since he was by far the most important person in my life, and he would always be.

I looked at Ramon and tried to give him a thankful smile. I swore to myself that I would never take anyone or anything for granted anymore. And so, Ramon's help wasn't something I would take for granted either.

"I can't thank you enough," I whispered.

Before I would start to cry again – I never thought I could be that sensitive – I wished him a good night.

"Goodnight, Luana," I heard him mumble.

Confused, I looked at him.

"Luna," I corrected him, and vanished.

Chapter 13

I couldn't explain how Tim was able to convince me to wait in front of Luna's school to talk to her. I knew this was dangerous, and usually I would've never done something as risky as that, but I guess, in the end, my curiosity and the urge to pretend to have a normal life for once got the best of me.

I still needed to figure out the connection between Luna, Luana, and me. But despite that, I realized again how deadly I was when we walked through the pedestrian zone (especially when we saw the little store that Tim and I went to). I was a safety hazard. A murderer. Still, some time had passed without any visions, and I was proud of myself, especially because I didn't try to avoid humans as much as I used to.

Tim was even more proud of me since I went outside without him talking me into it. It was the first time in my life that I went to a real party, and it was hard to try to act like it didn't scare me at all. But if there was one thing that I learned about handling my visions – I mean murders – was that everything was fine as long as I could repress my emotions. And even though I was 100 percent sure I didn't have any visions, the fear of being at fault for Finn's behavior that night grew from day to day.

My powers had changed so often that I couldn't tell for certain if it was possible for me to kill without having a vision at all. Maybe they had changed again and maybe now I was able to kill people without even realizing. Technically, I killed people for 19 years without knowing about it. But as long as Finn would stay alive, I couldn't be at fault, at least that was what I tried to tell myself.

Although I couldn't exactly say how many people were victims of my visions, since a lot of them were strangers, I knew from the people that surrounded me that my visions were certainly deadly. That's why I concluded that even if I couldn't find any evidences, the strangers that appeared in my visions would die as well. Like the cashier from the little store, who was another one of my victims.

So, if Finn made it, it would prove that I, for once, wasn't guilty. However, I couldn't explain his behavior that day because the main reason I was worried about him was that I barely saw him drink any alcohol that night. He got way too drunk, way too suddenly.

It was a normal Monday afternoon, I had worked all morning and figured out it was time to accidentally bump into Luna again to try to figure out more about Finn and his wellbeing and hopefully calm down my guilty conscience. The more I thought about it, the less I could stand being at home. I couldn't just sit here and do nothing and hope that all of my problems would solve themselves on their own. Maybe the old Ramon could do this, but this wasn't me anymore. I needed to take responsibility and try to actively change something.

If I wanted to live a normal life, I had to go outside and do something that normal people would do as well. So, I decided to go for a walk around the neighboring streets. Fresh air would be good for me, and in the best case, I would bump into Luna.

The fresh air couldn't completely free my mind from all of my thoughts, still, I felt a little bit better. I felt a little bit more alive. Lost in thoughts, I walked through the street that would lead me back home.

"Are you on your way home, too?" I heard Luna say behind me.

"More or less," I murmured quietly.

Actually, I didn't really expect to meet her here, outside. Would it be too weird if I asked her about Finn immediately? But her voice sounded normal. Neither negative nor sad, that must've been a good sign, right?

"Is everything okay?" she wanted to know and looked at me.

"Yes, it was a stressful day at work. What about you, are you okay?" I asked.

This change in topic was as perfect as it could've been. I wanted to pat myself on the back because this was just way too smooth to be true.

"Oh," she just said, and immediately her voice started to change.

This was bad.

This couldn't be good. If anything had happened to Finn, and if it actually was my fault, I would never be able to forgive myself for it.

"I guess that everything is okay with me," she said after a longer break, and it sounded like there were more words on the tip of her tongue, like she didn't want to end the sentence yet, but still she stopped. The name Finn was surrounding us invisibly, however clearly noticeable.

"And what about Finn?" I finally asked about the elephant in the room.

It felt relieving to know that I would soon have an answer to the question which had been bothering me for days. Still, I felt an unwell feeling in my stomach. Did I even want to know the answer to my question?

"He is still in the hospital, but he is stable."

It took me some time to understand what these words meant. I wasn't guilty. His weird and sudden change in behavior must've had another reason. Maybe I wasn't paying enough attention to him, and he really drank more than I thought he did. Maybe I just told myself that I didn't see him drink that much because I didn't have another explanation for his odd behavior, and it was always easier to blame myself than to accept reality.

"That's great news," I said.

This was definitely not the smartest thing I've ever said.

"Yes, it's almost a miracle that he could recover that well. When I was visiting him yesterday, he was exactly how he used to be," she blurted out while her face lit up again.

This is how it must feel if you had people that meant more to you than anything on this earth. A feeling that I wasn't all too familiar with.

"But why was it a miracle?" I asked her skeptically. If it was like a miracle, who knew if I wasn't the one to blame for his condition.

"That evening he was doing pretty bad. But this you know already. Apparently, his condition got even worse after we were gone. The doctors weren't so sure anymore if he would make it."

"That's strange," I said more to myself than to her.

"I agree. Especially since you were so sure that he wasn't in any all too big danger."

Suddenly, I felt hot and cold at the same time.

If she could remember my exact words, it could be that she could still remember all the other not-so-smart things I had said, and if she would start wondering why I had so many experiences with death and dead people, I needed to come up with a rather good excuse.

"Yeah, I was so sure," I pressed out between my lips and hoped that she wouldn't realize how tense I was.

"Can I ask you something and you answer honestly?" she asked, and sounded a bit insecure.

Now I felt even worse. I was sure that I would like to answer her next question as much as Faust wanted to answer Gretchen's question about his connection to religion.

"Sure," I just said, hoping that she wouldn't notice the shaking in my voice if I tried hiding it with a big smile.

"That evening, when Finn wasn't feeling well, you said something, and I don't know exactly what to think about it," she started, and sounded so innocent while saying it.

How could I be such a monster and drag her into this mess that was my life? I was a ticking time bomb. I was deadly and unpredictable. And when, not if, I explode I will drag everyone around me with me to doom, including her. When did I change that much? I had become so egoistic. Did I really want to destroy her life just to make my life a little bit better?

The scary thing about this was that I would answer this question with 'yes' without hesitating.

"What exactly did I say?" I wanted to know, and pretended like it wasn't a big deal and I forgot about it.

"Maybe I misunderstood you or my brain just made it up, it was a very long and stressful night, but I thought you said something along the lines of that you saw a lot of people die and since that night, I have to think about it a lot. I can understand if you don't want to talk about it because it's a personal topic and we don't know each other too well, but since we're friends now …" She didn't finish her sentence, still I knew what she was thinking.

She was insecure, and it would've been so easy to manipulate her, to gaslight her into believing I had never said these things, but it was time to get the corpses out of the basement.

"I'll answer that question," I started, and my voice suddenly sounded so strange, "but it's your own re-sponsibility."

I put the key into the lock of the main door and real-ized that my hand started to shake.

"Okay," she said, and followed me to the staircase.

"It's quite a long story so you better come and visit me when you have some time to spare," I said and couldn't prevent my voice from sounding absent.

"I'm free now," she said, and her voice sounded so secure and certain. As if she knew exactly what to do in that one moment.

"Come in and make yourself feel comfortable," I said after I unlocked and opened the door to my apartment.

Luna sat down on the couch, where she sat when she invited me to the party. If I had just stayed home that day. I wouldn't be in this situation.

Luna crossed her arms in front of her chest and looked at me. I was aware of the fact that it was my turn to say something that would explain the whole situation to her, but I didn't know where to start. I couldn't just say 'funny story, but sometimes I have these visions and they kill people lol' especially not when she was expecting a completely different story than the one I had to offer.

I cleared my throat.

"There are two rules that you have to follow when I start explaining everything," I finally began talking.

"Rule number one is that you don't think I'm insane, and rule number two is that you won't leave before I'm done. Let me explain everything. I don't want you to think wrong of me without knowing the full story."

She just nodded, and I was sure that after this little prologue, she must've expected me to be a mass murderer, which technically wasn't even wrong.

"What I'm about to tell you will sound unbelievable, and you'll think that I'm crazy, but I promise you that everything I'm about to tell you is nothing but the truth."

She looked at me expectantly, but she didn't say anything.

"Everything started when I was six. My whole family spontaneously met at my Grandma's place. It was the last time that we sat all together like that, and no one could've known that, especially not my Grandma...", so I started telling her everything. From my very first encounter with Luana up until her death.

"So, that's why you called me Luana," Luna threw in when she heard the name for the first time.

Completely overwhelmed and unsure of what to say, I continued with the story. The story, which included the death of a very good friend of mine. The story, which I was almost able to repress from my memory until today.

Luna had a really good poker face. Based on her expressions, it was impossible for me to tell what she thought, she didn't look scared nor like she was thinking I was crazy. No matter what she must've thought, she was incredibly good at not showing it. So, I continued to talk about the death of my mom, the beginning of my therapy sessions with Mrs. Müller, and my early move from home.

Then I came to the most recent events. I talked about the reasons for my shitty behavior, and for a brief moment, she looked like she could understand me. After that, her face went back to the unreadable poker face. I tried to not be distracted by it too much and told her about the sudden but predicted death of my Grandma, my hopes of living a normal life, and the disappointment I felt when I saw the book for the first time.

Luna stayed quiet and listened to me attentively. I still had no idea how she would react after I was done explaining everything, or if she would even react at all. Would she get up in silence and walk away, or would she even start laughing at me? Maybe she would be afraid and would avoid me, which would probably be the best solution for her, but I had no clue if I could handle this because it has been a while since I let anyone as close to me as I let her be.

I told her about Tim and his insane ideas of how to help me, the finally helpful words in the book, and my reappearing hopes, but I also talked about the first setback during our expedition to the city center.

Finally, I ended my story by explaining why Tim wanted me to let her into my life. Her similarities to Luana were undeniable, and I was sure that this couldn't be a coincidence. Additionally, I felt this weird connection with her – fortunately, I could stop myself from saying this out loud – which was another reason why it was easy for me to trust her.

"So, you are something like an angel of death?" she asked after I was done.

Even the sound of her voice didn't show any possible emotions.

"My Grandma called it Guardian of All Good, but your idea sounds not too wrong either," I answered nervously.

"What a euphemism," she answered quietly.

I had to chuckle for a second.

"Exactly my words."

She smiled for a second as well.

"And do you know how to cope with your visions or what you want to do next when it comes to the strangers your Grandma warned you of?" she continued asking.

"No, there are no further pieces of information about any of these things in the book, but Tim and I figured out that I can prevent having visions if I avoid being overly emotional. Stress is and has always been my main trigger. I was always so stressed just because I could have a vision. Such irony, I know," I answered, and realized how I felt more and more comfortable about this situation. If she thought I was insane, she wouldn't ask that many questions.

"I have one more question. You have nothing to do with Finn's trip to the hospital, do you? After everything you told me, it wouldn't be impossible that you did something to him, would it?"

She looked at me penetrably.

I sighed.

"That's pretty much the Gretchen question here, you know? Because I really don't know. I didn't have a vision, if that's what you mean, but I think his behavior was odd and unnatural," I answered slowly.

"So, even if you didn't have a vision, you still think it could've been you doing this?"

"Correct. My abilities have changed all the time. Think about the story with Luana that I told you. Back then, everything was different. Only when I turned 18 did my visions become unbearable and unpredictable. Back in the old days, I needed some kind of body contact, but now it's enough to simply look at a person. I would always expect them to change, and who knows, maybe they would change for the worse."

I observed her reaction closely and couldn't believe how chill she seemed to be about everything.

"Hmpf. That would make it even harder to control your visions," she thought out loud.

This hit the nail right on its head because it was my biggest fear that I had tried to repress in the past few days.

"Correct again," I confirmed.

"That would be super irrational and wouldn't make sense," she figured out.

When she saw my questioning look, she just answered: "In the book, it says that you'll be able to control your powers. It doesn't say how or how long it'll take, but it sounds like it's already determined, am I wrong? If your visions would change again, it would mean that they'll always change throughout your life, which would make them impossible to control."

She wasn't wrong about that, still I was speechless. How could she think so clearly after everything I had told her?

"Also, why should your powers change after your 18th birthday? You are officially an adult, and I'm pretty sure there has to be some invisible age line where your powers won't change anymore because they are fully grown. Or isn't it even 16 in most movies?" she continued talking.

"I never looked at it from this perspective," I admitted.

"That's why it's good that you have me," she answered, grinning. "What time is it, by the way?" she asked after a short break.

"It's almost 8 p.m.," I answered after looking at my watch.

"I think it's time for me to go back home. My mom is probably worried," she said, and sounded a little bit surprised. And so was I, neither of us had expected this conversation to take so long.

Understanding I brought her to the door. I still had no clue if she believed me or if she would start avoiding me.

Just before she left, she turned around one last time and asked me: "What exactly do you expect me to do now?"

This question hit me totally unexpectedly because I had no clue what exactly I could expect from anyone.

"I think it would be good for me to know if you'll avoid me or if you want to stay in my life, at your own risk of course. And maybe you even want to help me figure out more about what's going on with the strangers and the book of my Grandma," I summarized my thoughts.

She didn't say anything in response but turned around and walked down the stairs.

Chapter 14

D o you know the feeling of your whole world crashing down and falling apart, and it feels like you are carrying the whole weight of the remains on your shoulders, and you are about to break down? This is how I felt the evening Ramon told me everything. My whole worldview was destroyed, and the fact that I couldn't tell anyone about it just made it worse.

But what was even worse was the decision I had to make. I really could help Ramon, and damn, I was curious, and I didn't want to let him down, but on the other hand, every second I spent with him could be one second too much. Also, I barely knew him, which would make it much easier to avoid him in the future. So many thoughts were filling my head, but somehow I managed to keep calm and not let Ramon see how messy I really felt.

As always, when I was completely overwhelmed with everything, I ran a hot bath and locked myself in the bathroom for the next three hours. This usually helped me sort my thoughts and calm down. Most of the time, everything sounded more uncomplicated after a long bath. However, not today.

"Is everything alright?" my mom asked me after I sat down next to her on the couch.

"Yes, everything is fine," I lied.

"You know, if it's about the thing from this morning … It's totally fine if you are bothered by it," she said carefully.

I needed a few minutes until I could remember what she was talking about. But when I could finally remember, I felt bad. Even worse than before.

This morning, my mom told me that there was one of her colleagues at work who she really liked. Long story short, she found a father replacement for me and invited him over for dinner tomorrow. Although I didn't like the idea of that very much, it was by far my smallest problem at the moment. It was, in fact, so irrelevant that I even forgot about it. And now I felt horrible because my mom thought she was at fault for my weird behavior, even though she wasn't. But it was easier to let her believe that because I couldn't tell her the truth anyway. It probably made me a bad person, but I also doubted that I would get a free ticket to hell for such a minor lie. Still, I felt guilty for the rest of the day.

It was impossible for me to fall asleep in the following night. I had a lot of weird and confusing thoughts and dreams. Everything seemed to spin, shadows felt so much more threatening. If Ramon existed, who knew what other creatures would exist as well? And even though Ramon never proved that he had any special powers, I still believed every word he said without even questioning it. Was I naïve? Was I dumb, or was I simply running blindly after my destiny?

I looked at my alarm clock. If I would stop waking up every ten minutes, I could still sleep for two more hours until I had to get up. I turned around multiple times, but somehow my body just didn't want to properly rest; my mind was way too active.

Eventually, I decided I should use the last two hours of my night for something productive. I figured out that there was some homework I was supposed to do a few days ago, so I decided to try doing them. But I failed horribly. How should I be able to focus on anything ever again?

The following school day was long, and time passed slowly. During politics class, my tiredness reached its peak level, and I almost fell asleep. Luckily, Finn, who was finally back in school, could prevent me from actually dozing off. But I've never been so happy before to finally be able to go home from school.

This feeling of relief and happiness faded quickly after I realized that I wouldn't be able to hide in my room and maybe even fall asleep. No, when I got home, I would have other problems than my simple lack of sleep. At home, reality would await me, and I wasn't ready for it.

I wasn't ready to have a replacement father even if he was the nicest person on this planet. I wasn't ready to face Ramon since I had the feeling I needed to urgently make my decision on whether I wanted to help him or not. But I couldn't even think clearly, how was I supposed to make such an important decision? But I also needed to make my decision soon because what if he would make progress without me and decided that he wouldn't need me anymore.

What was I supposed to do? Helping him was like balancing on the edge of train tracks while laughing; it could be over at any time. Could I really decide against my own life and for Ramon, a person that I barely knew? Were other people actually more important to me than my own life, or was there no connection between these two things? How could I even help him? There was nothing special about me except for the fact that he sensed an unusual similarity between me and a five-year-old girl that had already died. Was there even anything I could do for him, or was everything just self-delusion?

On my way home, I purposely walked slower than usual to give myself a little bit more time. I put my headphones in my ears, turned the music on loud, and even went for a small detour just to avoid my mom and her new boyfriend for as long as possible. I hated changes sometimes. And these were just too many of them. Huge changes. Too many to be able to cope with them.

At some point, I couldn't think of any other possible way to stay away any longer, so I went home. I took my headphones out of my ears and looked for the key to the main entrance of the apartment complex. When

I finally found it and was ready to put it in the lock, the door opened from the inside.

"Oh, Luna. What a surprise," the old lady from the first floor exclaimed.

It might've sounded dumb, but her presence calmed me down for a bit.

"Yeah, I'm surprised as well," I stuttered, a little bit confused about what she had just said.

"We haven't seen each other in eternity. Probably since you moved here," she sighed.

It did sound like she was not getting a lot of visitors, even though this didn't make sense because she was super friendly and open, and I would expect her to have lots of friends.

"Right?! That was such a long time ago."

"Someday you need to come over to my apartment for some tea, and then you can tell me everything about your encounter with Ramon," she suggested and smiled.

It was not the first time that I was speechless in her presence. Why did she always know everything?

"Sure, I can do that," I answered politely.

"Thank you," she looked so happy.

Then her face turned serious again: "But now you should get home urgently. Your mom is already worried where you are."

"Oh, damn. I almost forgot about that," I suddenly remembered.

I said goodbye and sprinted upstairs.

"Where have you been? I was so worried," my mom greeted me when she opened the door.

"I'm sorry. I talked to the old lady from the first floor and lost any track of time," I tried to apologize.

Her face became even more stern.

"Yesterday, I tolerated your behavior, but today I don't think this is appropriate," she hissed.

"I'm sorry. I'll never let her distract me anymore, really," I affirmed.

I just wanted to get over the meeting with her new boyfriend as fast as possible. Also, I had no clue why my mom suddenly overexaggerated like that. Usually, we had such a good relationship with each other. I mean, it has always just been the two of us. I had no idea why she was behaving so weirdly today.

"Stop making excuses and go in the living room," she just said drily, but I didn't want to let this go.

If she had decided to be mad at me all of a sudden, I would at least like to know the reason behind it. We were no kids, but grown-ups who can talk about their problems.

"What excuses?" I wanted to know.

"Don't pretend you don't know what I'm talking about. And stop inventing stories about neighbors that don't exist."

I shot her a questioning look.

What was she talking about?

"You know that we don't have any neighbors on the first floor. The woman that used to live there had died six months before we even moved here, and since then no one else has moved in," she explained.

Her words sent a shiver down my spine.

"Oh, I'm sorry," I pressed out and went into the living room like I was remote-controlled.

Who was this woman? What was this woman, and what was wrong with me? I was sitting on the couch, more absent than anything else, and answered the questions my mom's new boyfriend had asked me politely. He seemed to be pretty okay, and I was sure that I would've probably liked him against all of my expectations if I had met him at another time. In another moment when my universe was not falling apart and spreading through space and time.

This evening, I made a final and very important decision; it couldn't get any worse than now anyway. It was time for me to discover myself as well as explore other things this world had to offer. It was time to open up my eyes to all of the things that I was sure didn't exist until yesterday. It was time to open my mind to the fact that there was more in this world than my eyes could see.

I only realized all of this when I was getting rid of my makeup in front of the bathroom mirror. The makeup that formed my mask. A mask that concealed my real emotions. After my mask had fallen, I could see myself for the very first time, and suddenly, it felt like I knew exactly what I needed to do. It was like I suddenly knew where I belonged.

I carefully listened at my mom's bedroom door, but it seemed like she was already asleep. Quickly, I grabbed my keys and ran out of the apartment into the staircase. My heart beat fast, and I had a lump in my throat. Adrenaline was rushing through my body. And even though I felt so uncomfortable, I knew it was the right thing to do. Never have I ever thought about something that much before.

Simply knocking on the door seemed like an impossible task. But I made it. After what felt like an eternity, I could hear steps approaching. A key. The door opened.

"I'll help you," she blurted out before he could say anything, "but under one condition; I'm not Luana."

Chapter 15

It was a cold day in winter, and he was meeting his friends to play outside. The incident of the past summer was still haunting him, and he couldn't stop feeling guilty about it. However, he continued living his normal life. He still had a lot of friends that would never know about this weird coincidence. He simply didn't feel brave enough to tell them. His mom was the only person he had ever told, and she tried her best to cheer him up. Not just once, but every time the memories came back up. Which happened. A lot.

He was sitting in his room playing Pokémon on his old Gameboy, which his mother had bought for him at a flea market. It was the only compromise she wanted to make since she was afraid he would damage a new Gameboy or accidentally drop it. He was just on his way to beat the second gym even though he had a huge disadvantage because he again chose the wrong starter Pokémon when the doorbell rang; his friends wanted to build a snowman.

Immediately, he saved the game and grabbed his scarf, his warm hat, and his snowsuit so he could stay outside for a longer time without freezing. It was not like there was a lot of snow in this part of Germany, but it was still pretty cold occasionally. The snowman ended up smaller than expected due to the lack of snow, but they didn't care. They felt like they had created something wonderful, and that was everything that mattered. In a friendly way, one of his friends wanted to give him a pat on the back and therefore touched his shoulder. But then, from one second to the next, he felt out of it.

Again, he felt the same twitching that he had felt the previous summer. The same tingle was striking through his whole body, and even though he had only felt it once before, it felt horribly familiar. He was too shocked to move, but his friends didn't realize it at all. They had no clue what happened in his mind. His view became blurry, and suddenly everything turned black. Again. Was he afraid? He couldn't tell. Everything happened too fast.

His view became clear again. He could see a branch. A branch full of snow. He saw his friend standing below this certain branch. A bird landed on the branch. A cracking noise. A scream. Silence. Darkness. Before he could realize what had happened, he had to observe the same scenario all over again. But one thing was different; this time it felt real. It was real. He had to watch his friend get hit by the branch right on the head. He died immediately.

I was all sweaty when I woke up. It was just a dream, I tried to tell myself, but that didn't change the fact that this event had still happened in the past. A shiver was running down my spine. I had killed him. It was all because of me that one of my friends had to die. I was a poor excuse for a human being.

I decided to take a cold shower to calm down. The cold water helped a bit, but still, my guilty conscience did not completely dissolve. I couldn't handle the fact that I was the murderer of so many innocent and special people. It was not the first time my visions haunted my dreams. And every time, I felt horrible. Every time, it felt exactly like back then when it happened. It felt so real.

I was never good at analyzing dreams, but I could imagine this dream to be some kind of warning to myself. Now that Luna had decided she would help me, I needed to be even more careful. It was not just Tim who was in danger, no, there was someone else who was at risk now too.

Although my situation has improved dramatically in the last few months, I still couldn't trust myself. What if Tim was wrong and my visions did not only depend on my feelings? It was way too early to fully rely on these kinds of theories. It was way too early to draw conclusions. Maybe I would never be able to control myself. The more I thought about it, the more afraid of the future I became.

What if I would never be able to control my visions and accidentally kill Tim or Luna? Or even worse, what if the unknown strangers my Grandma wrote about would suddenly appear? I was absolutely inferior, not just because I wasn't using my full powers yet but also because I had no clue what to expect. Of course, it was possible that the strangers were some kind of vampire or something like that, but it just didn't feel like that. It felt too unrealistic.

It would've helped if Grandma would've told me which page of the book would help me figure out who they were. Then, I wouldn't need to overthink everything.

I looked at my watch, it was almost 5 a.m. I yawned and decided I should eat breakfast. I wouldn't be able to fall asleep now anyway. Additionally, I had my 6 a.m. appointment with Mrs. Müller, which I couldn't wait to have. I mean, who wouldn't love going to a therapist, who instead of looking for solutions, made you feel like you were the problem?

I stepped outside the building and breathed in the lukewarm air. Even though it wasn't quite summer yet, it became pretty warm in the last few days. The air in the morning felt so fresh and untouched. I closed my eyes and took another deep breath. It was still a little bit dark, so it was impossible I would meet anyone here; I had all the time in the world.

I loved mornings like that. It was one of these moments when I could come out of my shell and finally see the world from a different perspective. Because sometimes this world wasn't as dark and unfair as my everyday life made me think. Sometimes, even if it was just for a tiny moment, this world could be beautiful. You just had to open your eyes and look for it, but then you could find peace in moments of absolute silence, just like I did that morning.

Unfortunately, this moment passed too fast, in my opinion, because I knew I couldn't just stand here forever. I had to fulfill my duties, and one of them was therapy with Mrs. Müller. No matter if I wanted to go there or not.

In a bad mood like always, I was on the way to her, and as always, I still had hopes that this time, it would be the last time I would go there.

"Good morning, Ramon," she chirped at me, and reminded me of the noisy bird that was sitting in front of my window every morning and tried to sing even though it sounded horrible every time. I wasn't a big expert when it came to birds, so I had no clue which bird would make such annoying noises, but eventually, I got used to it and gently named that little guy Vexator, which was Latin and meant harasser. I could get used to the bird, but I couldn't get used to Mrs. Müller.

"Good morning," I murmured.

Now I could feel how tired I really was. Usually, it was easy for me to get up early, but today I had issues staying awake.

"How did you sleep?" she asked as if she would care.

"As if I was in a coma," I lied.

I was not motivated to explore my feelings and possible issues today. In general, I was not motivated to ever talk to Mrs. Müller again.

"Did anything new happen in your life?" she asked, pretending she believed me.

This was a tough question. Internally, I was debating whether I should tell her about Luna or not. On the one hand, I didn't want to tell her anything because it was my private life because I wanted to keep Luna out of everything as much as possible because I wasn't even sure if Luna would play a major role in everything.

On the other hand, however, I wanted to tell her everything and rub it in her face that I was trying my best to live a normal life, which would bring me closer to the end of therapy. Secondly, Luna was way too similar to Luana, and I was sure they were somehow connected, even though Luna didn't want to believe it. This would be enough evidence to prove that I was not insane, and none of my diagnoses were correct either. But in the end, I decided against telling her.

"Nope, everything as usual," I answered, and added a short but fake smile to sound more believable.

Mrs. Müller also ignored this lie.

"What about your nightmares?" she wanted to know, writing something down in her ugly, bright yellow notebook.

"They vanished a few months ago," I answered calmly.

That was another lie. My nightmares still bothered me almost every night. Sometimes they were better to deal with, but mostly it was hell. Because every time I woke up, they reminded me that these dreams once were real. Everything was real. Which always led to a mix of shock and self-pity.

I couldn't even hear Mrs. Müller's next question. I saw that her lips were moving, but I didn't hear a word of what she said. It felt like I wasn't able to realize anything; in my world, there was just silence.

A loud beeping in my ear. A lot of black dots in front of my eyes. The dots grew bigger and bigger, the beeping higher and higher. I felt sick. I felt dizzy. Everything around me was spinning, and I couldn't do anything against it. Everything turned black.

When I opened my eyes again, I was blinded by a white, bright light. Out of reflex, I squinted my eyes. This time I opened them more carefully, but that didn't make the bright light disappear. I blinked multiple times in a row to try to get used to my surroundings. But nothing.

Was I in heaven? Very unlikely. In heaven, I wouldn't feel as shitty as I did right now, and neither would my limbs hurt. Another reason I couldn't be in heaven was that there was absolutely no reason for me to go to heaven. So, I was 100 percent certain the bright light was not coming from being dead. I guess I was just at the hospital.

"I dare you to ask me if you are in heaven."

I heard Tim's voice.

"I don't have to. Why should you be there?" I joked.

"Why should you be there either?" he countered, and I was finally able to look at him.

"Why am I here?" I asked confused.

"Do you want the long story or the short one?" Tim wanted to know, and I could hear how he tried to repress the happy undertone in his voice.

"Make it short, I'm afraid I won't be able to follow you otherwise," I begged.

My head felt heavy, and I was afraid it would burst. I was absolutely not in the position to listen to a long story. I just wanted to sleep, but at the same time, I felt as awake as I've never felt before in my life.

"So," he artificially cleared his throat, which made me smile for a second. Then he started the story: "You were having therapy, then you fainted."

This version was actually really short. I wondered how long the longer version would be. While I was processing his words, I started remembering again. He was right, I did faint, but it was different than the feeling I had before my visions. In general, everything felt so unfamiliar about that. I had never fainted before, so maybe that was just how normal people must feel.

"When I got the call from the hospital, I immediately rushed over, even though I was in a very important meeting," Tim bragged.

"Did you play League of Legends?"

I eyed him critically.

"Yeah, okay. Maybe the meeting wasn't that important. But I'm here. That's all that matters," he admitted.

"But why did they call you?" I wondered.

As if Tim would know that.

"I guess Mrs. Müller gave them my number because she knew you would prefer me being here over your dad. By the way, your dad was here too, but you were still asleep," he explained his theory.

That did, in fact, sound logical. I could feel the tension leaving my body, even though I didn't even know I was feeling tense before.

"Do you know why I'm here?" I asked after some time.

"The doctors say you are exhausted and stressed, and that's why you fainted," he said seriously. "But I have another theory," he added with a wide grin.

I raised my eyebrows and looked at him with my tell-me-finally-glance. During the time of our friendship, we got pretty good at communicating without words. Maybe that made our friendship even stronger.

"How well do you remember yesterday?" he asked.

"I don't know. I don't even know what date it is today?" I murmured.

"Yesterday, we lifted your abilities to the next level, like electrons during photosynthesis," he explained.

I had no clue what he wanted to tell me with this comparison, though. But that's just the way he was, super into biology and chemistry. He could be a real nerd if he wanted to. Deep down, I envied him. On the one hand, he was so smart and good with science, while on the other hand, he never lost the ability to believe in supernatural things.

"Ahhh," I said.

I actually remembered. After my conversation with Luna, I had called Tim and told him everything about it. Even though it was quite late, I couldn't stop him from coming over. Since there was another person in my life, I was more scared than ever of hurting anyone, and even Tim realized that, so he didn't care about my excuses but forced me to work on controlling and further exploring my visions. He didn't care if it was late at night or not.

"Your mind is your weapon," he had said, and demanded I should do something cool with it.

When I asked him what exactly he wanted me to do, he just responded that we should continue where we ended. Then he grabbed another glass and put it on the table in front of me.

"This won't work," he said eventually.

I just looked at him confused.

From the way he looked at me, I could tell that he enjoyed my confusion, but he decided to share his thoughts with me: "If my theory is correct and your visions are connected to feelings, you need something that triggers any kind of feeling, don't you?"

He was right. And because he was right and he knew this, he fumbled in the pocket of his jeans and pulled an old-looking photograph out of it. It was very wrinkly since he had to fold it multiple times to even fit it in his pocket. Triumphantly, he pushed the photo in my face so I could look at it.

A quick glance was enough to know what, or better said, who was in the picture. There were three children in front of a little snowman in the picture. One of the kids was Tim, the other one was a murderer, and the third one... The third one was dead. It was the picture that captured the day I had killed my friend. The last picture that he would ever be on.

Ashamed, I looked at the ground and wondered why Tim would show me this picture after all.

"Tear it apart," he demanded.

He didn't have to tell me twice. I could already feel the rage running through my veins, and then my body wasn't just tingling or twitching, I was trembling. I tried to focus on this feeling, to not let it go. I was so focused on this task that everything else became blurry. Everything happened so fast that neither Tim nor I could actually believe it. The picture was ripped into two halves, and I had precisely cut out one child and therefore separated it from the other ones: myself.

"Perfect. Because my theory is that your sudden exhaustion is caused by the active usage of your mind."

"Active?" I repeated questioningly.

"It was the first time something like this actually worked out."

"But what about the glass. It broke too?" I asked.

"Yes, but you weren't focused on breaking it. It broke because you were mad at me, and not because you were trying to break it," Tim explained.

Maybe I was just too exhausted to understand his conclusions properly.

"We need to observe this in the future, but for me, my theory sounds good," Tim added.

"You know what?" I asked him.

He just shook his head.

"I think you might have a point there, but now let's just go home."

Chapter 16

Not even two days after I had told Ramon I would help him, I received a WhatsApp message from him.

Hey, do you want to come over?

Immediately, I typed a short answer into my phone and went upstairs. Fortunately, my mom was visiting her new boyfriend, so I didn't even need to find an excuse for leaving the apartment. She didn't know that I got along with Ramon. To be honest, she didn't even know that I had met him at all (the previous times I went to his apartment, I took out the trash before I came to see him. Although she did wonder about my sudden interest in helping out with chores, she didn't say anything, maybe because she was afraid I would stop helping out).

She often complained about the fact that she knew all of the neighbors except for Ramon and started making up wild theories about why she had never seen him before and what could possibly be wrong with him. Our other neighbors didn't seem to know Ramon either; at least that was what my mom had told me.

At some point, I got tired of her shit-talking him without even knowing him, so I made up the theory that he might just work during the night. Almost disappointed about this somehow logical theory – that was obviously wrong, but she couldn't know that since she didn't know Ramon – she dropped all of her other theories and speculations.

The door opened before I could even knock (somehow knocking on his door became our thing. That's how I could show him that it was me in front of the door and no one else. I didn't know why, but I liked this idea somehow).

Confused I looked into the face of a stranger.

"Hey, you must be Luna," the stranger said.

"Ehm, yes. That's me," I stuttered still confused.

"Tim, I told you, you shouldn't wait behind the door," I could hear Ramon's voice from inside the apartment.

"Sorry but I was too curious," he responded, and then turned his head back to me. "I'm Tim, by the way, and normally I'm not as weird as I'm right now, but I heard a lot about you, so I got curious," he introduced himself, and held his hand in my direction.

Still, in disbelief, I shook it and tried to think of a good response to everything he just said.

"You heard a lot about me?" I wanted to know.

"Yeah, the whole connection between you and …– "

"It's great that you're here," Ramon said enthusiastically to drown Tim's words after he had pushed Tim to the side.

It wasn't even necessary because I could already imagine what Tim was about to say. Ramon still didn't give up on finding out more about the stupid connection between me and Luana.

The two stepped aside, so that I could finally enter the apartment.

"We thought six eyes could see more than four eyes," Ramon started with his explanation, "and since I'm desperate and I don't know anyone else except Tim and you, I thought you might be able to help us."

He ran his fingers through his hair and looked at me pleadingly.

"Of course, I help you. Like I told you before." When I said that, it looked like he seemed a bit relieved.

"Perfect. I already told you about my Grandma's book, but we still haven't solved every mystery of the book."

While he said that, he sat down on the couch next to Tim and signaled to me that I should sit down on the empty spot in the middle.

"Okay, but what do you hope to find out?" I asked while I sat down.

Not going to lie, it did feel incredibly awkward to sit right in the middle of them.

"We still don't know who wrote the book, and we still don't know who the strangers are that we should be aware of," explained Ramon.

To answer my question of where to find the book, he just moved his head in the direction of the couch table.

It was only then that I noticed a thick book. Carefully, I picked it up to take a closer look at it.

While I was skipping through the pages, Tim and Ramon explained everything they knew about the book in more detail, so I could immediately skip every nice fairytale and start reading the dark part of the book.

I tried to analyze every page as closely as I could, which wasn't easy since I could feel the observing glances of the two guys on me. I was pretty tense. I really wanted to help them, but after reading a few pages, I was afraid I couldn't tell them anything new. They had already found out so much about the book, and even though I liked reading and therefore had a few books in my hands, I couldn't find any difference to regular books.

"Do you want to drink something?" Ramon asked after some time to break the silence.

I denied, which didn't stop Tim from accepting his offer, even though I was sure Tim knew exactly where he could grab himself something to drink. While Ramon got up, I decided it was for the best if I would take a short break as well to rest my eyes so I wouldn't miss any important detail.

"It's challenging, isn't it?" Tim asked friendly.

"Yes," I sighed. "You guys have done some great work already."

"But apparently not good enough. Otherwise, we would be smarter by now," it was the first time since I had entered the apartment that Tim seemed thoughtful and stern. I thought he was one of these people that were always in a good mood and didn't take life very seriously. But apparently, I was wrong with that. Don't judge a book by its cover. What irony. But this gave me a new idea. I had to analyze the outside of the book. I would find something. I had to find something. Something about this book must be off, and I had to find it.

I looked at the very first page of the book, and when I couldn't find anything special there, I looked at the very last page. And actually, I found something. In the upper right corner, a small piece of paper was detached from the book cover. It seemed like the cover of the book was thicker after the last page of the book than before the first page as well. Under normal circumstances, I would've never seen this, but again, what even was normal?

"I think I found something," I said triumphantly.

"A piece of paper that wasn't glued down properly?"

Ramon, who was back with Tim's drink, eyed me skeptically.

"Do you want to bet I'll find something if we get rid of the paper completely?" I said fully convinced that I was right about what I found.

"I don't need to bet, but you can get rid of the paper," he said carelessly.

Excitedly, we all stared at the book while I slowly ripped the paper off the inside of the cover. Below the paper was a little flap made out of paper, which was almost impossible to find.

"Damn, you were right," I heard Ramon say quietly.

"Do you want to open it?" I asked him.

This was probably more important to him than it would ever be to me. Maybe he could find some personal value in opening this flap.

He just nodded and put the book on his lap. Even though he tried to hide it, it was obvious that his fingers were shaking while they were getting closer to the flap. After failing a few times – it was more difficult to open this than it looked – he made it.

He opened it slowly, and we could all take a look at what was hidden in the book's cover. Even before we could see anything, the smell of old lady perfume filled the room. What a penetrant smell. But judging by the face of Ramon, this odor was familiar to him. Inside the cover was a hidden envelope, which was probably the reason for the smell.

"You are a genius," Ramon exclaimed.

"Thanks," Tim said, and by that, he got rid of all of the tension around us.

"I didn't mean you, but you are obviously a genius as well," Ramon said while he opened the envelope and started reading the letter.

I had no clue what was written in the letter, and I was curious, but I could also understand that he wanted to read the letter himself first.

"What is the Prussian Reform Movement?" he asked after some time.

"I don't know why you need to know that, but it was a reform movement in Prussia to modernize it since Prussia lost half of its area to Napoleon, which made them realize they needed to improve something to keep up with the other great powers in Europe," I explained proudly. I've never been so glad before that I properly made my history homework about that topic.

"Prussia, you say," he murmured.

Until he looked up in shock.

"When exactly was this Reform Movement?" he asked.

"Ehm, I don't know. They lost the battle against Napoleon in 1806, and they lost half of their area in 1807, I think. Therefore, the Reform Movement must've started …– "

"What the fuck," Ramon didn't let me finish my sentence.

It seemed like this was all that he needed.

"What's going on?" Tim wanted to know.

"The letter was written by my Grandma, and she writes about herself and the mansion," Ramon stated.

Even before any of us could ask another question about what was wrong with that, he added: "She said she let the house be built in the year of the Prussian Reform Movement."

"And what's so wrong about that?" Tim asked us. Ramon and I looked at him speechless.

Finally, Ramon said out loud what I already figured out: "Stop thinking about Prussia! My Grandma wants to tell me that she has been alive since the beginning of the 19th century."

"What the ..."

Tim finally understood.

"This is getting weirder and weirder."

I could only agree with that.

"What else did she write about herself?" I asked.

"She wrote that she had special abilities as well and that she'll tell me about them when I'm old enough."

He put both of his hands in front of his forehead and screamed: "But she is dead, damn it."

A clinking noise made me look away from Ramon. I now stared at the table where, up to a few seconds ago, Tim's glass with water was standing. Now there was only a puddle of water and a lot of tiny glass shards.

Shocked about what I had just witnessed, I looked back to Ramon. He looked exactly as horrified as me.

"Now you can't say anything against my theory," Tim said with a wide grin on his face.

He was the only one in this room that slightly knew how to cope with what just happened.

"What theory?" I wondered after I could think straight again.

Was I really aware of everything that could happen to me when I told Ramon that I would help him? Probably not. The glass… It could've been something else. A head. My head.

Tim and Ramon explained their theory about the coherence of emotions and Ramon's abilities while they cleaned up the mess on the table.

"I think you owe me another glass," Ramon jokingly said to Tim.

Unfortunately, Tim had to go because he had something else to do, so it was just Ramon, me, and the book left.

"Do you think we'll find something else today?" he asked me.

"Yes, I promise," I said to cheer him up.

You could tell that the letter was messing with him more than he wanted to show. As a response, I heard something that sounded like a quiet thank you, but I couldn't tell for sure. Maybe I misheard him.

Again, I tried to focus on the pages, but I had kind of lost hopes of finding something else in the book. After finding the letter, I was sure we had discovered everything that was hidden in the book. If Tim and Ramon didn't know anything about the strangers, I couldn't find anything either. Of course, they were right to assume that six eyes would see more than four, but if there wasn't anything else hidden in the book than what they had already discovered, even six eyes couldn't find more than what was present.

To make him think that I didn't lose all of my hope and that I was actually trying to find something, I stroked my hands over the pages of the book (which must've looked incredibly dumb). From the corners of my eyes, I could see Ramon observing me. Maybe he had figured by now that I had no clue what I was doing but fortunately (or unfortunately? The silence started to feel awkward) he didn't comment on anything. I had promised to find something, and I would feel guilty if I really had to disappoint him.

My mom raised me to never make false promises if I knew from the beginning I couldn't keep them, but at that moment, I ignored it. I somehow didn't want to see him suffer anymore, and it was no secret that he was still a bit bummed by the letter.

I was about to give up and admit that I had no clue what I was doing, but just in that moment, my hands felt something rough in the middle between two pages. I lifted the book to look at it from another angle, but my theory was confirmed; someone had ripped out a page of the book.

"Could you find something?" Ramon asked immediately.

"Yes, I'm positive someone tore out a page of the book," I told him.

"My Grandma?", he asked.

"No, it's too well done. Someone doesn't want us to read that page."

"Why didn't we realize this earlier?" he thought out loud.

I couldn't answer this question because the only reason I could figure it out was all just a dumb coincidence. Of course, we could've paid more attention to the page numbers, but whoever had found the book before us knew what they were doing and used some kind of liquid to make some page numbers fade more than others. That just underlined my theory that it wasn't Ramon's Grandma.

We checked the other pages that had weird-looking page numbers and realized that this was not the only missing page.

"What are we supposed to do?" I asked Ramon curiously.

"I don't know, but I think it's time I learn how to control my powers," he whispered almost inaudible.

Chapter 17

Luna was a gift from heaven, as far as one believed in heaven or hell. Despite not being able to answer all of the questions we still had, she helped us figure out a lot. Now, it seemed less impossible that, in the future, we might be able to have all the answers we needed. We just needed to find the missing pages.

Luna came by my apartment almost every day after school, mostly just to quickly check on how I was doing and if we found anything new. Tim and I continued to work on controlling my abilities, and to my surprise, it worked way better than when we started. Everything somehow started to work out, and I wondered why I didn't let any other human into my life before, even though I already knew the answer to that question; if I had let anyone closer into my life before, maybe Luna would not be in it right now. Everything happened for a reason, and if she was the reason for it, I wasn't mad about it. It just felt right the way it was.

Once my situation was fully solved and I would be able to fully control my abilities, I would dig deeper into the past and maybe find out what exactly was going on with the connection between Luana and Luna, no matter what Luna thought about that. But now was not the time for it; I had other priorities, and maybe one day Luna would change her opinion.

I took a quick glance at my watch; it was just after 4 p.m. Luna would knock on my door at any moment. I didn't know why it all started, but it was nice knowing it could only be her when I heard a knock on the door. I didn't need to hide or second-guess if I wanted to open the door; I could just be myself.

On time, like always, I could hear her knocking on the door. It was incredible how fast you could get used to people being in your life. I opened the door, and she shoved a paper bag in my hand.

"Today is muffins Monday," as a response to my confused look, then she entered the apartment.

Still a bit off track, I followed her into the kitchen, where she had already grabbed two plates for us.

"Muffins what?" I asked.

"Muffins Monday. I thought you might need something sweet to eat today, and I kind of liked the alliteration. You can't imagine how long it took me to come up with that," she explained, shaking her head in disbelief that I couldn't recognize her ingenuity immediately.

"Of course, of course," I said as understandingly as possible.

"So, what's new?" she asked curiously after we had sat down on the couch.

"Unfortunately, not much today," I sighed.

"Then it's even better I brought the muffins – sugar makes people happy or something like this," she tried to cheer me up.

After we had eaten our muffins, I couldn't hold myself back from asking a question whose answer interested me a lot.

"Tell me," I started and looked at the ground. "Why did you decide to help me?" I asked her.

Since the day she told me she would help me, I always wanted to know why, but I never found the right moment to ask her. Maybe at the beginning, I was scared she would change her mind if I asked her this question too early. But the more I thought about it, the less I could tell what exactly I was afraid of.

"I had talked to the friendly lady from the first floor and came back home a bit late. My mom was pretty mad at me because I had to be on time so I could meet her new boyfriend. In her rage, she told me that no one lives on the first floor since the lady, who lived there, had died six months before we even moved here. I have no clue who I met on the first floor or why I met her, but that was the moment I realized that I was already in too deep. There was no turning back anymore," she explained.

"You didn't know the old lady from the first floor was dead?" I asked her seriously and raised my eyebrows.

"You knew it as well?"

She looked at me in disbelief.

"No," I admitted and started laughing.

"I didn't know she was dead either. I just wanted to see your reaction if I pretended, I did."

She threw the pillow closest to her at me, but I easily caught it.

"That's unfair. I bet you have other hidden superpowers like the vampires in *Twilight*," she said playfully mad.

"But what if I'm not the hero, what if I'm the bad guy?" I responded and laughed. "No, seriously, I can promise you that I don't have any other hidden powers. Unfortunately."

My voice got quieter at the end of the sentence, so I wasn't sure if she could even hear the last words. If I had other abilities like supernatural speed or strength, nothing would be holding me back. If I knew for sure I was superior to other people, I would've already been on my way to Grandma's mansion. I wouldn't be sitting here anymore.

Of course, I wouldn't know what would happen to me if I would go there – my Grandma didn't warn me for no reason – but with other abilities that were easier to control, I would expect myself to stand a chance against whoever would expect me there. The way things actually were, I didn't feel like I would stand a chance against anyone. How much I wished I had other powers. Actually useful ones.

I mean, there were so many dark creatures – and yes, I would count myself among them – why would I have to be exactly what I was? Why couldn't I be a vampire or a werewolf, even though these creatures were a bit stale, and I found the thought ridiculous to grow some extra hair during full moon.

I felt a hand touching my arm. Luna came a bit closer without me realizing it. She must've noticed that I was about to drown in self-pity. But not today, I told myself and tried to smile.

"Thanks," I whispered, and saw that her face lit up as well.

"Can you too answer me one question?" she asked, and suddenly she seemed to be a bit shy.

"As far as it's no history question, sure," I answered cheerfully.

"Why are you so convinced that Luana and I are somehow connected?"

I had to think for a brief moment. How should I explain to her that it was one of these feelings whose origin I didn't know; it was simply in my bones?

"I don't know," I stated.

What a great explanation.

"Maybe it's because you resemble each other. That might sound stupid because she was so much younger than you, so it's impossible to tell how she would look today if she wasn't... But I don't know, it really is just a feeling telling me the connection exists," I went on with my explanation even though I still wasn't fully happy with what I was saying. I simply couldn't describe my feelings.

"Is it possible that you just want me to be connected to her so you feel less guilty about what happened to her?" she asked carefully.

I looked at her, surprised by the sudden analysis of my mental health. Could she be right about that? Definitely.

"But your names sound so similar," I stuttered to defend my theory.

"Ramon," she said softly, "I can understand where you come from, but really, I would know if I had died before, I guess."

I sighed.

She was right about that, too. Maybe it really was just my mind trying to cope with the guilt I felt about my very first murder. Maybe it was a natural protection mechanism that prevented me from going insane.

"But how do you explain the fact that you can see the old lady as well? I mean, I can see her too. That can't be normal," I tried one last time.

She looked at me thoughtfully.

Silence.

I could see wrinkles forming on her forehead, and I could tell she was trying to think of a logical explanation for this phenomenon. It worked, I thought. She believed me, at least a little bit.

"Okay, good point. I have no explanation for this either," she said eventually, but before I could celebrate my victory, she added seriously: "But to make you shut up about this topic once and for all I'll prove that I'm not Luana."

I just nodded unimpressed.

"Let's start with the location of the mansion. You never told me where it is, but based on your Grandma's letter, I conclude it might be in eastern Germany or Poland."

When she saw my confused look, she explained: "This was Prussia in 1808."

I looked at her impressed.

How could she remember all of these historical things? I had history class in school, however, I was never really interested in it and got rid of it as quickly as I could. Now I wished I would've kept it because it would seriously help me figure out everything about my Grandma.

"However, I've never been to eastern Germany. Not even for a class trip, and even less did I live there. My mom and I only moved twice in my life, and one of these times was within my hometown, so it doesn't count. The only relevant move was last year when we moved into this building," she continued her explanation.

"Hm, but what if you just can't remember and your mom is silent about it because she knows more than you do?" I argued.

"I doubt it. Otherwise, she would be able to see the old lady from the first floor as well. Or at least she would believe me when I said I saw her," she completely destroyed my theory.

"But if you still don't want to believe me, I have one more contrary: I'll turn 17 in a few months. According to Adam Riese, Luana would be 18 if not 19. How do you want to explain that?" she asked.

"I can't," I admitted.

She was right. I didn't think about the fact that Luana was only one year younger than me.

"When is your birthday?" I asked to change the topic as fast as possible.

"13th of July, so in less than two months," she answered, happy about the switch in topic.

I answered something, but I didn't know what I really said. Everything about this situation was surreal. First, she could dismiss all of my arguments – except for one – and then … And then her birthday is on the same date as Luana's death day. Could this be a coincidence? In my head, I heard Tim's voice: *"Ramon, you have been through so much in your life, do you really still believe in coincidences?"*

Tim was right; I didn't believe in coincidences anymore, and even though I didn't tell Luna, I still held onto my theory. Maybe they weren't the same person after all, which was naïve to assume, even though there was a lot of evidence against it, but maybe they were still somehow related.

In the evening, Tim came over for practice since I had worked all morning. Of course, I told him everything about the conversation with Luna. The only thing I didn't tell him was the fact that Luna's birthday was Luana's death day. As expected, Tim tried to come up with a completely new theory, however, he failed horribly. Maybe there simply was no useful explanation. Or maybe it was because he didn't know the full truth.

At least practicing with Tim worked way better than expected. If we would keep on making progresses like that, I would soon be ready to aim for bigger challenges. And that was what we eventually did.

The days passed by, and after two weeks, I was able to close my window. Of course, I knew that this wouldn't help me fight anyone, but every success was a success, and it felt so damn great– especially after all these setbacks. If things would keep on going like this, then … then … well, what exactly would happen? Would I dare to go to the mansion? No. Even though I was curious, I couldn't bring myself to drive there. I was scared. Not just scared. I had panic.

I had panic when I thought about the memories that were expecting and throwing themselves at me there. I didn't know if I could ever be mentally prepared to go back. At the moment, there was nothing but curiosity that would lure me to the mansion.

Maybe we would find the missing pages in the mansion, but what even was their purpose? They would probably not help us more than what we already knew. Everything that we had figured out by now was enough for me. And even though I tried to convince myself of all of these things, there was this voice inside of me that demanded I should go to my car immediately and start driving. Away. Far away from all of the daily worries and struggles. But I stayed firm. Running away wouldn't help me. At least not right now.

Additionally, I needed to take into account that the mansion probably wasn't as lonely as it was supposed to be. I had to expect my Grandma's murderers to still be around there, otherwise, she wouldn't have warned me. It was difficult to think straight in a situation like this where nothing really made sense. But I had to wait and be patient. It was the only thing I could do. Also, Tim was right, and me actively using my mind exhausted me too much for now. Although it had improved a little bit, I still had a long way to go.

I woke up to the ringing of my cell phone, and I was even kind of happy about it, because as usual, I had only dreamt weird things. Then I took a look at the time; it was still night. Yawning, I picked up the call.

"Tim, do you know what time it is?" I greeted him tiredly.

"Wait, let me check," he just responded.

"Why are you always calling me in the middle of the night?" I wanted to know.

"3:43 a.m."

"What about that?" I asked confused.

"You asked me for the time," Tim explained.

It was definitely too early for me to understand Tim's humor.

"But jokes aside, I found the ultimate challenge for you. If you can do this, you can do anything."

"Aha," I didn't sound convinced.

Tim sighed audibly on the other side of the call.

"You are not into it?" he asked almost a bit offended.

"Yes, I'm in, but not at 3 a.m. It's night."

I tried to make him understand that it was way too early for me to function. I didn't know anyone who liked being disturbed while sleeping. However, I didn't know a lot of people either, so I couldn't say if this was a good excuse.

"See you in 10 minutes," he said cheerfully, and hung up on me.

I sighed annoyed, then I started my way to Tim.

"I'm glad you came. So, let's talk about my plan. Do you see this door?" he greeted me and pointed at his bedroom door.

"Good morning to you too," I answered.

This didn't seem to disturb Tim at all.

"So, your task is to close this door," he explained his ultimate challenge.

"But we did this so many times before?" I reminded him.

"Yeah, but let me finish."

He looked so enthusiastic about it.

"You have to close the door and keep it closed while I, on the other side of it, try to open it," he finished his explanation happily and grinned proudly as if he had just invented a time machine.

"Okay, the sooner we're done, the sooner I can go back to bed. Let's start," I agreed to his plan.

I knew Tim for long enough, he wouldn't have accepted a no anyway as soon as he was into something the way he was into this ultimate challenge. So, he went into the bedroom and got into position.

"On three," he screamed from the other room.

I would really hate to be his neighbor in moments like these, I thought, and chuckled. Then I tried to focus on closing the damn door. I failed.

"Emotions," Tim said admonishingly, and went back into the bedroom. "Next try," he shouted.

Again, I tried to really concentrate and think of something that could help me trigger the emotions I needed, but everything that came into my mind was useless. Something needed to trigger me. There must've been something that could've made me close that door.

Desperately, I tried to go through my memories, but there was nothing that made me angry in the past weeks. So, I tried using other, older memories of Mrs. Müller and how she always looked down on me during our sessions. I felt something changing. I felt the familiar tingle rush through my body. I was about to make it, I knew it. My forehead wrinkled, and the only thing I focused on was the door in front of me. Everything but the door became a big blur. It all happened so fast that it was not noticeable to anyone who would've watched me. No one could see what was happening inside my mind. Nobody could even imagine what was going on in there. It was working, I thought. Then the door was opened again, and Tim was standing in front of me. Frustrated, I threw my head back.

"That was already great," Tim praised me.

"But not good enough," I pressed out.

"But it was a good start. It was way harder this time to open the door. Only a few more tries, and then you got …– "

"Have you ever thought that my power might have limits? Maybe that's all I can do," I interrupted him harsher than I wanted to.

"Such bullshit. Your limits only exist because you create them. I mean, look at you. Your powers have already blown up every existing limit. Let's try again, and then you'll see that I'm always right."

He didn't let me drag him down and went back into the bedroom.

That was utter nonsense. Why should it work this time? I sighed. Then I focused my view on the door. It was naïve to believe things would work out that easily. I really liked Tim, but this time I was simply annoyed by his stubbornness. Why couldn't he just give in for once and agree with me? Why couldn't he give up as easily as I could?

At first, I didn't realize that my body had already started tingling. My view was blurry as well. It had never been as easy as it felt right now. Don't give up just yet, I told myself, and tried to maintain this feeling. I was scared to lose my focus. I was scared of failing again. I could feel that I was about to do it, but a tiny spark was missing. Suddenly, everything returned back to normal, and the blur in my view vanished. Damn. Another failure. I waited for Tim to appear in front of me, but he wasn't there. The door didn't open. Maybe Tim didn't know I was ready and still waited for me to give him a sign.

"You can come out now, I'm done trying for today," I called him.

"I would love to but it's not working," he said incredibly proud.

"What? Why?"

"You did it. You are keeping the door closed," he tried to explain.

"What am I doing?" I repeated stunned.

I couldn't believe I actually did it. A feeling of happiness filled my body. I really did it. Finally.

Finally, I made something happen that could actually help me in the future. Finally, I was ready. Ready to explore my Grandma's secrets.

"Can you let me out?"

Tim brought me back to reality.

"Oh, sure," I answered.

I just had no clue how I should do it. It couldn't be too difficult; I mean, I was the one that locked him in there in the first place. I took a deep breath. Luckily, I didn't have to focus as much as I had to at the beginning, and suddenly the door burst open so quickly that Tim almost fell to the ground in front of me.

"Congratulations, you are officially prepared for the real world," he said while applauding.

I would still hate being his neighbor.

I couldn't tell if it was the lack of sleep or the ongoing euphoria, but without really thinking it through, I grabbed my telephone when I came back home. It was 7:30 a.m. which was late enough to reach Mrs. Müller. Clearly confused about my call, she picked up.

"You might wonder why I call, but I thought about it for quite some time, and I concluded that I want to end therapy for good. I'm prepared for the real world," I blurted out without letting her speak at all.

Maybe it was a mix of both, the lack of sleep and the euphoria, otherwise, I had no explanation for quoting Tim.

"Okay," she responded confused.

Pause.

I had no clue what else I was supposed to do. How were you even ending therapy for good? Probably not like this.

"But you have to know that your insurance won't pay for another therapy in the next six months. Additionally, I won't be able to support you for the next two years in case you would need professional help again," she warned me.

But I couldn't care less about anything. I planned to never go to therapy ever again, and if I really needed therapy in the future, I would surely not go back to her.

"So, are you sure you really want to end it?"

I've never been more confident about anything before.

Grinning, I spoke the final words: "Yes, I'm really sure."

This decision was long overdue, and after everything that had happened in the past months, I wondered why it had taken me so long to realize that this was the right thing to do. Maybe it was hard for me because I had promised my mother to go to therapy even though I was sure she wouldn't be mad if I hadn't started therapy, especially not if she had met Mrs. Müller. Although not everything about Mrs. Müller and the time we had spent together was bad, she just had questionable ways of treating her patients.

I wasn't a therapist, but I was sure that it was unprofessional to try to force diagnoses on someone if you simply didn't like the way they behaved. And I was sure that it was her task to take her patients seriously, which she didn't do. She had belittled me when I told her about my visions. If she only had seen me today, she would have taken back every word she said. But ending things with Mrs. Müller wasn't the only thing that was long overdue.

It was Friday, even though it was still early in the morning, but it was Friday. From the time I used to live with him, I knew that Friday was my dad's day off work. So, I entered my car and started driving to the neighboring city where my father lived.

It felt like an eternity that I had seen him, and if I thought about it, I really hadn't seen him since I had moved out one and a half years ago. How could I avoid him for so long? Did I really think everything would be easier if I lived a lonely life? This way of living had no future.

"Ramon," my father said astonished, when he opened the door and saw me standing in front of it. Then he started crying and hugging me tightly. It was the first time I realized that not only did I suffer from my way of living; he had been suffering too. But I was so focused on myself that I never really thought about whether I was hurting others with my behavior or not.

When he stopped hugging me, I realized that he had aged quite a bit. His hair was much grayer than I remembered it to be, and his face was full of wrinkles. He had dark circles below his eyes from all the sleepless nights he had because of pain in his joints – at least that was what kept him awake before I moved out. Automatically, I felt even guiltier. Why did I push him out of my life just like that? Why did I do this to everyone?

He offered me to stay for breakfast, and I thankfully accepted.

"What did I do that you honor me with your visit?" He wanted to know after he took a bite of his sandwich.

"It was long overdue. I'm so sorry. I ..."

I made a break.

I was tired of lying to everyone. I was tired of making up new excuses every time I talked to someone.

"I had a difficult time, but now everything is going to be different. Better. I'm not even going to therapy anymore," I answered eventually.

That was a good start. A good start to tell him the truth, which he deserved. He was my father, after all.

"You ended it yourself?" he asked.

"Of course, she would've never given up on me, but I was so sick and tired of her constantly repressing me," I justified myself.

"I'm proud of you," he said and smiled.

I couldn't tell what exactly he was proud of since there was not much happening in my life that anyone could be proud of. At least nothing that he could know about.

"I told you from the beginning that she was weird, but you finally figured it out on your own," he added as if he could read my thoughts.

"Yes, it was long overdue to do all of these things."

He nodded while getting up, then he left the kitchen. I still couldn't believe that he still lived here. In the house that we all grew up in, it used to be so full of life.

My older sister was the first to leave us. She was 13 years older than me and moved out when my mom was still alive. Then my mom left not just this house but this world. It was only my dad and me until I eventually left him too. So many times did I feel lonely in the past without ever wasting a thought on how my dad must've felt. Left by everyone he loved. Lonely and alone, living in a house that was way too small for a family of four but too big for one alone.

Without saying a word, he came back and handed me a piece of paper. I looked at him in confusion but began to read what was on the paper. It was my Grandma's will. What should I do with it? I had already gotten everything she wanted me to have.

Still, I read everything. Unexpectedly, I didn't know about everything I inherited from her.

"But why didn't you tell me earlier?" I asked my father.

"You weren't ready to manage the whole mansion on your own," he winked at me.

I was confused and speechless. Every time I thought things couldn't get any more confusing, something happened that proved me wrong again.

So, I had inherited the villa, but why did he just tell me about it now? Did Grandma want me to have it now so I wouldn't go there too early, or did my father know more than he was supposed to know?

I couldn't answer any of these questions. Yet. But one thing I knew for sure; nothing could stop me from driving to the mansion.

Chapter 18

"Are you busy today?" Finn asked me when we left the school building together.

"Sorry but I'm already seeing …– "

"Ramon, I get it. It's okay," he interrupted me annoyed.

"I'm really sorry but …– ", I tried again.

"But he asked you first," he ended the sentence for me. "You might not realize it, but you neglect us. And all of this for the neighbor who treated you like a piece of crap."

Was he right about that? Did I really neglect Finn, Jane, and the others?

"You are never free if I ask you spontaneously, you don't even come to our parties anymore. You don't join our study group, and during the breaks at school, you're always so lost in your thoughts that it's impossible to have a real conversation with you. Damn, I don't even remember when we hung out for the last time," he continued.

"I don't join the study group because there is no exam to study for. I don't know if you missed it, but summer vacation starts in around a week," I tried to remind him.

What a crappy argument.

"I don't hang out spontaneously because other people have asked me first. It has nothing to do with you …– "

"But with Ramon. I just never thought you would neglect all of us immediately just because you have a boyfriend," he sounded sad, while he said that.

"Nothing is going on between Ramon and me," I answered outraged.

This conversation was ridiculous. Finn looked at me like he was about to add a very sarcastic 'of course'. Even though he kept his mouth shut, the way he looked at me in disbelief made me even angrier.

"Do I have to ask you months prior if you might be able to hang out because you have such a busy schedule?"

His voice was full of mockery.

"I think a week prior should be enough," I answered ironically.

Finn laughed.

That was what I liked about him the most. He could blow up fast, but he could calm down even faster. All the tension was gone.

"Are you free next weekend?" he wanted to know.

"I think I can save you a spot, I just need to check my calendar."

It wasn't until then that I realized that I had really let my school friends down. It was pretty nice of them to still want to hang out with me, to be fair. If I were them, I would've completely ignored me and given up on the friendship by now. I really needed to take better care of my friends. I should spend more time with them. Sure, Ramon was also a friend of mine, but maybe it would be good for once to spend some time with normal humans. Maybe it would even distract me. Thinking about other things might be healthy for me. It could even help me lose some tension. Recently, I've always felt so tense about everything.

Also, it was probably nice to spend some time with people where I could be certain I was not at risk of getting killed, even if they would want to. It wasn't like I didn't trust Ramon, more like the opposite – the fact that I helped him proved that I wasn't afraid of him – but there was always a risk, and the risk was never zero.

Every time I had these thoughts, I tried to think of Tim. Ramon and Tim have been friends forever, and still, Tim hasn't been murdered. And especially now, when he was getting better and better at controlling his abilities, the risk of being killed would get lower and lower.

"I think Friday should be perfect," I answered after flipping through some pages of the book I had in my hand to pretend it was my calendar.

"Great."

He grinned.

"I count on you. We're going to another party."

Then he left me, so I couldn't change my mind or say anything against it. He never said anything about a party. If I'd known about this earlier, I might've canceled from the beginning. Somehow, I didn't feel like celebrating anything or even thinking about partying. Not after all the things that Ramon had told me.

I reminded myself again of the fact that I wanted to spend more time with my friends. Distraction would be good for me. I would go to the party, and I would enjoy myself. And no one could stop me from doing that.

Like every day (except for last Friday), I spent my afternoon at Ramon's apartment. This time, he had peculiar good news for me. Of course, everything had happened on the weekend when I couldn't visit him because my mom had the horrible idea to camp for a whole weekend with her new boyfriend. As a family. I've never been a huge fan of camping, but the fact that her new boyfriend and his son were part of it made everything even worse. After this weekend, I had a new understanding of one *bring me the horizon song*; there was a hell, and I had seen it.

"And what do you plan to do next?" I asked curiously.

"I guess, it's time to go home," he answered lost in thoughts.

"But you won't go alone, will you?"

"To be honest, I didn't really think about it," he admitted.

"If you go, I'll come with you. And I bet Tim will come as well," I said almost demanding.

"But what if it will be dangerous?" he asked and looked worried.

"Then it's even better if we're three people. We can defend each other. And we can try to search the lost pages from the book," I tried to convince him of my naïve idea that everything was going to be alright.

"Okay, okay, you convinced me. You can come with me," he gave in while shaking his head. "You two are too stubborn, I can't fight you anyway."

"Perfect. When do we start?" I asked quickly before he could change his mind.

"I was thinking about next weekend, so we have enough time for planning."

I thought for a second: "What about Saturday?"

"Sure, I'll ask Tim, and then we can talk through the details," he said.

"How long do you think you'll stay there?" I wanted to know.

"As long as possible."

This answer was enough for me. I would've never admitted it, but I was incredibly excited to see the mansion, which Ramon had told me so much about. It was the place where everything had started.

Everything fitted perfectly into my schedule. I had only one week of school before summer vacations would start. I would spend some time with Finn and my other friends, and then I would go on *an incredibly tremendous journey.*

The week flew by, and before I could even notice, it was Friday, and I was on my way to a party. I had already packed my backpack for the next day.

I was looking forward to the day finally being over, but I still had no clue how I should tell my mom that I was going on a road trip with two – for her – strangers for an unknown amount of time. Usually, we never had any secrets from each other, but since she had kept her new boyfriend one for some time, our relationship has changed. If she was allowed to have secrets, so was I. That was just fair.

Maybe it would be the smartest to tell her everything after I'm already gone, because if I would ask her if I could go on this trip, her answer would 100 percent be a 'no'. But I had to go on this trip. And I couldn't ever tell her the true reason why this trip was that important to me.

Of course, there was more to it than just Ramon's powers. Since my mom had her new boyfriend, the situation at home got worse. We got into fights more often, and I realized that I was feeling worse mentally with every passing day that I spent in that apartment. But if I was with friends – especially Ramon – all of this didn't matter anymore. Maybe I really needed space, especially from my mom. And with space, I didn't mean I needed one apartment between us. I needed a federal state between us. At least.

It felt like the only solution for my relatively small problem. However, I not only needed space from my mom but also from myself. So, I could find myself again. As philosophical and paradoxical as this might've sounded but to feel happy again, I had to go away from here. Additionally, I have never been on a journey with friends, and I was way too curious to see the mansion. Things that my mom would never understand, and it would probably just lead to more fights, and I really didn't need that. Not now.

The party was odd. It wasn't a bad party after all, it was a regular party; the only problem was me. I couldn't get a grip on all of these people celebrating without any worries when there were more important things to do. Maybe they could call themselves lucky because they didn't know the things I knew. Would I be happier if I didn't know that much?

Everything passed by in front of me. I saw people that were dancing, but I wasn't dancing. I saw people that were drinking, but I wasn't drinking. I didn't even know why I was at this party because I was seriously bored. It wasn't my world. At least not for today.

"Are you okay?" Jane asked after she sat down next to me.

Like the previous parties, I had made my way to a rather quiet corner where I just sat and observed the other party guests.

"Yes, of course. Why wouldn't I be okay?" I answered confused.

"You are so thoughtful today," she said carefully. She was right. Not everything was okay. I was scared of the journey I was about to go on, but I was still looking forward to it. At home, everything was falling apart, and my meetings with the dead lady from the first floor occupied me more than they should.

"Maybe my life isn't that okay after all," I started. Then I told her about my situation at home and how difficult it was for me to accept the new boyfriend of my mom. I obviously didn't talk about Ramon. But it was therapeutic to be able to cry about everything that I had tried to repress in the past months.

I noticed how I felt way better after I was done talking about all of these things, but I also realized how much I missed my school friends. There were different kinds of friendships, I was sure of that. I could talk about everything with Jane and Finn, and I was sure that they would understand me. With Ramon on the other hand, I didn't talk much about my problems because they simply felt so irrelevant in comparison to his life. However, this didn't make our friendship less valuable. Having friends was just weird.

In the meantime, Finn had sat down next to us. Jane looked at him with a stern glance so I could avoid him asking me as well if everything was okay. Because I knew if he had asked me, I would've told him the whole truth. And if I would've told him everything, I probably would've cried.

Luckily, he understood Jane's glare and simply hugged me. Neither Jane nor Finn said anything, and I stayed silent as well. It was not like it was hard to stay silent when the music in the background was so loud anyway. But it really felt good to be silent together.

Earlier than planned, Finn dropped me off at home. He didn't drink any more alcohol since the incident. Quietly, we drove on the empty country road that led home.

"Do you want to talk?" he asked carefully.

"I don't know," I admitted.

"A lot of stress, huh?" he tried again.

I nodded.

"What do you think about going on a day trip next weekend or so?" he suggested enthusiastically.

I was glad about the change in topic, but I hated that I had to disappoint him again.

"I'm going on a journey tomorrow," I mumbled as an answer, and hoped he didn't understand me.

"Where do you go and with whom?" he asked still in a good mood.

"With Ramon and Tim, he is the best friend of Ramon."

I just answered his question partially because I had no clue where exactly we would go, or how long we would stay, or if it would be any dangerous. Neither did I know if I would ever come back. We couldn't know what would expect us there.

"Aha," he said, and I could see how all the happiness had vanished from his face.

"For how long?" he pressed out.

"I don't know. As long as we think it might be necessary. We're doing some kind of road trip," I lied. Technically it wasn't even a real lie. The trip would take some time, and we would be on a road, which could be called a road trip.

"You don't even know how long you'll be gone?" he asked confused.

"No," I admitted, "it's a very weird and abnormal road trip, and we don't know enough to even start this adventure. But how do you say, the journey is the real destination."

Damn. I told him too much. He would have questions. He would wonder what I meant by calling the trip weird. And if he would ask, I would be done. But he didn't say anything. He was silent.

"What do you think right now?" I asked carefully.

I couldn't stand seeing him angry.

"I just wonder what is so special about him."

Silence.

I wished I could tell him another lie just to calm him down again. To say something that he would appreciate, but that wouldn't tell too much either.

"I don't know," I answered after a long break, "it's difficult to name it because I don't really understand it either. I wish I could tell you everything, but I can't. I promised Ramon not to do that...– "

"Then don't," he said coldly.

I flinched.

He has never been that cold and distant with me before.

"I'm sorry," I murmured and wished I would sink into the car seat. I just wanted to go home. I just wanted to vanish out of this car. Out of this situation.

"We're there," he interrupted my thoughts.

"Bye. I really hope we'll see each other again soon," I said, and I really meant it.

It wasn't until then that I realized how afraid I was of the strangers and how poorly the odds were of even coming back alive. Maybe I was ready to travel for some time, but I wasn't ready to leave all of this – my friends and my mom – forever behind. I wasn't ready to die, even though I was ready to accompany Ramon wherever we would go.

My head was filled with a lot of different emotions that I couldn't even name. Finn didn't respond at all. He didn't even look at me. Apparently, he waited for me to close the car door so he could drive home, but I didn't close it.

Hurt, with tears in my eyes, I looked at him. I couldn't let him go like that. I didn't want to let him go like this.

"I promise I'll talk to Ramon and I'll explain everything to you when all of this is over," I tried to calm him down.

"Why then? Why not now?"

"Because we first need to figure out some things, okay? Trust me. I hate having secrets."

"Okay," he said and paused. "I do trust you."

I smiled.

"Be careful," he added.

Then I closed the door and made my way upstairs.

Chapter 19

It was Sunday morning, and the ringing of my alarm woke me up at 5 a.m. I had exactly 15 minutes to get dressed and sneak out of the apartment. I had already packed my bags yesterday, and we agreed to have breakfast somewhere along the road.

As always, I was running late, but having a good night of sleep seemed important to me. After all, I had no clue how much time we would spend on the road, and I couldn't fall asleep in a car.

Quickly, I put on some comfortable pants, grabbed my bags, and sneaked out of my room. It was still dark in the apartment since my mom didn't have to work and she loved to sleep in on her weekends. And our blinds were pretty good at keeping the light out.

Carefully, I made my way through the apartment, I even stopped myself from turning on the light to not risk waking up my mom. The moment I almost fell because of a shoe that was lying on the ground, I decided it was for the best to turn on the flashlight of my phone. This flashlight wasn't all too bright and just helped me to find and put on my shoes without further incidents.

Then I had to face the biggest challenge; opening the door to the staircase. Carefully, I turned the key in the lock and hoped that my mom was sleeping tightly so the jingling keys wouldn't wake her up. It worked. I slipped out of the door and closed it behind me. Then I took a deep breath and went down the stairs without even looking back.

Tim and Ramon were already waiting for me outside. They had started packing the car with luggage and food supplies. I could sense the tension in Ramon's face from far away.

"Wow, you guys are so busy that early in the morning," I greeted them.

"Yeah, we already checked the best route to get to the mansion as well," Tim said, who just carried a fishing net and a baseball bat to the trunk of the car.

I critically observed him.

"Just in case," he explained when he noticed my stare.

"Tim, I've told you to leave the bat at home," Ramon sighed slightly annoyed, and sat down on the driver's seat.

Tim closed the trunk after he had stored all of his things inside. Everything was now packed, and we had a plan to follow; it was time to start. Tim and I looked at each other until we realized that we hadn't discussed who would sit in the passenger seat. Quickly, we both ran to the passenger door and tried to open it, but it didn't work.

"If you can't agree, you both have to sit in the back," Ramon informed us.

"That's no need to lock us out of your car," Tim grumbled and sat down in the back seat.

I followed, and Ramon started the car. We were on our way to the mansion. Finally.

We left our street and turned into a usually quite busy street with a few stores on each side of the road that were obviously closed at that time. But even the street was so much emptier than usual. If you looked at the houses, there were no lights on, most people were still asleep or had their blinds down or both. It was only when we drove onto a federal highway that the sun started rising.

Even though it was pretty early, it was already quite warm, and the air smelled fresh and clean, like summer. It didn't take long for us to reach places that I had never seen before in my life. Cities where I had never been to and technically where I shouldn't be at the moment. Technically.

Suddenly, I realized that I still hadn't told my mom where I was. If she would wake up, she would just find my bed empty. Quickly, I typed in a message on my phone where I tried to explain that I was on a journey with friends, and I hoped that she wouldn't ask any more questions. She would be pretty angry, that was for sure, but she wouldn't be able to stop me anymore. We were already too far gone by now.

We had left the gray city behind; in front of us was our new beginning. I felt like the main character in Kafka's parable *the departure*. I didn't care about the destination as long as it was far away from here. Away from the old city, where no one could understand me, especially not my mom, because no one knew the things that I knew. How must this feel for Ramon? Or Tim? Nobody knew what we knew, and nobody would be able to ever understand us. Even I couldn't understand Ramon at first. But now I could.

We continued driving slightly to the north, and I felt some kind of tension in my chest. If we didn't change the highway soon, we would end up in my hometown.

I hoped we wouldn't get any closer because I was done with that city and the people inside of it. Even more than I was done with our new city. I had let go of my past, but getting closer to it would only rip open old wounds.

Ramon drove very focused and calmly, and I felt secure in his car. I still couldn't believe how it was possible for him to be so calm under these circumstances, but I was grateful he was chill. It was enough that I was nervous. Tim sang along to every song on the radio as loud as he could and didn't seem to be bothered by us. I had no clue how he could remember all the lyrics. But maybe he just listened to the radio a lot, contrary to me.

We passed so many bigger cities on our way to the mansion that I highly doubted we were on the fastest way. Because I would expect the fastest route to be on highways and not through any city. But it was beautiful. I could take so many impressions with me that I would capture in my mind for the rest of my life.

Most cities were the prettiest when it was still early. The streets were empty, and we could pass through them fast. The sunrise between the skyscrapers was simply spectacular. I wished I had a better phone camera or a normal camera because maybe I would've been able to snap a pic. I've always had a good eye when it came to aesthetic things; I just never had a camera with me. I couldn't say if one should envy me or if I was the most useless photographer on this planet.

"God, Tim, can you stop singing?" Ramon complained while he was entering another highway.

"*In this business, leave God alone!*"

I complained as a joke. At this moment, I didn't know if any of them would understand my joke.

I tried to observe Tim's reaction, but he just sat there in silence and looked confused.

"Did you just quote Goethe?" Ramon asked from the front seat.

"I thought it was fitting," I answered.

Ramon laughed.

"Okay, then let me test if you know this quote."

"I have German literature as a specialized course in school, you can't make me look like a fool," I said motivated.

"*Someone must have been telling lies about Josef K. …–* "

"That's all you have to offer?" I interrupted him challenging.

"*For without having done anything wrong he was arrested one fine morning.*"

I finished his quote.

"Not bad," Ramon said, and whistled through his teeth.

"Kafka, *The Trial*, is easy to guess and of course, a brilliant book."

Tim looked at us, still in confusion.

"Nerds," he said laughing and zoned out of the conversation.

"Okay, I have another quote," Ramon said after some time.

"Go for it."

"*Shall I compare thee to a summer's day?*"

"Shakespeare. *18th sonnet*," I answered shortly.

"Damn, how are you doing that?" he wanted to know.

"I would love to say she is googling but she isn't," Tim joined the conversation again, "you both are just freaks, that we can agree on."

Tim was right, it was probably not that common to guess famous quotes from certain authors.

We didn't even pass the halfway mark of our trip when we ended up in our first traffic jam.

"We're lucky. We could've ended up in a traffic jam way earlier," Ramon said.

It still didn't change anything about the not-so-great mood in the backseats. And if that wasn't enough bad luck, my mom decided to call me. My first instinct was to hang up on her and throw my phone out of the window, but I decided against it. If I wanted to be treated like a grown-up, I needed to act like one first.

"Hello?"

I greeted her carefully.

"WHERE THE HELL ARE YOU?"

I heard her raging from the other side of the phone.

Automatically, I held the phone a bit farther away from my ear, so my eardrum wouldn't rupture.

Then I answered calmly: "I'm on a road trip with friends. Exactly like I texted you."

"Aha," she just responded.

Silence.

"With who?"

"With Tim and Ramon – our neighbor from the fifth floor."

Silence. Again.

I could picture her going into the kitchen and boiling some water for tea because that was what she always did when she was angry.

"Come back, immediately!" she demanded.

"No, I'm not coming back. We're already on our way for too long to turn back," I argued.

"Oh, you'll turn back. Do you even know them that well? They could be criminals or murderers, or something like that," her voice had switched from angry to worried.

"Yes, I know both of them. Even pretty well, but I could never tell you about it because you were way too busy judging Ramon although you had never met him."

Silence.

I had no clue if she was even angrier now or if she was calming down.

"When do you plan on coming back home?" she asked neutrally.

"I don't know yet."

"When do you plan on coming back home?" she repeated sternly.

Apparently, she didn't like the answer I gave her.

"In a week," I responded.

And then she said something way worse than any reaction of hers I could've imagined. Something that hurt me more than anything else.

"We'll talk about this when you come home. Things can't go on like that," she sounded disappointed. Without saying goodbye, she hung up on me. Another person that I had disappointed. Again, another person that was angry at me, and this time I couldn't do anything to calm her down.

"You didn't let her know that you would come with us?" Tim asked after the conversation with my mom had ended.

I just nodded.

"She is probably worried."

"You are right, it wasn't my smartest decision ever, but I was angry at her, okay?"

I tried justifying my behavior.

Luckily, Tim didn't say anything else about the situation. I didn't need another person that would be judging me at the moment. I was already judging myself enough.

If that wasn't enough, the traffic on the highway got even worse. We could only move slowly, and the mood in the car kept on getting worse as well (or was it just me?). However, we decided we would stop at the next service station to eat something.

Luckily, it didn't take too long until we could find an exit leading to a service area. Next to the huge parking was a small meadow with multiple chairs and tables on it. It was absurd that this patch of grass could exist in the middle of loud noises and exhaust gases.

Hungrily, we ate our breakfast without saying all too much.

"Actually, we should wait here for a little while. There is still a traffic jam on the highway, and it's kind of nice to just sit here,"

Tim sighted and squinted his eyes. The sun was high in the sky, and it got pretty hot.

"Oh, especially all the car emissions are great for us," Ramon answered calmly grinning.

"It was just an idea," Tim murmured, but started grinning as well.

I could feel how my mood got better the further away we got from home, and I could sense that Ramon was feeling the same. Or was he feeling better because we got closer to his actual home?

Even Tim had changed since the beginning of our trip. He got way quieter – which was probably the lack of sleep – still, he seemed cheerful to me. Could a short trip like ours change us that fast? Could it really make us happier?

In the end, we took our time and kept sitting at the table on the meadow, waiting for the traffic jam to dissolve a bit. Eventually, we got bored, so we decided to continue our trip.

"The music is horrible," I blurted out after I had heard the same shitty pop song for the 10th time today.

"If I would've known the radio music was that shitty, I would've packed a CD," Ramon said calmly.

"The music isn't that bad," Tim tried to argue.

I looked at him sternly.

"Okay, you are right. It's pretty bad," he finally admitted.

"How much time did we lose because of the traffic?" Tim asked out of nowhere.

"We have all the time in the world," Ramon replied.

"Perfect. Then we take the next exit and buy a proper CD somewhere," he demanded.

Amused, I observed them. They were such a great team, no one could deny that. They were good for one another.

As Tim demanded, Ramon took the next exit, and we quickly entered one of the stores that sold electronic devices and CDs.

"What do you think about that one?" Tim asked, and held the latest *Bravo Hits* CD in his hands like a trophy.

Ramon and I looked at him skeptically and just shook our heads. A little bit disappointed, Tim put the CD back where he had found it and helped us look for one that everyone would enjoy. In the end, we bought one with old rock songs that were perfectly fitting to a road trip, according to Tim. Additionally, Ramon took the time to go to the next gas station because it was way cheaper to refuel the car in the city than on the highway.

After we had fixed our music issue, the mood in the car got better as well. Tim sang along to the music again, and I enjoyed the view out of the window. We were back on the highway, and even the traffic jam was over now, so we could drive without further interruptions.

I was stunned by the number of green fields and forests that we passed on our way. I had never thought Germany could be that pretty; I had always expected all the pretty places to be outside of this country. It must've been such a one-sided view, but I had never seen anything particularly pretty in Germany. However, I didn't know many places in Germany either; we had never traveled anywhere.

I had never seen other places than my hometown and the current city we were living in. For vacation, my mom and I drove to the closest camping area because camping was so much better for the environment, and we would destroy the environment if we would drive long distances by car. She never cared about me. I wanted to see the world, and even more, I hated camping.

After the sun was almost setting, we exited the highway and entered a small village. I couldn't tell why, but it felt like we were almost at our destination. All the small and colorful houses made me feel comfortable.

We continued driving through the narrow streets for some time until there were no houses anymore. The road now led up a small hill that was completely covered by a forest. If I didn't know it better, I wouldn't expect any houses on the tip of the hill.

In the meantime, it got pretty dark, and the first stars were visible through the treetops. I had never seen such a pretty night sky. Were we really still in Germany? I let down the window on my side so the chilly and fresh air could get inside the car. Spruce, pine, or larch – I couldn't tell what exactly I was smelling. I took a deeper breath. Everything here felt so unreal. It felt like we weren't supposed to be here, which technically was true, at least for me. Carefully, I got my head a bit closer to the window to feel the fresh air on my skin. After this long day, I needed this to cool down a bit.

Finally, the street looked like it was about to end. In front of us was one last curve that was separating us from the mansion. We were finally there. Against all expectations, Ramon didn't say anything; he drove in silence.

"Are we there yet?" Tim asked as a joke while we drove the last meters to the mansion.

Everything looked exactly the way I had imagined it. The mansion was old and huge, maybe a little bit bigger than I had expected. The entrance looked inviting despite the rotten plants and the broken stone steps in front of the door. Just the stone façade, in combination with the huge windows whose shutters were closed, looked a lot creepier than inviting in the dusk.

Actually, the whole mansion was saying only one thing; stay the fuck away from here.

Chapter 20

It has been too long since he had travelled back there. He wished it wouldn't have taken him that long to finally come back. He had never felt that happy and carefree before. It was overdue to finally feel something again. Grinning, he went up the stone steps that led to the mansion. The air smelled like pines and strawberries. It was a miracle that the plants he had planted with his Grandma were still alive after all these years. He took a deep breath. Welcome home.

Tim was very motivated because he had already started carrying the bags from the trunk to the front door. He looked like he was enjoying himself. I observed that Luna followed him with some camping lanterns that she had borrowed from her mom. After everything, we couldn't be sure if we would have electricity or water in the mansion. It had been empty for more than six months.

I looked inside the trunk, which still had Luna's backpack, more lanterns, Tim's baseball bat, and lots of food in it. With so many bags, it didn't really feel like traveling to a familiar place. It felt more like traveling abroad forever. I grabbed the bags with the food supplies and followed Tim and Luna to the door. They were already waiting for me to finally unlock the door.

I was the first one to enter the mansion. Immediately, I could smell the familiar scent of my Grandma. This is what it must feel like to come home. Carefully, I looked for the light switch to turn on the golden chandelier that used to enlighten the entrance area. I didn't really expect it to work, but after a quick electrical hum, the darkness surrounding us vanished. I was confused for a second, but I didn't think twice about it. I was just glad that we had light for now.

Followed by the others, I tried the light switch in the kitchen, which worked as well. And even the tap was working after multiple tries. I wouldn't particularly want to drink that water, but at least we had running water.

I put the bag of food in the kitchen and started unpacking it. It felt like I had just come home from grocery shopping. All of this was mine now. Technically, it had been mine for over six months, I just didn't know it.

We continued emptying the trunk, and I still couldn't convince Tim to leave his bat in the car. He could be so stubborn. Like me.

After we had carried everything inside, we made our way upstairs to explore the first floor of the mansion. The stairs had become fragile over the years, and I wouldn't trust the banisters with my life either, but somehow, we managed to make our way upstairs without anyone getting hurt. The high walls inside of the villa could probably seem a bit threatening, but to me, they felt familiar. The paintings on the wall in their golden frames looked at me reproachfully. Until today, I didn't know who these people were or why my Grandma hung them up in the first place. But one thing I was certain of; I would never throw them away.

Hypnotized, I went down the aisle to my right and stopped in front of the last door. I took a deep breath, then I pushed down the dusty golden doorknob. The door opened with a small bump. I had to cough. Judging by the amount of dust that was welcoming me, it could only mean that this door hadn't been opened in a very long time. To be more precise, for 13 years.

It looked like Grandma had never entered the room again after I had visited her for the last time. Maybe she thought it would be enough if she would clean the room when she could be sure I would come and visit her; but I never came. Ever. Until today.

After the death of my mom, I hadn't seen a purpose in visiting her. Luckily, she came over a lot. She wasn't a replacement for my mom, but she had become one of the most important people in my life.

The light in this room was working as well. With a buzz, my blue-green lamp in the shape of an airplane turned on. It didn't shed too much light, but it was enough to be able to see. I looked through my old room. My glance wandered to the wooden, green wardrobe that was standing on the opposite side of my loft bed. Below the bed was a tiny shelf filled with all kinds of toys and books. The storybook had always been right there as well. It was kind of absurd that my Grandma didn't want me to know about my powers while at the same time kept the answer to all of my questions right under my nose. But maybe that was the best hiding spot because no one suspected anything about it.

My whole room was a contrast to the elegant furniture in the mansion. However, my Grandma thought it was important that I could decide myself how I wanted my room to look. She wanted me to feel at home here if I would come over for a visit. And I felt more at home here in the room of my early childhood than I felt in my apartment. Now that I was back here, I couldn't understand how I could have stayed away from this place. Now that I was back here, I actually didn't want to leave. Never again.

Maybe it was weird, but it was the first time in my life that I felt like I belonged somewhere. I hadn't felt like this since Luana's death. I mean, how should I feel like I belonged anywhere when I did everything to keep other people away from me. But now, everything has changed. Or was it just me who had changed? I couldn't really tell. But at least I could tell that my whole philosophy had changed. I had friends – not a lot, but I was able to open up to people again, which was a huge progress. Also, it had been some time since I had a prediction. I was able to control myself, and all of this thanks to Tim, who never gave up on me, even though I had given up on myself so many times.

I couldn't tell if I felt more connected to Grandma here or if it was because I was so far away from home, but I could comfortably tell that I felt understood. I couldn't tell why this place here was so special at the moment because it was possible for me to avoid it for so many years. But maybe it was just the fact that I had always preferred this place over my actual home until the incident with Luana. If something was important to you, it would always be important to you.

I realized all of these things while I was standing immovable in the middle of my old room and staring at my bed.

Maybe this here has always been my real home. Maybe I have just been a visitor in my own apartment. Or maybe I felt more at home in the mansion because they got rid of the playground next to it after all these years. It was easier to repress my memories without looking at the crime scene. Maybe I felt less guilty because I had met Luna. So many maybes, and so few answers.

"Do you have a vacuum cleaner somewhere?", Tim asked, interrupting my thoughts.

Caught in the act, I answered: "Yes, in the broom closet. But I'm not sure it still works."

He vanished as quickly as he came, and I followed him. It was best for me to leave that room as well, otherwise, I would start crying after my innocence and childhood.

Carefully, I closed the door behind me. Also, Tim would probably need my help to find a vacuum cleaner.

I surpassed him and showed him the way to the broom closet, which was on the other side of the large hallway.

"These paintings are somehow creepy," I heard Tim say behind me.

The closet was by far the smallest room in the whole mansion. I searched for the vacuum cleaner, which was harder than it sounded because I couldn't find the light switch. Finally, I could find the vacuum cleaner and some other cleaning devices, which I couldn't name. They would be good for something, probably. Then I helped Tim clean the kitchen and a few of the guest bedrooms. Because of her fear of spiders, Luna had decided she would try to cook something for us. I guess she had the most pleasant job that night.

It was already late, but we definitely needed to eat something. Exhausted, Tim and I sat down at the table in the kitchen after we were done cleaning. Our food tonight was no Michelin-star-like meal, it was something rather simple but perfect for the first evening of our huge adventure; we had pasta with ketchup.

"How do you like it here?" I asked to break the silence.

"It's quite cool. I didn't know it would be that huge, but please hang down these creepy paintings when you move here," Tim said, and impaled his pasta with his fork.

I flinched.

Of course, I had thought about moving into the mansion, but I hadn't fully decided yet. It sounded so weird to hear these words from someone else. In my head, everything sounded easy, but once said out loud by someone else, I started to panic internally.

"If I move in", I corrected him, "I'll probably hang them up in the guest bedroom, where you'll sleep when you come and visit."

Tim looked at me beggingly.

"Please, don't do that or I won't ever come here again."

"What about you?" I asked Luna who looked like she was lost in her thoughts.

"Me? Oh... Hm... I don't know yet. Everything doesn't feel real and unbelievable. The house is really pretty and everything, but there are too many spiders," she responded.

I smiled encouragingly at her.

"That's why Tim and I cleaned the bedrooms."

After dinner, we brought our sleeping bags into the rooms that we had cleaned before. This was the moment when we would separate for the night.

I took the dust cover off the bed – luckily my Grandma was always prepared for visitors, but maybe this was even a common thing for people who had a lot of bedrooms. Because of the dust cover, all the beds were clean and free from dust; we could just hop into them and start sleeping. And that's what I did.

I let myself sink into the soft mattress and turned the light off. The clock on my mobile phone showed me that it was past midnight, but even though it was already late, I suddenly didn't feel tired anymore.

I knew that I was exhausted, but my mind was too awake. I turned around multiple times, but I couldn't fall asleep. After what felt like an eternity, I could finally fall doze off.

And that was the first night in the mansion.

Chapter 21

The warm sunbeams that fell through the not-completely sunproof shutters woke me up. I probably didn't sleep much, but at least I had no nightmares keeping me awake, which was pretty rare. It took me some time until I realized where I was and that it wasn't all just a dream.

I stretched my limbs and walked over to the window to open it. The birds were singing, and the sky was blue. When I opened the shutters, the scent of the forest entered my room. Without even realizing it, I grinned widely. I was happy. Finally.

When I went downstairs, Tim and Luna were already waiting for me in the kitchen. They had already eaten.

"What is the plan for today?" Luna asked curiously when she saw me.

"I thought we're looking through the mansion to see if we can find some hints regarding the missing pages of the book," I answered casually and sat down.

Secretly, I hoped to find out more about my Grandma or even me as well. I still felt like I didn't know everything. Also, I hoped to find some clues about her cause of death. She only told me that she would die, but nobody could tell me how. I hadn't asked for it, but I was sure that my dad didn't know more than me anyway. Even in the newspaper death announcement – which my dad had printed in some kind of regional newspaper for some reason – it didn't say a proper cause of death. Everyone suspected her to have died because of her age, but I couldn't believe that. Not after receiving her letter.

The mansion must be full of secrets, and I was more than ready to discover them. I hoped we would even find them because, as far as I could tell by now, Grandma was great at playing hide and seek.

"I would say we start looking in the rooms that we didn't clean last night, how exciting," Tim said and was ready to start. Then he hesitated: "As long as you don't feel uncomfortable when we look through the private things of your Grandma."

I shook my head and bit into my toast.

So, we spent all day long looking through the rooms in the mansion, one by one. But we couldn't find anything. It was disappointing, for sure, but we couldn't change it. The last room we wanted to check for today was her office. I had never stepped a foot in there that's why it felt extremely odd to go inside. Tim and Luna followed me. They were probably as surprised by the room as I was.

Everywhere were moving boxes full of paper. The boxes had notes pinned to them, which I couldn't read because the letters had faded over time, and it even seemed like it was written in another language. The violet curtains in front of the window were dusty and had holes in them. A moth probably had the time of its life in here. The bottom of one side of the curtains was hanging over an old globe, which covered the globe partially (no need to explain that the globe was dusty as well).

There was a desk that, in contrast to the rest of the room, was tidy and clean. On the desk stood a bottle of my Grandma's favorite perfume. She must've written her letter to me from here. There was exactly one shelf in this room, which was also filled with papers. Some of the shelf racks were, however, completely empty. On the ground in front of the shelf were a lot of books, some of them were open, others closed.

If I had thought about going to bed early tonight before, there was no way I would be able to follow that plan. In this office were so many things that we needed to check through, we could be happy if it wouldn't take all night long.

To work faster, we divided the room into three areas, one for each, to search through. My third included the desk and the shelf, while the others had to look through multiple boxes full of papers.

The desk was absolutely irrelevant; there was neither a secret hiding spot (or it was too secret, so I couldn't find it) nor any other papers that could help us. All I could find were different kinds of envelopes and fountain pens (yes, my Grandma preferred them over ballpoint pens). At least I was quickly done checking the desk and could start looking through the shelf.

"I think I found something here," Tim said from one corner of the room.

He was looking through one of the smallest boxes in this room. Immediately, Luna and I rushed toward him to look at what he had found with our own eyes. It was a death notice taken out of a regional newspaper.

"Did your Grandma know her, or why else would she keep this?" Tim asked confused.

I had to swallow and noticed that Luna looked at me pitifully.

"No, they never met. I have no explanation for this," I answered, grabbing the piece of paper.

My hand was shaking, but I tried to ignore it. What else was this woman hiding? In situations like this, I wondered if I even knew her at all.

"We can put this to the side for now and look for further evidence regarding Luana," Luna suggested and carefully took the paper out of my hand to lay it on the windowsill. Internally, I was thankful. Looking at Luana's death announcement wasn't good for me, and apparently, she could tell that as well.

I kept on looking for other peculiarities, but at first glance, everything seemed normal. It was simply a lot of paper (and a lot of books). Nothing special about that, I thought. Carefully, I picked one of the books up from the ground and took a closer look at it. Against my expectations, the book didn't have a title on the cover, and even then, it took me a few seconds until I realized that this wasn't a normal book but a photo album. All of these books were photo albums.

I decided to look inside. There were pictures of strangers. A lot of strangers.

Who were these people, and why did she know them? Confused, I flipped through the pages until it became more and more absurd. On one photograph was a feminine-looking creature that could only hardly be identified as a woman. Instead of arms, she had wings that were full of colorful feathers. But that wasn't everything not human about her. Her feet were no feet; she had claws, but her legs were human-looking. Her nose was pointy, and on her head were a lot of feathers.

It was a harpy, and no, I didn't mean the bird. I wished I had figured this out all through my knowledge about paranormal creatures, the truth was, however, that I only knew it because I loved watching *Yu-Gi-Oh!* as a child.

"I think I found something as well," I said automatically.

Immediately, the others appeared behind me.

"What is this supposed to be?" Tim asked and sounded exactly as confused as me.

Without asking, Luna picked up another photo album from the ground and looked through it.

"That's interesting."

I heard her mumble and somehow, she sounded more interested than confused.

Finally, she put the book back on the shelf where it probably belonged and looked at Tim and me triumphantly.

"What? It looks like you didn't know that your Grandma had some kind of hotel for supernatural creatures."

My eyes widened.

"What?" I blurted out in disbelief.

"Well, the pictures were all taken in front of or in the mansion, look!" She pointed at the photograph I was looking at.

"I immediately recognized this room in the photo because that's the room I slept in last night," she explained to us.

"But why do you think she had a hotel? This can't be a coincidence, can it?" I continued asking.

Somehow, I couldn't imagine any of this being true. How should my Grandma have a hotel for magical creatures without anyone noticing it? How could no one in our family know about that, or was she really that good at keeping secrets?

"In the other album were some old bills in addition to the photographs and an old letter addressed to your Grandma. I just had to read one letter until it became obvious that she was managing a hotel here." She answered this question, and suddenly everything made sense.

The house was big, too big and I had always wondered if my Grandma enjoyed living here all by herself. It was hard not to feel lost in this mansion when you were all alone. But not just that. In the last months, I had learned so much about my Grandma.

She was very tactical. I bet she had other reasons to use the mansion as a hotel, and if everything was true that I had learned about this world, then she must've somehow profited from doing that. Maybe it was some kind of symbiosis between my Grandma and other creatures. My Grandma offered them shelter as long as they were in the area, and they offered something to my Grandma. But what? She didn't need any money.

"Okay, I think I'm starting to understand what's going on," I said and scratched my forehead. "But why did she do this? She didn't need money," I added.

"I can't answer this question. But I would agree that she didn't do this for money. Her prices were way too low. I doubt she even made any money with it," Luna confirmed my theory.

Silence.

We all thought about the reasoning behind this.

"Maybe she did this to study supernatural creatures," Luna offered an idea.

More silence.

I already started to befriend the thought that we would probably never know for sure when Tim suddenly said: "Protection."

That was all he said, but immediately I knew that he was right. After the letter and the knowledge that somewhere out there were strangers that wanted to see my Grandma dead, this sounded quite plausible. The strangers might've been after my Grandma for longer than we knew, and since it looked like she was help-less on her own, she needed other creatures to help her out.

"Tim, you are a genius," I praised him, and even Luna seemed to prefer his theory over hers.

"Is this something supernatural?" Tim asked, show-ing us another photograph.

It was a woman with long brown hair and dark blue eyes. She didn't look supernatural; she looked ordi-nary. Like any average woman in her 40s or early 50s. Somehow, she looked familiar, and I wondered if I might've seen her in one of my visions and therefore murdered her. I couldn't remember every single per-son that I had killed, and I didn't want to remember the fact that I was a murderer as well. Maybe I had seen her in the city center at some point in time. This would explain why she looked familiar to me. Why would I remember anyone's face that I had just seen for a brief moment?

"No, not at all," Luna said quietly.

Immediately, I looked at her. She looked so pale and shocked all of a sudden. And while I looked at her, I finally remembered why I knew this woman – it was Luana's mother. Before I could tell Tim why I knew her, Luna beat me to it.

"That's my mom, and if she was supernatural in any way, I would know it for sure." She was in a rage.

I had no clue if I should say anything about it. If I should add why I knew this woman or if I should let it go again. Since Luna looked like she was already suffering enough, I decided not to say anything about the photograph. She didn't want me to talk about the connection to Luana, so I wouldn't talk about it anymore, but one day I would find out the truth. Not for me. Not for Luna. But for Luana.

The day ended more promising than it had started, however, I still felt like there was more to discover. Every answer we could find led to even more unanswered questions. Everything about Luana became more and more strange. I was 100 percent sure by now that my Grandma knew something about the incident. However, I had only talked about it with my mom, and this was only months after it had happened. Even if she had talked to my Grandma there was no way, she knew it in time to save the death notice from the newspaper. It had happened way before she could've known about it.

Also, why would she even save it? Who did such things? I didn't keep the death notice of my mom; I didn't even read it. But even if I would've kept it, it would've been okay. She is, I mean was, my mom after all. Luana, however, must've been a stranger to my Grandma. And the picture of her mother was making things even weirder than they already were. Where did she find the picture, and what was the connection between Luana's and Luna's mother?

The only thing that I could tell for certain was that the strangers that went after my Grandma were stronger than I had expected. It was obvious they had to be strong because otherwise she wouldn't be dead. But it looked like they were after her for a long time, and she wouldn't have built an army out of supernatural creatures just for the joke. The strangers must be supernatural as well, with abilities that we couldn't even imagine.

Chapter 22

That night, I was lying awake for a long time again. No matter how often I turned, I couldn't fall asleep. There were too many questions filling my head, which made me restless. After what felt like an eternity, I couldn't stand this feeling anymore, so I decided to leave my room.

Carefully, I made my way into the kitchen and boiled water so I could drink the first tea I could find. I wasn't even that much of a tea drinker, but Tim was. Without him, I would've never thought about packing tea for a journey like this. Especially not when the journey was in the middle of summer. But right now, I was grateful he was as stubborn as always.

After my tea was done and I could get rid of the tea bag, I decided to drink it in the winter garden of the mansion. When I visited my Grandma, we always ate our food in the winter garden since the view into the forest was absolutely calming and breathtaking. When I arrived at the winter garden, I got scared for a second. Someone was sitting there.

Someone had taken a chair and placed it in front of the huge windows, so I could only see the back of that person. In the darkness, I couldn't even tell who was sitting there. It must've been one of my friends, but still, it felt a bit weird. Carefully, I tried to get closer to figure out whose silhouette I was looking at. I was almost behind the person until I could tell for sure who was sitting there. I could breathe again. It was just Luna. There was never any reason to worry.

"Hey, you have trouble sleeping as well?" I asked and grabbed another chair to sit down next to her.

I could tell that she was twitching for a second, I guess she didn't expect anyone else to be awake.

"I always sleep poorly if I'm not home, but here it's even worse," she responded.

"Why is it worse here?" I wanted to know and carefully put my mug on the table behind me.

"Well, everything is so big and overwhelming. Of course, I mean that in a positive way, but it's also somehow scary," she admitted, and her voice got more and more quiet until the end of the sentence.

"I think I can imagine how that must feel," I admitted.

Her view, which was focused on the forest, now wandered to me.

"I didn't expect you to answer something so serious," she said grinning.

"I'm always good for surprises." I had to grin briefly as well.

Silence.

None of us said a single word. Still, the situation wasn't tense at all. It was nice sitting here and staring out of the window. I couldn't think of any other person I would rather be with right now.

"It's ironic," she broke the silence and I looked at her, "I should be able to sleep better because even at home I feel like a visitor."

I didn't know exactly how I should respond. I had never talked to someone like that. I would've loved to give her a hug and let her tell me the whole story, but I didn't know exactly if this was a normal reaction among friends or what else I was supposed to do. Luckily, it wasn't even necessary to say anything because she kept on talking on her own.

She talked about her problems at home with her mom and her new stepfather. It was kind of refreshing to listen to someone else's problems. And it secretly made me happy that she trusted me enough to share important details of her life with me.

"Is this why you wanted to come with me so badly?" I asked after she was done talking.

She didn't say a word but nodded.

It would be possible to kiss her at this moment, but it was probably weird, so I repressed the completely weird urge to do it.

"And that's why you didn't tell your mom?" I wanted to know.

"Yeah," she responded, "and because I was afraid, she wouldn't let me go on this trip. I know how important it is to be here for you, and I didn't want you to go alone. It could've been dangerous, and especially since today, I'm glad I'm here."

She didn't look at me while she said all of these things.

"I'm glad I'm not alone," I answered.

"How will we continue in the future?" she asked suddenly, and looked at me.

"I don't know. I guess we'll continue looking through the villa and maybe we'll find some more things and then… " I didn't finish my sentence because I had no clue how to finish it.

I didn't know what would happen after we were done here. I didn't know what I was supposed to do with all the knowledge we had and the one that we would get. I didn't even know exactly what we were looking for.

"And then?" she further asked.

She managed to ask exactly this one question that I couldn't answer. Because if I wanted to answer this question, it meant I needed to think about it at first, and I didn't want to think about the future at the moment. Everything was fine the way it was. I didn't want to prepare myself for disappointments, and I didn't want to go back to our hometown because I found my home here. It has always been. I really tried to think of an answer.

"I think if we don't find anything here, we have to drive back home," I said out loud.

"So, you also don't want to go back?" she analyzed me.

Now it was me who just nodded in silence.

"But what happens if we find something?"

Another question I couldn't answer.

"Then we're smarter than before and make our decisions based on the newfound knowledge, I guess," I tried to find a vague answer.

"If you knew who the strangers are, would you try to find them?" she asked carefully.

"I think so. I want to know why they were chasing after my Grandma," I murmured.

It was obvious that I didn't stand a chance against a group of strangers whose powers I didn't know, still, it seemed important that I would find them and get my answers as far as it was possible.

"I think you won't find them. I think they'll find you first," she said her thoughts out loud.

I shivered.

"Why do you think that?" I answered staggered.

"They were after your Grandma for a reason, and it's way too odd that multiple pages are missing from the book. I doubt your Grandma got rid of them. Whoever did this just doesn't want to be found," she reminded me.

And she was right about that. Damn right, even. Again, silence took over.

"Do you think you'll come back here?" she broke the silence for a second time and sounded a bit worried.

"And open a hotel for magical creatures? Maybe." I grinned while I said that. I had never thought about changing my current job. I had never even thought about opening a hotel for supernatural beings. I had never really thought about inhuman things at all.

It was bizarre to live in a world where we were surrounded by the supernatural – maybe even in our daily routine – still we didn't realize it at all. Were we just blind, or did we purposely decide to look away?

"I didn't mean it like that," she said and pretended to hit my arm.

"Huh? You didn't?" I asked ironically. "What did you mean then?"

"I mean, you like being here, probably even more than you like your apartment. Will you move to the mansion without opening a hotel for anyone?" she rearranged her question.

"What would you do in my position?" I tried to avoid actually answering.

"I think I would do it," she responded after a short break.

"Then, you can imagine what I'll do," I lowered my voice at the end of the sentence.

Actually, up to this moment, I was uncertain what I should do, but it felt like the only right thing to say and to do. I would come back here. For good.

"Yeah, it would suck if you would go away, though."

I smiled.

"That won't mean I'll be dead. You and Tim can still come and visit me whenever you please."

"Do you think you'll get lonely?"

"Probably."

"I wish I could talk you out of it, but I know I would do the same if I were in your position. Talking you out of it would just be egoistic."

It surprised me that she was opening up so much. Again, she left me frantically looking for something to answer.

"You want to talk me out of it?" I just repeated perplexed.

Immediately, I got angry at myself for asking such a dumb question.

"Yes, I don't even know why, but somehow being with you comforts me," she laughed as if she didn't really know what she had just said. "Also, you are different than all the other people I know. But not in a bad way, in a good way," she added, and sounded exactly as confused as when we first met, and she introduced Finn as her friend-friend.

"And your problems are so different than mine, somehow more severe. Wait, that sounds weird and mean," she stuttered.

Maybe she even flushed, I couldn't see it anyway, it was still too dark. She needed a few seconds to find her words again.

"It's simply nice to be with someone that makes you forget about your own problems for a little while," she finally said.

"That sounds way better," I answered amused.

I didn't say or show it, but her words meant so much to me, and maybe she did exactly what she didn't want to do; convince me to stay.

"You and Tim," I started, and took a deep breath. What I was about to say wouldn't be easy to say.

"You make me a better person than I am."

I could feel her grin.

"It was about time you realize that," she answered in a way I would've probably answered as well.

Suddenly, she turned her head away from me and looked into the forest.

"Are you okay?" I wanted to know and looked out of the window as well.

"Yes, everything is great. I just thought I had seen someone, but I guess I was wrong. I might be more tired than I thought after all," she explained.

"Maybe you should go back to bed?" I suggested.
I wasn't tired at all, and maybe I didn't want her to leave just now, but it felt like the right thing to say.

"Maybe," she said softly. "Can you tell me something about your Grandma?"

Confused about her question I stuttered: "What should I say? I don't even know her that well, apparently."

"You should not tell me who she was, but how she was. It doesn't matter if you knew her that well. All that's important is that you never forget the way she treated you. The how is more important than the who."

I wasn't prepared for such a philosophical answer, however, I had to admit that she was right. It shouldn't matter if she was the person I thought she was or not. All that mattered was that I would never forget all the time we had spent together.

So, I told Luna about my Grandma and that she always read books to me. I told her about the time we drove to IKEA to buy furniture for my room in the mansion and that she let me decide exactly what to buy. I even told her about how we always plucked strawberries in the garden and how proud she had been that her garden was full of flowers and life. When I looked at Luna, she had fallen asleep. I still couldn't tell for sure, but her breathing had slowed down, and she didn't answer my question about whether she was still awake or not.

Quietly, I stood up just to notice that I hadn't touched my tea so far; it was probably cold by now. Then I looked for a blanket to cover Luna with. If she was already sleeping in such an uncomfortable position, she should at least not get too cold.

I went back to the kitchen to warm up my tea again. It didn't work as well as I thought, so I went back to sit down on the chair next to Luna to drink my lukewarm tea and look into the forest to try to stop my thoughts from going wild.

Finally, he had arrived at his destination. It has been a while since he was here for the last time, but at the same time, he couldn't know he would be back here that quickly. Since he had started his mission, he knew that their traces would lead him to the mansion one day.

However, he first needed to inform the others so they could prepare themselves for what was about to come. They needed to hurry up a bit, otherwise, their plan wouldn't work. The plan, which they had been working on for years. They had only this one chance, and it must happen now. Even though it was quite a surprise to find them at the mansion that soon, but it could only be to their advantage.

Their target wouldn't be able to fully control his powers after only six months. He wouldn't be a huge danger to them. Immediately, he went back to the others. Tonight was the night of the nights, and he would finally be free. Forever.

Chapter 23

I must've fallen asleep while talking to Ramon because when I woke up, my neck hurt pretty badly – it was a horrible idea to fall asleep on a chair – and Ramon was gone. A very loud noise, similar to the sound of a squeaking door, had woken me up.

I was confused and sat straight in my chair. From the corner of my eye, I could see a shadow vanishing through the door. Now I was even more confused.

If Ramon had just left the winter garden, who was responsible for this horrifying noise? Without further thinking, I hurried out of the room and tried to follow Ramon undercover. I didn't know why exactly I didn't ask him to wait for me so we could check out the origin of the sound together, but for some reason, my gut feeling told me it was better to lay low and hide.

Ramon walked down the stairs, and I tried to keep up with him without falling down. It felt super weird to shade him like that, especially since I was sure it was not him who kept any secrets in this mansion.

Ramon turned into a small passage that neither Tim nor I had stepped into so far, to be honest, I didn't even realize it existed until that moment. My gut feeling was escalating even more. This was so weird; I didn't like anything about this situation. Whoever or whatever was behind this door was none of us.

Adrenaline was rushing through my body when I opened the same door that Ramon had disappeared through just a few seconds ago. I was still careful, so he wouldn't notice me.

The door was heavier than it looked, but nothing would prevent me from following Ramon. I simply had to do it, especially now that I knew we weren't alone in this mansion. It would be too dangerous to let him go anywhere alone.

Behind the door was a long corridor whose stoned walls were lit with torches. Normally, I would've wondered if open fires like this in a secret corridor were a good idea or not. It sounded pretty dangerous to me, but I tried to repress that thought. I couldn't risk getting lost in my own thoughts; I couldn't risk being caught because I was thinking too much. Nothing was allowed to throw me off my mission.

Maybe it would've been smarter to wake Tim, but I was afraid we would lose Ramon for good if I did so. There was no way we would've found this hidden passage without him. Damn, what a dilemma!

It was difficult to stay close to Ramon because of the torches on the wall, but since the corridor was mostly straight and without any crossings, I could allow myself to keep up with a bigger distance without risking losing him. Damn, what was I even doing here?

The air in the corridor was musty, and I could feel goosebumps raising on my arms even though I couldn't feel the coldness. My body was way too pumped with any kind of hormone to feel anything.

After some time, I reached a spiral staircase – which was made out of stone, surprise, like everything around me – which led even further down. If it wasn't for the torches, I was certain I would've fallen down the stairs since they were surprisingly moist.

It was absolutely headless to walk down these stairs since the walls were high, and it was impossible for me to see what or who was in front of me until the other person would see me as well. I had a huge disadvantage here. But I tried to repress this thought too. The staircase went on forever, or maybe it was just a feeling because I wasn't known for being the most patient person ever.

The ceiling was covered in cobwebs, which made me feel very uncomfortable. I would've loved to just turn around, but I wasn't doing this for me; I was doing this for Ramon. Even though I had no clue how I should explain to him that I shaded him until now, but I had enough time to figure out what to say. For now, it was important to figure out where the strange noises, which had stopped by now, came from.

The further I went down the stairs, the colder it became. And in comparison to earlier, I could feel the cold around me now. I exhaled, and I could see the air in front of me, even though it was supposed to be summer. I had lost all sense of time, and I had lost track of Ramon as well. I didn't even know how far ahead he was by now. I just felt lost. Maybe this was all just a bad dream, and I would wake up any time. A little bit dazed by the coldness, I pinched my arm; I wasn't sleeping.

I also noticed that I was so lost in my own thoughts that I barely realized I had almost reached the end of the stairs. It was only when I heard the voices of some people that I snapped back into reality.

"What do you want?" I could hear Ramon's voice. He didn't sound very excited. Wherever I was at the moment, it had to be the origin of the strange noise. Carefully, I searched for a little gap in the stone wall that was big enough so I could catch a slight overview of the situation.

Apparently, the stairs led to a room that looked like a regular basement. There were shelves filled with cans and bottles next to the walls. There even was a rusty sink in one corner of the room. On the opposite side of the stairs was another corridor. In general, nothing looked extraordinary or even supernatural about this room.

Three older-looking men were standing right in the middle of the room, one of them had a long, gray beard. Their sense of style looked quite old-fashioned. I had never been much into fashion trends, but they didn't look like they were wearing clothes from this century. Maybe not even from the last.

"What a delightful question! We already knew you would ask this," the man in the middle answered.

He had incredibly full lips that reminded me of a fish and barely any hair on his head. Only the sides of his head had a few white hairs growing out of his skin.

"You don't have to be particularly intelligent to figure that out," Ramon responded coldly.

I smiled.

How could he be so much like himself in a situation like this? Now, the right man, who had a long gray beard and deep, dark-looking wrinkles on his face, took a step closer to Ramon.

"You better behave!" he sounded angry, and his voice sent shivers down my spine.

"Antonius, calm down! We have a plan to follow," the stranger on the left warned him. He was tall, wore a long cape, and had a short, curly beard.

"I know, Titus, I know," the man who seemed to be called Antonius answered and stepped back again.

Who were these people? What did they want?

Ramon looked exactly as confused as I felt at the moment.

The guy with the curly beard, Titus, cleared his throat and started talking: "What we want is simple."

The others didn't say a word but looked at Ramon expectingly.

"We want you."

"Aha," Ramon sounded skeptical and distant.

"Let us finish," Titus tried again, but as far as I knew, nothing he could possibly say would convince him to follow these three strangers.

"Unfortunately, I'm not interested in any physical relationship with you guys, but I feel flattered," he shrugged.

"Maybe you can understand us better if we tell you who we are," Titus said, unbothered by Ramon's ironical words.

He then stepped in front of the others.

"Or do you not want to know who we are, Ramon?" He looked at him penetrating.

Although it shouldn't shock me that they knew his name – after all that we knew, they were clearly aware of his existence – however, I didn't like the way he said his name.

"If you have something to say, say it," Ramon said casually.

"Lucius!" Titus demanded.

The stranger in the middle went forward and stopped right in front of Ramon, who automatically stepped back. Should I do something?

"To understand us better, you should know who we really are. We, the three of us, are magicians. The darker kind. We all came from the same circle, a circle that rejected us because we weren't magically enough for them. They despised us simply because of our DNA. No matter what we did, we were never good enough to keep up with the other wizards, so we had to go our own way. From this day on, we concentrated on dark magic. This, however, was not a natural ability that we could have or not have, no, it was exactly what we needed to feel powerful and superior. We made different pacts with lower demons that should help us control our dark magic, but in the end, nothing was really useful to us. Still, we didn't give up, and taught us everything ourselves. As you can see, we aren't that different, Ramon. We're outsiders as well. We don't fit in; we felt like we didn't belong, and we failed so many times. Just like you," Lucius explained.

"Tragical story. But what do you want from me?" Ramon said totally untouched by Lucius's story.
He wasn't allowed to get manipulated by these weirdos. Whatever they had planned, it couldn't be good.

"We just want your help with some sort of purification. We want to get rid of all those who didn't understand us. We want revenge on those who tried to outsmart us, and we want to create a new and pure world without any other supernatural creatures. A perfect world that will be ruled by us. That's why we made our way here when we realized your Grandma was about to depart from this world. We knew she was hiding something, something powerful. Who would've known it would be you? We ripped the pages out of the book because we knew you would come here eventually," Lucius responded.

"Yeah, no chance I'm going to help you. And now, go away and stop bothering me!"
Ramon was about to turn around and leave when another creature stormed out of the corridor. Within

seconds, another person appeared in front of Ramon. This all happened so fast that it was impossible for this stranger to not have inhuman abilities.

"If I was you, I would think about this again," the person said with a pleasantly deep voice.

"I thought about it. I stick to my decision."

The person held Ramon and pushed him in the direction of the magicians. Ramon stumbled and fell on his knees, which the new guy seemed to enjoy since it was easier for him to prevent Ramon from running away now.

I should go back and get Tim. Definitely. I couldn't do anything against them, there were simply too many of them. And even though I knew what I had to do, I couldn't bring myself to do anything. I couldn't look away from what was happening in this basement.

It had become colder and colder, and I could only hope the chattering of my teeth wouldn't seek anyone's attention.

"So, what exactly do you want from me?" Ramon hissed.

"We don't demand much. And we're even kind enough to let you choose. Either you help us kill all those who were against us, or you can simply hand us the spell book of the grand Myrddin," Titus offered surprisingly gently.

"What's the catch?" Ramon wanted to know.

"There is none," answered the stranger, whose name we still didn't know.

Now that the situation was calming down a bit, I noticed that the stranger was a guy around the age of me, or Ramon. If he was older than me, he couldn't be that much older. His hair was dark brown, almost black, which fitted well to his dark eyes. Just the way he looked made me think that he could impossibly be younger than 18. He might even be good-looking if he wasn't allied with the magicians.

"There is always a catch," Ramon pressed from between his lips and tried to free himself. Caused by that, the stranger held him a little bit tighter, which I could only tell because his arm musculature was tensed. Ramon's face changed into an expression of pain.

I couldn't even imagine how much pressure must've been on him at that moment. Why did I feel like I was paralyzed?

"Then just enjoy the fact that there is no catch. And now make your decision!" the stranger demanded.

"I don't even know what book you are talking about. I'll certainly not give you anything," Ramon responded annoyed.

"What a shame. I always thought that out of all the people in the world, you would understand us. We are not the bad guys. We are the ones that want to protect others from all evil, and we need you. You are the deadliest weapon that exists. Isn't there anyone that you would love to get rid of? Anyone, that did you wrong? Anyone, that didn't want to even try to understand you?" Titus said empathetically.

It was more than obvious that he was hinting at Mrs. Müller. He clearly tried to manipulate Ramon.

"Even then, I wouldn't wish them death. Otherwise, I would've already ended their lives. In opposition to you, it isn't a question whether I can or cannot do it but whether I want to do it." Ramon provoked them.

I couldn't tell what the stranger was doing, but Ramon's face looked even more in pain than before.

"We can kill other people too, just not in huge masses the way you do it." Titus was absolutely unbothered by Ramon's behavior.

"Then why do you need my help anyway? Especially after you killed my Grandma."

He tried again to free himself. Again, he failed.

"That's not true," the stranger said, "it wasn't them who killed your Grandma. It was me."

"That's not making things better."

Ramon looked tense.

I didn't know what he was thinking, but it looked like he had a plan. For a moment, nothing happened, and everyone was silent. Then, all of a sudden, one of the shelves fell over loudly. But the stranger was fast enough to dodge it. Ramon used the momentum to try and get up, which he almost managed to do. However, as soon as he started getting up, the stranger came back and pressed him back to his knees. It broke my heart to see Ramon like this, and I started to panic.

"Nice try," the stranger laughed.

"Matt, restrain yourself!" Titus demanded.

Matt just rolled his eyes but didn't respond.

It seemed like Titus was the leader of this weird cult, and Antonius and Matt were his passive-aggressive minions. Which role Lucius would play in their dynamic, I couldn't tell so far. It did, however, surprise me that someone like Matt was submissive to Titus. He seemed so much stronger and more powerful than all of the three magicians combined. I mean, I had no clue what or who Matt was, but it was clearly visible that he was not a wizard.

"What happened to your Grandma was a mistake, we're heartbroken as well. She was a great woman," Titus said and wiped away an imaginary tear from below his eyes.

"And as a sign of our condolences, we want to make you another offer: you help us, and in return, you get everything you want. Your freedom, your parents, your Grandma, and everyone else that you have lost," Lucius offered.

So, I guess he was the one doing the trades? Interesting tactic, but it wouldn't change anything. I knew for a fact that Ramon could be as stubborn as me.

"You can't do that," Ramon responded, looking at the ground.

"Of course we can. If we were magicians of white magic, we surely wouldn't be able to bring anyone back, but since we were smart enough to learn dark magic, we can do anything you please. It really is that simple for magicians like us," Lucius explained.

"But if you are that powerful, why do you need me in the first place?" Ramon countered.

"Because nobody is perfect, and neither are we. That's why we need either you or the spell book. It's your choice which one you offer to us." Lucius sounded calm and neutral.

"I don't even know where the book is," Ramon said desperate.

"Yes, you do. You just forgot about it. Your Grandma was a smart woman, you know. You are the only person that knows where to find the spell book. Your Grandma had received this book from the great Myrddin himself. It's the most powerful existing spell book, and you are the key to everything. So, you'll stay out of trouble your Grandma made you forget you ever knew where the book is. Would you please allow us to look inside your head?" Titus explained calmly. Somehow, he reminded me a bit of my grandpa.

"I have to allow you to look into my head?" Ramon repeated confused.

"Of course, there are certain rules we need to follow. When it comes to that, we're like vampires that need to be invited into your home to be able to enter it. Your head is the house, and for us to enter, you need to let us in." Titus laughed amused by Ramon's lack of knowledge about mythical creatures.

"Good to know, because I'll never let you in, in this case," he answered in exactly the same calm voice that Titus has used all the time.

"So, you don't want to see your Grandma again so she can answer all of your questions? Maybe I misjudged you, but if I was in your position, I would do everything to unite my family again," Lucius threw in. I could see Ramon's facial expression change, as if he was actually considering this offer. But I wasn't the only one noticing that. The magicians could tell that their manipulative tactic was starting to work.

"We'll give you everything you ever wanted," Lucius repeated.

What a son of a witch, he knew exactly what he was doing. Suddenly, Ramon's facial expression changed again.

"No, I don't want my family back. I can't be egoistical when the whole world would be put in danger because of me, that would be wrong," Ramon said determined.

Titus's face darkened again, while the face of Lucius turned into a wide grin. You didn't need to be good at human knowledge to realize that nothing good could come out of that.

"We already expected you to deny our offer. Some people are simply good," Lucius looked like he was disgusted by anyone being good. "For being the deadliest weapon in this world, you have an incredible amount of human feelings," he ended his sentence.

"Everyone submits to us eventually," Antonius said, and laughed horribly. His laugh sent shivers down my spine and raised the hairs on my neck.

Whatever they had planned, it had been planned for a long time and in every detail. Whatever they had planned, it would make Ramon join them, that was for sure.

"We didn't need to look for long to figure out much about you. We let Matt spy on you, and it worked perfectly. Through his observations, we were able to analyze you and figure out your weakness, better said who is your weakness." Lucius took over the conversation once again.

I could see the shock and fear in Ramon's face.

"We were prepared for you to deny our offer," he explained further.

"Great, because that's what I'm doing," Ramon said confidently.

"That's what you think yet. But listen to our last offer," Lucius answered just as self-confident.

"We have been nothing but nice to you, and still you disrespect us, even though you are the one on his knees. You are in no position to treat us that way. We tried to lure you to our side diplomatically, but you pushed us away. So, listen to our last offering or deal with the consequences," Antonius threatened.

My heart beat faster. I couldn't even imagine what else they would offer to him. I had no clue what they were willing to do to drag him to their side. I had no clue what Ramon would do next, I couldn't say if they were breaking him or not. He was so certain he would not join them, but the magicians sounded certain as well. And depending on what their last offer was, I couldn't tell if Ramon even had a fair chance to deny it.

My breathing became more panicked, and I stepped away from the wall. I didn't want to see what was going on anymore. I tried to calm myself down, but I had no clue what I should do. Looking away felt like the only thing I could do.

In biology class, I had learned that there were two possibilities if you would end up in a threatening situation: fight or flight. I was more of a person who was running away from everything than a fighter. And this situation just proved that I wasn't meant to fight anyone. I would've loved to somehow be able to help him, but I didn't know what to do. And now it was too late. It was too late to go back up and find Tim. It was too late for everything. And this was only my fault. If Ramon would join the magicians, it would be all my fault. Damn. Damn. Damn.

After my breathing had normalized again, I decided to further observe the situation. I did feel like a weird lurker that was looking at an accident from the first row without helping at all, but I knew I would go crazy if I didn't see what was going on. There was still a small hope inside of me that I would stop being paralyzed and start doing something to help. Maybe a miracle would even happen; I wouldn't know if I wasn't looking.

Since I had looked away, nothing had changed. I probably didn't step back for as long as I had thought. It had probably only felt that long because I was about to collapse.

"Are you ready to listen to our ultimatum? It's your last chance. Choose wisely!" Lucius said calmly and with a wide grin. Then he went down into a squatting position, which looked kind of funny. His face was now at the same height as Ramon's, and I was certain they could look each other straight in the eye.

"Join us, give us the book, and in return, we'll let Luna live," his voice was friendly and gentle while he was uttering his threats. It almost sounded like he had said something completely normal. It was absurd. Exactly as absurd as what I was doing in reaction to that.

I could see how Ramon's facial expression had changed. I could see that he was about to accept their offer. So, I ran. I ran down the last stairs without thinking at all. I didn't care if I was quiet or not while doing that. I could feel my heartbeat in my ears, so that I couldn't hear anything anymore. Eventually, I stood in the same room as the others. Like in slow motion, I ran toward the magicians and threw myself with all of my strength at Lucius, who immediately lost balance and fell to the side. I saw the shock in

Ramon's eyes, and I saw that he was about to say something.

But before he could say anything I just said: "Don't worry about me. Worry about yourself because if you accept their offer, you just wish I would be dead."

I could see a tiny smile flit over his face. I could see how Matt was packing Ramon by the shoulders and throwing him away. I could see how Ramon's head smashed against the wall. And I could see Matt throwing himself at me. Then everything turned black around me.

Chapter 24

I couldn't have been unconscious for all too long because, when I woke up again, nothing had changed around me. The scared and shocked glance of Ramon and the confused glances of the others were all focused on me. No one – especially not me – understood what had just happened. It took me a moment until I realized what I had done. It took another moment until the others surrounding me realized that I was awake again.

Matt, who was kneeling next to me, grabbed me below my arms and lifted me up against my will. I was now standing again. Ramon's face, which was a bit more relaxed once he realized I was awake, darkened again.

"Everything is going to be okay," I said and tried to reassure Ramon that he shouldn't, under no circumstances, accept their deal. They were batshit crazy.

Matt twisted my hands with so much force against my back that I felt like they would fracture at any time. My face changed in pain, but luckily, Ramon couldn't see this because Matt had already started to push me in the direction of the same corridor he had come from earlier.

Contrary to the other passages that had let me here, this one wasn't lit up at all, it was completely dark. I lost all sense of orientation and stumbled blindly in front of Matt. None of us said anything, and we had already gone far enough, so I couldn't hear what happened in the basement. The further we walked, the more uncomfortable I felt.

At the end of the corridor, I could see a light. Was it daylight? No, it seemed way too artificial for that. I hurried up, hoping to use the moment of surprise to free myself from Matt, but it didn't work. It felt almost like Matt knew what I was about to do before I even started. Instead of freeing myself, I just stumbled again and fell down. My head hit the ground since I couldn't use my hands to catch the fall. I couldn't even feel if there was blood involved or how badly my head was hurt.

Suddenly, I had a genius idea: I could play dead and hope that Matt would buy it. So, I ignored Matt's demands to get back up.

As good as it was possible, I tried playing the role of a dead body, and I was almost sure it would work until Matt leaned closer and whispered: "Are you done relaxing on the ground? I can hear you breathe."

Before I could come up with the idea of simply holding my breath to play dead even better, he added: "Don't even think about holding your breath."

Discontented, I followed his orders and stood back up. My head ached more with each step I took. and with every step, the source of light in the distance got a bit closer.

Eventually, it turned out that the light was coming out of another room that was completely empty, besides a few torches on the walls. Matt grabbed an iron chain that was connected to the wall and fastened it to my hands. I was too weak to do anything against it.

"What are they doing to him?" I blurted out suddenly.

"I don't know," Matt answered and shrugged. "But I don't care either," he added, as if it wasn't clear before that he didn't give a damn about anything.

"But you must know what they want from him?" Now I was confused.

"No. I just have to do my task. It's their plan, after all, I just follow their orders."

I still looked at him in disbelief.

"But why?" I wanted to know.

"Because they promised me freedom," he said coldly.

"So, they switch you for Ramon. How selfish of you." I was bewildered.

Matt smirked briefly and said: "I don't think you are in the position to call anyone selfish here."

That hit me. He was right. I was exactly as bad as he was, if not worse. So, I decided it was best to stay quiet and plan what to do next. But I couldn't think of anything that seemed somehow doable. I was so dumb and actually thought I could hijack their conversation without any consequences, even though I hadn't really thought about anything at all; it was more of a reflex or impulse anyway.

Suddenly, one thought came over me, which I was able to repress before, but now that my adrenaline rush was slowly fading and even the cold could find its way into my body, it was impossible not to think about it.

The things the magicians had told Ramon, they haven't said them for no reason. They were following their devious plan. They had always followed it. And I was part of everything. And if Ramon would be able to get away from the magicians, which was what I hoped for because everything was better than working with them, it was still unclear what would happen to me. Or maybe it was crystal clear, and I just didn't want to realize it. The odds were high that they wouldn't let me live. And when I realized that, I couldn't stop myself from crying.

I didn't want to die, really. I had left this phase of my life behind, I had gotten over it and I was finally glad to be alive again. I had so many people in my life that I didn't want to leave behind. And as cliché as it might've sounded, but I didn't feel ready to die, I was way too young. There were so many things I wanted to do in my life. The first point on my bucket list, for example, was growing up. I couldn't simply die here. Not a week before I would turn 17. I couldn't let my mom be angry at me and then just die, she would always blame herself.

I noticed that Matt was eyeing me critically and said to himself: "I really don't understand you humans."

He sighed.

"What's your problem?" his voice sounded cold and if I wasn't already shivering, I would've surely started now because just the tone of his voice was the whole winter all at once.

"Are they going to kill me?" I uttered, still crying.
I didn't even dare to lift my head, which had rested on my knees by now. I didn't care that the ground in this basement was as wet as everything else here. The moistness was drilling through my clothes.

Matt started to laugh out loud, almost as if I had made a great joke. When he calmed down again, which took some time, he just shook his head in disbelief.

"You really have no clue, do you?" he finally said.

I managed to look at him questioning.

I gulped.
My throat was sore from all the crying, but this was my smallest problem.

"So, you throwing yourself at Lucius was just stupidity? I've heard so many things about humans, but this surpasses everything." Again it sounded more like he was talking to himself than to me.

"It would be more helpful if you would explain what's going on instead of insulting me," it took me all of my strength to make this sound as firm and demanding as possible. In the end, it didn't sound anywhere near as good as I had hoped, still, it seemed to work.

"Okay, okay, little one, I'll talk," he smirked.

Then he took a break.

"I don't know everything but all that I know is that these three guys in the basement here won't do anything to you. They don't do the dirty work. As you might've realized by now, this is my job."

The way he talked down on me made me furious.

"Why should I know that? Because you are their little puppy?" I provoked him.

His face turned dark from one second to the other, but as fast as he got mad, it lit up again.

"No, because you've already seen my powers in action."

When should I have seen his powers? Today was the first time in my life that I had seen him.

"You might not remember because it wasn't you who was affected by them."

I was even more confused, but Matt seemed to have found joy in my unawareness.

"I give you another hint," he grinned and exposed his perfectly white teeth. "Let's put it like this, my powers aren't always deadly."

He looked at me as if I should've known the answer by now. But I had no clue what he was talking about.

He puffed in annoyance: "How many hints do you need?"

"If you would give me good hints, I wouldn't need that many," I hissed.

I hated that he was treating me as if I was stupid.

"Because you won't understand it otherwise, I have to start telling you the story. Ironically, it didn't happen long ago, but that's okay. Going to school doesn't mean you must be smart, huh?"

I clenched my hands to fists. How did he know so much about me?

"However, I was at this party – a really good party by the way. And do you know who else was there? That was a rhetorical question, you don't need to answer this. So, you were there. And your little friend there", he moved his head in the direction of the basement room, "he was there as well."

My eyes widened in shock. The more he said, the more I remembered. It was the night Finn was absolutely miserable, so the doctors could only save him last second.

"You," I screamed and jumped up.

I wanted to make a step closer to jump at him, but the chains were holding me back. I tried to pull on them, but it didn't change a thing.

"This should be the best example for you to understand how my abilities differ from Ramon's. It's way too easy to manipulate humans so they can become part of something bigger. But that's what you all want, don't you? You all want to give your life some kind of purpose or sense," he was just shaking his head while looking grossed out.

"If Finn would've been manipulated by Ramon, then…" I wanted to ask, but Matt interrupted me.

"Then he would've had zero chances of surviving."

"That's why they want Ramon to join them," I concluded.

"Congrats," Matt said and applauded. "You finally understood something."

I threw a mean glare at him, but he didn't seem to care.

"How did they find out about Ramon?" I blurted out.

He shrugged.

"I don't know. Probably because of this weird book or something like this."

He walked a bit closer to the corridor and looked in the direction of the basement room.

"What are you doing?" I asked confused.

"I'm waiting for my call," he answered as if it was something completely normal. Then he came back into the room and sat down on the ground.

"But how do you know?" I wanted to know.

"Don't tell me you've never heard about supernatural hearing?" he answered and laughed.

"So, you can hear everything," I concluded.

"Sure, you can't?" now it was him who looked confused. He really seemed to have no clue what humans were able to do and what they weren't.

"I can hear everything, every step. Every single scream," he said after a while.

"And what else can you do?" I tried to ignore his attempts of provoking me.

"I can see incredibly far, I can run fast …– "
He started naming a few of his powers, but I interrupted him.

"Do you sparkle in the sunlight as well?"
He glared at me in a mix of confusing and bewilderedness.

"Why should I sparkle in the sun?" he asked neutrally.

"Well, I thought you might be a vampire," I explained my train of thought to him.

"You've never met a real vampire, haven't you?" he concluded.

"No, but in books…– "
"These books don't know anything. They were written by humans for humans. It's all just fantasy and has nothing to do with reality, keep that in mind. Most humans don't even know supernatural creatures are real." He laughed, and I couldn't tell if he was laughing about me.
His laugh echoed through the room and was thrown back to us by the walls until it slowly started to stop. Then an uncomfortable and unfamiliar silence filled the room. A silence that made me sink into my thoughts and feel the cold in every part of my body. How could it be that cold despite being summer?

The chattering of my teeth had filled the room for some time. Suddenly, Matt's face changed. He looked focused and concentrated. Then he jumped up and went back to the entrance of the corridor. He stopped for a few seconds, as if he was thinking about what to do next.

Then he quickly glanced at me and said: "I have to go. Just wait here and don't move. I mean, it's not like there is anything else you can do anyway."

He winked at me provokingly, then he vanished into the darkness, and left me all alone, frightened, cold, and chained. Now it was me who was the puppy.

Chapter 25

Everything happened so fast, and I couldn't realize what was happening. In one moment, I was on my knees in front of the three magicians, and in the next one, the magician closest to me was on the ground, and I was thrown against a wall with so much power that I was confused that I wasn't the one who was fainting. While everyone was focusing on Luna, I used the time to get a bit closer to them. Of course, I could've run away, but it didn't feel like the right thing to do. Even though Luna had told me that I shouldn't save her.

Although it was what she had asked for, I wouldn't leave her hanging down here, and I wouldn't join the magicians either. I couldn't say if I was angry at Luna since she appeared down here out of nowhere, even though it was too dangerous for her, or if I should feel relieved because she had probably prevented me from making the worst mistake of my life.

Also, I had no clue how I should get in control of this situation, but there had to be a solution somewhere. A solution that wouldn't involve killing any of the magicians. I didn't want to kill anyone ever again, but I needed to be prepared for the worst to happen.

After Luna woke up again, Matt carried her away. I wanted to say something, but my mind was completely empty. I had no clue what to tell her, nothing was relevant enough to might be my last words to her. They vanished in the dark corridor, and I couldn't do anything but watch them until they were completely swallowed by darkness. I thought about running after her, but I was sure the magicians wouldn't let me do that, and even if I was able to outrun the magicians, there was still Matt. And let's be real, I didn't stand a chance against Matt. So, all I could do was wait and hope that they wouldn't do anything to her.

"Where did they go?" I asked seriously.

"Just down the corridor, nothing special. But you apparently made your decision on what side you want to be," Antonius who became more and more talkative with time answered.

"Yes, and nothing will change my mind," I said. Okay, I had to concentrate. I needed to get rid of them and hope that Matt would come back here somehow. Why was Tim not here? I needed him so badly. If he was here, he could distract the magicians, and maybe even Matt and I could try to save Luna. I sighed. Unfortunately for me, Tim wasn't here. His genius plans couldn't save me now; I was on my own.

"When will you understand that you already are one of us?" Lucius asked.

"Never!"

"But look at you. You are sacrificing the life of another person not just a strange face in the crowd, but a friend of yours, only to not join us – the ones you call evil. Don't you realize that nothing is that easy? There is more than black and white. While trying not to be evil, you became the bad guy," Lucius argued.

Maybe he was right. Maybe I should simply give them the book and concentrate on saving Luna. How bad could the spells in the book be? After all, they couldn't be as horrible and deadly as I was, and no one could prove it was me who gave them the book. NO. What was I even thinking? I wasn't allowed to let these people into my head. I shouldn't let them mess with my emotions. I shouldn't even take them seriously.

There had to be a reason they wanted this book, and this alone should be reason enough to not give it to them. I would be able to help Luna somehow else.

"You just have to give us the book, that's all we ask for. It's just a spell book – a former present for your Grandma. You won't be able to use it anyway, you are not a wizard, Ramon. It would be a shame if the book wouldn't be used at all," Titus tried to talk me into giving in.

"No," I shook my head, "you won't get anything from me."

"We didn't put so much effort into finding you just to get back home empty handed," Antonius screamed and jumped toward me. "Now give it to us!"

I stepped to the side to dodge his attack, if you could even call it an attack. Slightly confused, I looked after him. Did he seriously want to fight with me now? I was expecting them to maybe curse me with some spells or something like that, but I didn't expect them to get physical. I quickly looked around to see if I could find anything helpful, but there was nothing.

"Antonius," Titus called him back, "you know exactly that we're out of the age where we can fight." And this felt like the secret codeword for Matt because, as soon as Titus had said this, Matt reappeared and threw himself on top of me.

He was so fast that it was basically impossible for me to dodge his attack, and the next thing I realized, I was thrown against the wall, again.

"That's all you can do? It's starting to get boring, you know," I pressed out in pain while standing up.

In answer to my question, he picked me up by the collar of my shirt.

"Is this enough for you?" he said after he held me like this for some time.

I couldn't say anything, couldn't breathe, couldn't move. I couldn't do anything.

Okay, okay, okay. I needed to focus. I wasn't especially strong, or fast, or anything, but I had another advantage. I needed to get Tim down here somehow. Then we still didn't stand much of a chance, but it was bigger than if I stayed alone down here. And even if I didn't have a plan for what to do, Tim would probably have one. He always had one.

I tried to visualize Tim's bedroom as detailed as possible in my mind. Then I focused on the door of the room. I just had to open and close it; maybe that would wake him up. It had to work, there wasn't any other plan. If I didn't do it now, I wouldn't have the time to do it at all. I tried to use all of my power. I noticed my view becoming darker. The familiar tingle rushed through all of my body, and then everything went back to normal.

I couldn't tell if it worked or not. I had never tried to move something that was as far away as Tim's bedroom at the moment. Additionally, we were in a basement below the ground, maybe the reception for my visions was bad. All I could do was hope that it had worked.

The longer Matt held me like this, the more I had trouble breathing. I panted, which caused Matt to let me down on the ground again. I took a quick breath, then I ran to the shelf that I had thrown over earlier and grabbed the first few things that I could use for my defense: an empty bottle and a can of salt.

I saw how Matt came closer again, however, he was taking his time, maybe he wanted to observe what I was up to. There was just one problem; I had no clue what I wanted to do now. Without thinking, I put my hand in the can and spread a line of salt on the ground in front of me.

"Don't get any closer," I shouted threatening.

Matt, who was now on the other side of my salt line laughed at me. If I just had Grandma's book with me, I would know exactly what to do. But I didn't have it here.

"You know that salt is just a myth, don't you?" he asked me.

I didn't respond. Instead, I held the bottle at its neck and hit it against the wall. Shards of glass were flying around. But that was exactly what I wanted to happen. Now I had something in my hand that I could use as a weapon.

"So, what are you going to do now?" skeptically he raised his eyebrows.

I stretched my arm out in his direction as far as possible, still holding the pointy leftover of my bottle in my hand as a warning: "Stay away from me!"

"You would never do that. Just look at you. You have the power to kill all of us right here right now and still you prefer playing with a bottle, pathetic."

I didn't move, but I knew he was right. I WAS pathetic. I had killed so many people that it didn't make much of a difference if I would kill one or two more. Still, I couldn't do it. I didn't want to do it.

Anger about myself, about Matt, about the whole situation overcame me, and I managed to act quickly and brush his hand with my bottle weapon as he was about to pass my line of salt. His facial expression changed for a brief moment. Blood dripped out of the cut, but he didn't seem to care. Unbothered, he hit the rest of the bottle out of my hand. Carefully, I stepped back. Quickly, Matt picked up what used to be my weapon from the ground and again reduced the distance between us. I took another step back, but I also knew that I didn't have much space until I would end up in the corner of the room. I overestimated the size of the room, and this step was one too much. I was trapped. There was no escape.

Matt held the end of the bottle close to my throat.

"Any last words?"

"Not today," I countered.

Matt was raising his arm with the bottle still in his hand. He ignored all the panicked screams of the magicians. I didn't even dare to look at him. My glance was focused on the bottle. I saw how it was moving toward me at high speed. I needed to do something now.

I focused. I didn't have much time. No matter what I was about to do with this bottle, it had to happen fast, and equally important, it had to work. I tried to project all of my emotions onto this bottle. I felt my body react. The shard had almost reached my throat. I felt my view getting blurry. The bottle started to cut through my skin. I closed my eyes. I felt the pain. I heard a scream but couldn't tell if it was my own. I took a breath. Realized, I was bleeding. Realized, I was breathing. Realized, I was still alive.

I dared to open my eyes again. Automatically, my hand wandered to my throat, which, to my surprise, was still intact. Before Matt could cut through my throat with the bottle shard, it had exploded in his hand. The only thing I carried from all of that was a small cut. Nothing life-threatening. Everything was fine; my plan had worked.

The three magicians screamed something in a, for me, foreign language. I used this moment where Matt was distracted to punch him in the face with all of my power. He stumbled back for a bit, however, he caught himself faster than I would've preferred.

I had to somehow get out of this corner otherwise, I would be doomed. Fortunately for me, I remembered that my mom made me go to multiple self-defense courses when I was a kid. Even though this here was a rather peculiar situation and I was inferior to my opponent from the start, I had hopes that this knowledge could come in handy.

Matt came closer and raised his hand again, but this time I wasn't surprised by his superspeed anymore. I already knew that he was incredibly fast, so I could prepare myself in comparison to the first time he had hit me. I could get used to his speed.

His fist came closer. I ducked and tried to disturb his balance with my foot. This time it was me surprising him, which helped me escape from this unfavorable situation in the corner. Without any plan, I ran into the middle of the room just so no wall behind me could stop me. I noticed that everything around me was spinning, and I was feeling weaker and weaker with every passing second. It wasn't until then that I realized the full impact this fight had on me.

I tried to get into position so I would be prepared for Matt's next move, but I wasn't even able to stand straight. Every move dared to throw me to the ground. I saw a blurry silhouette running toward me, the dark clothes made me realize that it was Matt. But even he wasn't as fast as he used to be at the beginning of this fight. He still looked better than me, though.

I blinked multiple times, but nothing changed. My eyes didn't want to see clearly anymore. I was panicky, there was no way I would be able to dodge him anymore. Matt came closer, and I tried to see more clearly. I failed. I could barely notice his fist going for my face again. Just in time, I crossed my arms in front of my face and therefore blocked his punch. Unfortunately, this didn't change the fact that I was in incredibly strong pain. Part of me was relieved I could block him, but the other part wondered why Matt was still so powerful while I couldn't even walk anymore without the risk of falling.

I wasn't prepared for Matt to punch me with his other fist as well. With a loud noise, his fist hit my face, and for a moment, everything was dark in front of my eyes. The next moment, I was lying on the ground in pain. Carefully, I fumbled through my face. I felt blood, but everything else seemed to be still intact. It must've been a miracle because I was sure his punches would break multiple bones.

I was still trying to find the source of the blood but before I could find it, Matt picked me up and made me stand on my legs again before he made his final hit. I was too numbed from the pain and all of the blood that was running down my forehead – maybe I never liked looking at blood – which was why I couldn't dodge him. I felt a metallic taste in my mouth. If I had hurt myself in the mouth or if it was just the blood from my forehead, I couldn't say. I didn't have much time to further think about it either because Matt's arm was speeding toward me again.

This time he didn't aim for my head but a bit lower, right below my ribcage. I had heard before that a punch on exactly this spot, the solar plexus, would be especially painful, still, I had never had the urge to feel this kind of pain myself.

Within a second, all the air I had in my lungs vanished, and I panted in pain. It was way more painful than the punch in the face. In general, it was more painful than anything else I had ever experienced. I gasped for air, but I couldn't breathe. It was ironic that I was surrounded by air and still I wasn't able to breathe it in. I was literally breathless. However, I strongly doubted it was the kind of breathlessness that Helene Fischer meant in her song.

I sank to the ground, knowing that my brain would be out of air soon and eventually shut down if I wouldn't be able to breathe. Matt just observed this scenario, maybe he didn't even know how much power was behind his punch. The magicians were also just watching. Silence filled the whole room, but I couldn't hear anything anyway. Finally, my lungs were able to soak up the air again, and the roaring in my ear became quieter. I could feel a piercing pain in my lungs while breathing in and out, but this was my smallest problem now. I knew I wouldn't be able to stand up.

"Do you have enough, or do I need to punch you again?" Matt wanted to know.

"I still won't tell you anything," I panted.

"You are tougher than I thought," Matt eyed me, and I was almost sure this was a hidden compliment. Not that I would care about that anyway.

"Maybe but I still won't help you," I tried to sound as casual as possible (but I still sounded pathetic).

"Interesting," Matt murmured.
It seemed like he didn't know what to do with me now.

"Am I interrupting this party?"
My glance wandered to the beginning of the stairs. Tim was standing there with his baseball bat, which I had tried to talk him out of taking with him. Matt looked exactly as confused as the magicians.

"There is another one?" I heard Lucius ask.

"I guess I overlooked him," Matt justified, but they seemed to be too much into their plans to listen to him anyway.
Tim came closer, which Matt tried to prevent. However, he was too exhausted and nowhere near as fast as at the beginning. From far away, I could see that

there was sweat running down his forehead. How human. Maybe Tim and I did stand a chance after all.

"Who are these wimps?" Tim asked after he had reached me.

"I'll explain everything to you later, they got Luna," I answered.

"Okay, I'll distract them, and you free her. I hope your powers are enough for that," Tim whispered his plan.

I nodded exhausted, and hoped that he wouldn't overestimate me.

"What if something happens to you?" I wanted to know.

"This won't happen. That's why I have this bad boy." He looked at his baseball bat. Then Tim ran toward the three magicians with his bat.

Immediately, Matt came after him. This was the distraction I needed to sneak into the corridor unseen. As long as my legs could carry me, everything would be fine.

I had to lean against the wall while I was moving because otherwise, I was afraid I would lose my balance, but still, I ran as fast as possible to the corridor. As expected, the corridor was dark, and I couldn't see anything, but this was the least of my problems. I knew I didn't have much time or strength. That's why I had to run as fast as my shaking legs let me.

My hands were fumbling on the wall for support but also to lead the way for me until I could finally see a light in the distance. I didn't know if what I was doing was smart or not, but I couldn't just not do it.

"Luna," I called her as loud as I could.

Immediately, I started coughing. My lungs still haven't fully recovered from the punch.

The walls threw my own words back at me, but besides the echo, there was another noise. I could hear a quiet "I'm here".

Motivated by that, I kept on running toward the light (there wasn't any other direction anyway), and with every meter I came closer, I became more hopeful that this would end well. Finally, I could reach my destination, a small room that was lit by torches on the walls. There was no furniture or anything else in this room but the torches and Luna.

Luna was chained to the wall. I immediately made my way toward her but broke down just in front of her. I had no strength left in me.

"You are bleeding, are you okay?", she asked worried.

Until now, I didn't have time to worry much about my look, but now that I thought about it, I must've looked quite horrifying. At least half of my face was covered in blood, my hair was sticky, and my clothes were drained in a mix of sweat and more blood. I was at my personal rock bottom, and there was no way to hide that. Whereas I didn't even leave a scratch on Matt, the one wound I had caused him has already fully healed.

"Everything is fine," I said.

I needed to use my arms as support to keep looking at her and not completely breaking down.

"Somehow, I can't believe that," she eyed me still worried.

I wished she wouldn't have to see me like this.

"It's all good. I just need a minute," I pressed out and tried to control my voice as much as possible. If I couldn't stop my body from shaking uncontrollably, I wanted my voice to sound as firm as possible.

"It's okay. Take your time," she responded gently, and I knew that she meant it exactly the way she said it. She had risked her life to save me from myself, every second that I needed to free her wouldn't change anything about her situation. Nothing would be able to stop me from saving her, and she knew that.

I gave her a weak smile.

"Thank you," I whispered, because I wasn't able to speak louder than that. My body was weakened, and the piercing pain in my head and chest didn't want to stop.

"I don't know why, but I have the feeling that these three didn't tell you the full story. There must be more to them than what they admit," she started babbling.

I tried to lift my head a bit to look at her, but the pain was getting stronger. My body was signaling me that what I was doing was a bad idea; still, I kept on looking at her.

"The way you look makes me think that Matt has way more strength than he has used against me. Which means it would've been easy for him to kill me. I mean, that was their threat, wasn't it?"

"Maybe he didn't want to do it?" I suggested.

She just shook her head.

"It's not about wanting or not wanting. He follows the orders of the magicians. I don't know if you see it like me, but I think it's strange that they threaten to kill me but, in the end, they didn't do anything to me; as if they had never planned to murder me."

"Yes, I completely understand what you mean," I lied.

To be honest, I had no clue what she was hinting at. The pain made it impossible for me to focus on what she was saying, but I was sure that everything would make sense once she would explain it to me when I was not in pain.

"Do you have any idea how to get out of here?" she asked eventually after a few minutes had passed.

"Nope, I think we need to improvise, and, in the end, everything is going to be alright." I added a fake smile to cheer her up.

I knew it was about time that I would have to free her, but I also knew that I had no power left in me. I just couldn't focus on anything.

"Are you really okay?" she wanted to know.

"No," I answered honestly while trying to repress the tears that were forming in my eyes.

I was desperate. I didn't know what to do, but mostly, I was angry at myself because I couldn't get a grip on myself for just a second to open her damn chains.

"Look at me, okay?" she said gently, and I lifted my head another time.

"Everything is going to be fine, okay? No matter if you free me now, or in a few minutes, or even tomorrow. Everything is going to be fine, repeat it!"

"Everything is going to be fine," I pressed out of my mouth, then my arms couldn't hold the weight of my body anymore, and I broke down completely.

But instead of everything turning black, I saw the silhouette of my Grandma in the distance. I ran toward her, trying to reach her, but she seemed like she was unreachably far away from me, so I had to stop to get some air.

At this moment, she turned around and moved toward me.

"You cannot always run after everything and wish you would reach it faster that way. Sometimes you have to take some time for yourself otherwise, you'll break down," she said when she finally reached me.

Then she put her hand on my shoulder: "So, what are you waiting for?"

I twitched and woke up again.

"How much time did I lose?" I asked her frantically. I was afraid Tim wouldn't be able to keep Matt distracted forever.

She looked at me in confusion: "What do you talk about?"

"It doesn't matter," I said, and grabbed her hand only to be able to focus on the lock of the chains. With my newfound energy, I managed to focus until my view was only occupied by the lock of the chains because everything else had become blurry. A tingle. A clicking noise. Then the lock opened, and before I could realize that I did it, Luna threw herself in my arms.

I wasn't prepared for that to happen, so I almost fell to the side. I also tried to hide the pain I felt in my chest during her hug. We stayed like this for a moment.

"Thanks," she whispered, and brushed a stray of hair out of my face. "So, it won't stick to the wound," she added shyly.

I smiled exhausted.

Opening the lock was more exhausting than I had thought in the first place.

"Thank you," I said while still smiling.

There was a weird atmosphere in this room. I couldn't tell what exactly it was, but I liked this feeling. I liked this kind of tension. It wasn't until then that I noticed her freckles, they had faded over the years, but they were still visible. Maybe it took me so long to realize this because I had never been that close to her face before.

"Can we please talk about why your Grandma needed a room like this with chains and everything?" she suddenly asked.

I laughed about what she said, and then I did what I should've done a while ago; I gathered all my courage, closed my eyes, and kissed her. I could tell she was a bit surprised about it, but so was I.

"I think it's time to go now," I said after the kiss.

She nodded, and we went through the dark corridor back to the room where I had left Tim. The closer we came, the bigger my fear grew. What if they did something to him? He only had his baseball bat, which wouldn't do much to Matt.

"Don't forget, everything is going to be okay." I heard Luna say next to me.

I took a deep breath, I could finally breathe properly again, and nodded. Even though it was dark I knew that she could sense that I agreed with her.

To our surprise the three magicians were lying unconsciously in one corner of the room and Tim sitting in another corner.

"Where is Matt?" I asked immediately.

"You mean the tall, scary guy?" Tim asked. "I made him run away," he bragged.

"Somehow, I can't believe you."

He now stood up and walked in our direction.

"Okay, maybe I didn't have to do anything. He just vanished because he was tired of obeying these three guys," he said, looking at the magicians that were slowly waking up again. "Kind of shitty of him but better for us," Tim added.

I was astonished.

How could he change his opinion that quickly? First, he fought for the magicians, even risking his own life by doing that, and from one second to the next, he was running away.

"Where is this good-for-nothing fool?" Antonius asked the other magicians.

"Gone," Tim said casually.

"Did he…?"

Titus sounded panicky and frantically looked for something in the pockets of his cape, the others mimicked that behavior.

"Yes," all three screamed in unison. They looked very unhappy.

I was confused, but I actually couldn't care less about the well-being of these three guys. They were probably pissed that Matt had run away, but this was none of our concern. The opposite was true, Matt running away was the only way we could get out of here more or less unharmed.

"Change of plans," Titus called out.

The three magicians walked toward us until they finally stood right in front of us.

"You might think you defeated us, but we'll come back," Antonius threatened.

It looked slightly ridiculous since he was more than a head tinier than me. Also, without Matt, the magicians weren't as frightening as before.

"It's not over, and remember, the next time we'll see each other, you'll be begging us to let you join us, and then we'll get what we asked for," Lucius said.

Antonius pulled something out of his pocket, it looked like a tiny Erlenmeyer flask, which I had last seen in chemistry class when I still used to go to school. Before I could react, he emptied the flask right in my face.

"Until we meet again," Titus said confidently.

Then the three of them vanished as quickly as they had come here.

"Are you okay?" Luna asked immediately.

"Yes, I'm just confused," I answered, still starring at the place where the magicians had stood just a few seconds ago.

"Let's quickly clean your wounds to avoid nasty infections," Luna sounded seriously worried about me.

"But let's first get upstairs again. I don't want to be here any longer," I answered, and tried to hide the fact that I wasn't as okay as I wanted them to believe.

I didn't know what was in that flask, but it couldn't be anything good, that was for sure. Only time could tell what this liquid would do to me if it was doing anything.

However, some things were simply more important than the content of the flask at the moment. We needed to get out of our moist clothes, especially Luna and I were incredibly wet.

Carefully, we made our way upstairs again. Tim and Luna supported me because I was still pretty weak from all the fighting with Matt. After tonight, I still had so many questions left unanswered, but we did know the answers to the most important questions.

We finally figured out what had happened to my Grandma, and we knew who was involved in killing her. We also knew who the strangers were and what they were looking for; me.

And I was certain that even though Matt had left them, they wouldn't give up until they would get what they had asked for.

Chapter 26

Making our way back to the mansion was harder and took longer than we expected, but it wasn't impossible. It took a lot of strength for either of us. We all had fought our own battle down there with the magicians. And each of us did our part to save our lives.

"Now we clean your wounds," Luna said while making sure I was sitting down on the sofa in the living room of the mansion.

"Does your Grandma have some kind of alcohol or something like this?" Tim asked suddenly.

"I don't know but why do you want to drink now?" I asked him visibly confused.

Still in pain, I touched my head to try to help me think. Since we came out of the weird basement, my headache had only gotten worse. I couldn't tell if it was because I had used my powers so many times in a row or if it was connected to the flask of the magicians instead.

"I'm not asking for me. We could use alcohol to disinfect your wounds," Tim explained slightly laughing.

Damn, I could feel how my concentration and ability to think clearly and logically had faded because of the pain I was in. I tried to remember if my Grandma could've had alcohol hidden somewhere, but I had never paid attention to that when I was here. I was a child after all, why should I have cared about alcohol?

"If we can't clean your wounds here, we need to get you to a hospital asap," Luna said.

"Rather not. Let's just drive back home, and on the way back we can buy something to clean the wounds. If I feel worse at home I can still go to a hospital," I begged them.

I didn't know why I wanted to avoid the hospital at all costs, but to be fair, there was no way we could explain what had happened to me. And if it really was about my powers or the magicians' brewed stuff, they would be overwhelmed with that anyway. If we would really bring me to a hospital and tell them we had fought magicians and another magical creature in my Grandma's hidden basement, they would only lock us in some kind of asylum.

Tim and Luna hesitated for some time, but eventually they decided it was best to follow my plan. Within seconds, they packed all of our things and stored them in the back of my car. Before that, Tim had given me one of my T-shirts to stop the bleeding on my forehead.

In my condition, it was impossible to drive, so Tim had to stir my car for the first time in my life. I could only hope he wouldn't crash it or something like that since the insurance was only in my name and I wanted to avoid spending money on things like that. Then again, if we would have an accident, I guess the insurance company would be the least of our problems.

Without saying anything, I laid down on the back seat, hoping the police wouldn't stop us on our way back home. I had no clue how legal it was to sleep like this while the car was driving.

Still, I tried to distract myself from all the pain I was in, but it was unsuccessful. In the end, I simply fell asleep and didn't wake up until the end of the trip.

Worried, I looked at Ramon, who had fallen asleep on the backseat of the car. His wounds seemed to bother him more than he was willing to show. I had no clue why he wanted to drive home now, but I could understand that he wanted to avoid going to the hospital. However, I was scared he wouldn't make it until the end of the drive.

Maybe I was being overly dramatic, but he was doing pretty badly, and he definitely overused his powers. I had no clue about how exactly using his powers affected him, but I knew he was always feeling a bit under the weather after he had actively used and controlled his abilities. And this night, he had used them more than ever before.

"Do you think he is going to be alright?" I blurted out.

"Of course, but he'll probably need some days for himself before he is back to normal."

"Can you promise that?" I asked almost begging.

I needed something in this moment that I could hold on to, even if it was just a false promise; it was better than nothing at all.

"I promise."

I knew that Tim wasn't a doctor, and even if he was, there was no guarantee Ramon would be alright. It was impossible to know what was going on and how things were about to evolve. But it meant something to me that he at least pretended everything would be okay in the future.

It was still dark outside, and it felt like the night would never end. I had no clue how much time we had spent in this horrible basement or how long I had been held hostage by the magicians. I had lost all track of time, and our phone batteries had died a long time ago. We didn't even know what time it was at the moment.

This must've been how people in ancient times had felt. Where they didn't have mathematicians that calculated the time and even the year. A time before time even existed. It was incredible that something like time has always been there, but at the same time, was invented by humans.

My thoughts were drifting off, but this helped me to calm myself down and distract me. I still couldn't believe what had happened that night. It was too much to cope with. That was why I admired Tim. He always seemed to be so chill and loosened up about everything, still he was incredibly helpful. Now that everything was over, he was back to being his usual calm self, as if he wasn't worried about anything. It felt like he had already found a way to cope with everything. Obviously, I didn't know what exactly he was thinking, maybe he was as messed up as me, but from the outside, he just seemed like always. Maybe that was what we all needed; someone calm who would bring us back home safely.

Even if it was hard to admit, I was looking forward to being home again. We continued driving through the night, and it felt like the sun would never rise again. Even when we were less than 30 minutes away from home – it felt weird to call this place like that, especially since I was ready to get as far away as possible from it just a few days ago – it was still dark.

We couldn't even stop on the road to buy something to clean Ramon's wounds because all of the stores were closed. I tried to remember if we would have anything helpful at home, but I couldn't think of anything.

Eventually, we made it; we arrived back home. Carefully, we woke up Ramon, who became conscious pretty quickly (luckily). We had to support him a little bit while bringing him back to his apartment on the fifth floor. It took a while until Ramon managed to unlock his door, but he made it. We decided to bring him to the couch, then we looked through his apartment to see if we could find anything to clean his wounds.

We already knew he wouldn't have alcohol at home, but maybe he had a med kit or something like that, even though there was no reason why he should have one up here. But everyone kind of had some med kit at home.

Suddenly, I had an idea. If anyone had this at home, then we must've had it somewhere.

"Tim, google what else we can use to disinfect wounds. I'm going to look for a med kit in our apartment," I called and left the apartment before he could even respond.

Now, the real adventure would start. I had to sneak through the apartment without waking up my mom. Again.

Quietly, I unlocked the door and didn't fully close it – to avoid making more noises – after I had entered the apartment. This would make my escape easier and more silent as well.

Immediately, I went into the bathroom because that was the room where I would expect a med kid the most. Desperately, I tried to look through different drawers and shelves, but I couldn't find anything.

"Luna? Is it you?" I suddenly heard a voice in the hallway.

I had forgotten to be quiet since I was frantically searching for the med kit.

"Yes, it's me. Don't worry," I answered, and hoped this would be enough for her and she would go back to bed. But she didn't. I could hear her steps coming closer. Then she turned on the light in the bathroom.

"Why didn't you turn on the light? And why are you even here already?" she wondered.

From the sound of her voice, it was impossible to tell how she felt. She sounded neither angry nor surprised; she sounded like usual. That was a good thing, wasn't it?

"I didn't want to wake you up," I answered quickly, and hoped she would forget her other question.

"But why are you here?" she repeated.

"Do we have a med kit?" I murmured.

"Of course. You are looking in the wrong drawer. It's here," she went to another shelf, and handed me a plastic bag.

"Why do you need it in the first place?" she wanted to know skeptically.

"Thank you so much. I promise, I explain everything to you later, but right now is pretty bad," I shouted and ran out of the bathroom.

Then I left the apartment.

When I arrived at Ramon's apartment, Tim had already cleaned his wounds with regular water. He said that the internet claimed that water would be more than enough to prevent him from getting an infection. I really hoped he was right about that. I only knew that he got these wounds from fighting Matt. I didn't know any more details, but it couldn't be completely excluded that some dirt had gotten in it. Since we didn't have anything else but water to disinfect the wound, it had to be enough.

Quickly, I opened the package of the first dressing I could find in the med kit. Why were these things all wrapped in plastic? Tim helped me wrap it around Ramon's head. It felt like he knew what we were doing, in opposite to me. Maybe he had googled it while I was gone.

"Thank you, guys," Ramon said tiredly.

Tim and I decided it would be for the best to let him rest from now on. Tim also promised me to stay for the night so he could help Ramon change his clothes and be there in case he was feeling worse. It helped me calm down enough so I could walk back downstairs. I even forgot for a second that I had promised my mom to tell her the truth. But I had no clue which version of the truth I would tell her. There was no way I could tell her the full truth; it was not my position to share Ramon's secret with anyone without asking him first whether it was okay to talk about it or not.

Secretly, I hoped my mom had already gone back to bed and would forget about everything, but as soon as I entered the apartment, I knew I wouldn't be able to get around talking to her.

The apartment was well-lit, and my mom was waiting for me in the kitchen, drinking her tea.

"I think it's about time we talk," she sighted and stirred her tea.

"I fear you are right," I answered, and sat down on the other side of the table.

"Why are you already back, you were only gone for four days?" she wanted to know, and sounded like someone would ask you about the weather; somehow friendly but still distanced.

"Four days?"
I repeated and counted the days in my head. It took us one day to get to the mansion, and then we looked through the rooms on the second day. In the night, there were those weird noises. These were three days, and not four.

Then I understood. It was no surprise anymore that the night felt like it lasted forever. The noises must've started in the early morning hours before sunrise. The long way to the basement, observing the magicians, all of these things must've taken multiple hours. Then I was chained for an unknown amount of time, and our way back took some time as well. It sounded incredible, but it was the only explanation. We had lost any sense of time down in the basement, so we didn't realize that when we left it, the sun had already set again.

The serious conversation with my mom went surprisingly better than expected. She wasn't even half as angry as I thought she was. Apparently, the replacement father had protected me, so I wouldn't be punished all too much for my behavior. I had to be a bit more responsible and help my mom by doing some chores, which was absolutely no problem for me. It was way better than being grounded for life, which was the punishment I had expected.

At the end of the day, she was happy that we all came back home – more or less – unharmed. I guess it also helped her that I reassured her, we would never do such a trip again because there was really no way I would go back to this mansion.

I had explained as much as possible about Ramon and the first time we met to my mom. Of course, I left out all the details about his mood changes because that would just lead to more questions, which I wanted to avoid. I only told her all the superficial stuff, but that was enough for her. It was the first time in a while I could be honest with her again.

I mean, just because I didn't tell her the full truth didn't mean I had lied. It wasn't until then that I realized how much I had missed talking to her like that. The conversation, however, didn't change the fact that my mom wasn't a big Ramon fan, which was mainly caused by the fact that I basically ran away with him and Tim. I guess no mother would like this to happen to her kid, even though it was my fault and not theirs. Additionally, it wasn't helpful that I came back with some bruises on my arms and face.

I could be happy that she didn't see Ramon's condition after we had come back from the mansion, otherwise, she would've probably forbidden any contact with him, and it would've been super difficult to find an explanation for his wounds.

***

After I had talked to my mom as honestly as I could, I had to make her meet Ramon coincidentally so she would finally realize that he wasn't as bad as she thought. When Ramon was feeling better – he needed multiple weeks for that and a trip to the hospital – I made them meet each other quickly on the staircase. However, it felt that after this encounter, my mom disliked him even more than before.

She didn't try to actively forbid our friendship, but I could tell she wasn't happy about it either. It felt like she was, for some unknown reason, afraid of him.

Things with my school friends, especially Finn, went surprisingly smoothly. I managed to find the perfect balance between spending time with them but also spending time with Ramon and Tim.

I didn't know how much I had missed out on in the past. Julius had his coming out – which was according to Finn about time – and was now dating a guy from another school. I didn't know him so far, but Julius had already promised we would get to know him soon. He would probably bring him to my birthday party, which would not be a party but a small gathering among friends.

Even though my birthday was a few weeks ago, I didn't find time to properly celebrate it because I wanted to wait for Ramon to get better and look less wounded. I really wanted to invite him and Tim so they could get to know my school friends a bit better if they wanted to.

Chapter 27

Finally, exactly one month after my regular birthday, it was time for my party. Since the weather was nice, Finn had offered to host the party at his place. His family was living in a house with a nice garden, and I loved some good barbecue, so I immediately accepted his offer.

On the day of the party, Tim, Ramon, and I drove together to Finn so they wouldn't get lost on their way. Also, I wanted to further observe Ramon; he still looked weaker than usual. I couldn't really believe him when he said he was doing fine, because he didn't look fine.

We were the first people to arrive – despite Finn, of course – and shortly after us, the others arrived as well. Julius really brought his boyfriend so we could meet him. In general, the mood was great and harmonic. Tim and Ramon integrated themselves well into my friend group, so no one felt excluded. It was the perfect evening.

While we were on our way back, I noticed that Ramon was shaking a little bit. Tim didn't seem to notice because he didn't talk about it at all and happily said goodbye when we arrived at our apartment complex. He had become such a good friend of mine as well. It was odd how friendships could just exist. I couldn't even tell when the friendship between Tim and me had started, but that was irrelevant. All that mattered was that we were friends. That's the fun about friendships, they just happen. Tim drove away, and I eyed Ramon skeptically.

"What?" he asked, and tilted his head.

"You're shaking, don't even try to deny it. I saw it with my own eyes," I confronted him.

"I'm perfectly fine. It's just a bit cold." He tried to justify his behavior.

I raised my eyebrows.

"It's summer," she answered, "if you are cold, then something is seriously wrong with you."

Then she opened the front door and went up the stairs. I looked after her for a second, then I followed. She had caught me, but I wouldn't let her know.

I would rather lie than tell her the truth. And the truth was that I was still feeling miserable, and if I wanted to be really, really honest with myself, I had to admit that it was getting worse with every passing day.

My nightmares had come back, and I could barely catch any sleep. I was restless and couldn't focus on anything anymore, no matter what I was doing. But the worst feeling was that it felt like I was repressing something bad. It felt like something was about to happen – something so horrible that it would make everything else that went horribly wrong in my life look like a children's birthday party. I couldn't imagine what was about to happen, but I was certain it would happen soon.

Technically, it was too risky to even talk to her friends when I felt that way. I didn't even know myself anymore. But I had to risk it because I wanted to keep up with the illusion of being okay. Maybe I just wanted things to be alright so badly that I also tried lying to myself.

I was so focused on my thoughts that I didn't realize she was standing in front of my apartment and waiting for me.

"I'm sorry, but you are not going to get rid of me," she said, and waited for me to unlock the door.

I knew that I was not in the right place to start a discussion, so I didn't even try.

"I'm fine, really," I lied, and sat down on my couch exhausted.

"Then prove it," she demanded.

"How should I prove it?" I asked desperately.

I didn't want her to know how I felt; I wanted to keep her out of all this. Whatever it was, it would be better for her the less she knew, and it would get better, hopefully.

Maybe it was just a side effect of my predictions. Every time Tim and I had actively worked on my visions, I was feeling like shit for some time. Why should it be different now?

"It would help if you would stop shivering, but you can't, can you? Because something is wrong," she explained.

"Who cares if I'm shivering. I'm fine," I tried again.

"Is it because of the magicians," she asked after a short break.

"Why should it be connected to them?" I wondered.

"Well, they threw something in your face and …"

"Exactly, they just threw it on me. It can impossibly have affected me. In every book, people have to drink magical potions to be affected by them. I didn't drink anything, and I'm positive none of the liquid went into my mouth when they threw it," I interrupted her.

"First of all, screw the books. What do they know anyway?" she started, "and secondly, you were hurt. The potion just needed to be thrown at your wound, and it could enter your blood system. That's simple biology."

Unfortunately, she was right about that, but I didn't tell her.

"This doesn't mean anything," I said, and wiped my face with my hands. While doing that, I accidentally brushed the wound on my forehead, which was still visible and would probably turn into a scar.

Touching it, even if it was just slightly, still hurt. I twitched.

"Of course, it doesn't need to mean anything. But I think the magicians had a plan when they threw the stuff in your face, and I'm trying to figure out what they want to happen," she said my exact thoughts out loud.

"You are right," I admitted.

Her face lit up.

"I think they are up to something as well. But this here might just be the side effect of my vision. There is no need to worry. It's all normal and will go away on its own soon," I tried to calm her down.

"But it's been such a long time since we were at the mansion. Don't you think it would've vanished by now?" she tried to argue.

"I guess it's because I've never used my powers as much as I did that night. Maybe the side effects are all added on top of one another," I explained my theory. At least that was what I told myself to calm down.

"Everything is going to be okay, did you forget about that?" I repeated her words from that night.

"I wish I could believe that," she looked at me pene-tratingly.

"I couldn't believe it in that night either."

I loved that we knew what the other person was referring to when we talked about that night.

It was fascinating, and relieving we didn't need to add more details to talk about the same topic. Because I was sure we both would prefer to forget about that night.

"But everything worked out," I added.

She still didn't look convinced, but she didn't say it out loud.

We spent more time together until she went back to her apartment. I had no clue what this was between us, but I liked it. Was I insane? Probably.

Chapter 28

A few days had passed, and I barely heard anything from Luna. She almost didn't text me, and if I texted first, she took some time to respond, which was unusual for her. She was one of these people that answered within seconds. I wondered if I had done something wrong, but I couldn't explain why she would suddenly behave like that. And I couldn't remember doing anything wrong either.

One day, I heard loud noises from the staircase. I was curious, but I stayed in my apartment. I didn't want anyone to think I was spying on them. I tried to distract myself, so I looked out of the window.

In one of the parking lots downstairs was a big moving truck. Luna's mother stood next to it and discussed with one of the guys from the moving company. Now, I was completely confused. I observed what was going on for some time. I saw how more and more furniture got packed into the truck. I saw a strange guy that was opening the car door for Luna's mother. And I saw Luna getting out of the house.

She looked back as if she was looking for something or someone. Quickly, I took a step back from the window, even though it was basically impossible that she would be able to see me. And as quickly as she moved into this apartment complex, she moved out.

Somehow, I couldn't get my grip on what just happened. At least it explained why she barely texted; she had probably been too busy packing boxes.

One day after her move, my doorbell rang. Confused, I went to the intercom system and stayed quiet.

"Ramon? Are you there?" I heard Luna's voice from the other side of the intercom.

I didn't say anything but pressed the little button, which would open the door for her. When she arrived in front of my apartment, she basically threw herself in my arms and didn't say a word.

I wasn't prepared for that, so I stumbled a few steps back to find my balance again. Maybe this had suffered a bit since the night in the mansion.

"Are you okay?" I wanted to know after she still didn't let go of me minutes later.

"Of course," she stuttered and immediately let go of me.

"We moved out," she started while we sat down in my living room.

"I know. I saw the moving truck," I just said.

Everything about this conversation felt odd.

"Oh," she responded. "However, I hate it. It's all bullshit, but I can't say anything against it. The new boyfriend of my mom seems to be fine; he helped her calm down while we were at the mansion. And even if I want to hate him for not being my real father but just a replacement, I just can't," the words were coming out of her mouth unhinged.

"I'm sure it's going to be fine. Sure, he isn't your dad, and he doesn't want to be anyone's replacement. I think it's just about accepting him as the new boy-friend of your mom, nothing more," I answered, and couldn't stop myself from smiling.
It felt too good to talk to her. She was good for me. I was a better person with her.

"I never looked at it that way," she said astonished.

"Where did you move, by the way?" I wanted to know.

"To the other end of the city. I swear, I hate it there. The bus connection is horrible, and I can't even walk to school by foot anymore, but I also don't want to change schools. Otherwise, I have to repeat the last school year, and I don't want that. Can I maybe move in with you?" she joked.

"I highly doubt your mother would be very happy about that," I grinned.
I knew that her mother wasn't the leader of my fan club, but I couldn't care less. Maybe she was even happy to move away so I would be able to see Luna less than when we were still neighbors.

"But I would be," she blurted out.

"Oh, really?" I asked laughing.

"Sure, the way to school would be so much shorter," she responded smiling.

"Of course, it's all about your way to school," I said ironically.

"What else should it be about?" she confirmed and started laughing. "But seriously, I already miss living here," she added.

"Hey, in a year you are 18 and then you can move wherever you want," I tried to cheer her up.

"So can you," she said.

"I know but I won't."

"Why not? You have, in theory, the possibility of living wherever you want. You can run away from here, and there is no reason for you to ever come back. You have a car, a driver's license. If I were in your position, y'all wouldn't ever see me again. Why do you even stay?" she asked in disbelief.

"Because being lonely is worse than being here," I answer shortly.

"I know how it feels to be alone, I've been like this for my whole life," I added.

She probably wouldn't get it, but I was glad to be here. I was glad I could be among other humans again. Of course, driving away sounded tempting, especially now that I was able to travel without risking killing anyone, but for some reason it had lost its charm. Nothing was more attractive to me than staying here, at least for the moment.

All the things I had imagined I would do once I was able to live a normal life didn't matter anymore. I wanted to stay. I had changed a lot within the last six months without even noticing it. I couldn't say when it started, but I could say that Tim and Luna had a huge impact on it.

"But you can go away without being lonely. There are so many people on this earth, you would find... "

"Do you want to get rid of me or why are you saying that?" I laughed.

"No, it shouldn't sound like that," she stuttered.

"I'll say this only once, and if you don't listen, it's your loss. I won't repeat it," I started.

She nodded.

"Of course, there are humans everywhere on this earth, but do you really don't understand, or do you don't want to understand? You and Tim, you only exist once, and that's here," I ended the probably most cheesy thing I had ever said and would ever say in my life.

Luna didn't say anything but kissed me. I tried to think about what this could mean since we had never talked about our kiss in the mansion. For some reason, we pretended it had never happened, I didn't even talk about it with Tim.

I tried pushing all of my thoughts away so I could fully concentrate on the kiss, and in this moment, everything was perfect. And I felt good. Even happy. I finally felt like I belonged somewhere.

Suddenly, he noticed a strange tingle twitch through his body. Wrinkles appeared on his forehead, and his view turned pitch black. When he was finally able to see again, he was somewhere else. An unfamiliar place. He could see mountains and a camp with two tents. Then he could see her. Luna was running around a path that was next to a steep hillside. It looked like a hiking track. Behind her was another person, someone he didn't know.

The strange guy stumbled and tried to hold on to Luna so he wouldn't fall down the hillside. Unfortunately, Luna wasn't prepared for that. She lost her balance and fell. Cause of death? Probably a broken neck. A quick but painless death.

As usual, it ended as fast as it had started. Shocked, he moved back a bit and, therefore, interrupted the kiss. He couldn't believe what just happened.

"Are you okay?" she wanted to know worried.

"Yes, it's all perfect," he answered stiffly.

So, this was the event that was connected to his weird feeling. The event that would make all the other bad things in his life look like they were nothing and irrelevant. And again, it would all be his fault.

Acknowledgements

I'm not a woman of many words (even though I just wrote a whole novel), still I think it's very important to thank everyone who helped and supported me during this project.

First of all, I need to thank my friend Maren, who made this absolutely stunning cover art. I fell in love with it the second I saw it. It turned out so much better than I could've imagined it, and even after all this time that lies between the publication of the German version of this book and the English version, the book cover never fails to amaze me.

Then I need to thank my friend Judith, who helped me during my writer's block. She always encouraged me to keep on writing my book. She was also the first person that I had told about my idea of writing a book, and she always believed that I could do it. Additionally, she came up with this awesome and mysterious title. And without a title, this story might have ended up unfinished in some folder on my desktop. Who knows?

Another huge thanks goes to all the other people that read parts of the book in English or in German to give me feedback. A special thanks to my friend Catie, who is a proper English speaker and therefore read and corrected the English version of my book.

You guys really carried me through this project, and without any of you, I wouldn't be able to publish my book at all, no matter in which language.

Then I want to thank my boyfrench Kilian, who doesn't speak German (yet) and therefore inspired me to finally start translating my book from German to English. I had tried it so many times before. And I gave up every time because nothing ever felt good enough for me. It really pushed me that I wanted him to read one of my books.

Another motivation for the translation is my Twitch chat. Huge thanks to the sexy pigeon gang, who at least pretends they want to read my book and listens to me ramble about the progress I made.

But my very last thanks goes to YOU. Because the fact that you read this book is the best support I could ever receive. It really means the world to me.

And if only one person that doesn't know me in real life reads this book, then I reached everything I ever dreamt of.

Maybe it's important to mention that after this mean cliffhanger, there will obviously be a second part (I've actually been working on it since 2020, but life got in the way. And it might take some more time until it'll be translated into English, but it will happen, I promise). The story of Luna and Ramon isn't over, and neither is my story. This here is only the beginning.

I know my book isn't perfect, but I think it has the potential to become someone's favorite book. I just need to find that person ☺

As a little treat that you made it this far, here is a cute picture of Goose and Yuki (two of our seven birds). They totally supported me while translating this book.